MW01147980

Sometimes Ridiculous

UMBERTO TOSI

Copyright © 2018 Umberto R. Tosi

All rights reserved.

ISBN:
ISBN-13:

All rights reserved. No part of this publication may
be reproduced, distributed, or transmitted in any
form or by any means, including photocopying,
recording, or other electronic or mechanical
methods, without the prior written permission of the
publisher, except in the case of brief quotations
embodied in critical reviews and certain other
noncommercial uses permitted by copyright law.

Published by Light Fantastic Books

Chicago, Illinois

DEDICATION

To my daughters Alicia, Kara, Cristina and Zoë,
and my inamorata, the artist Eleanor Spiess-Ferris,
for their inspiration and support.

SOMETIMES RIDICULOUS

CONTENTS

SOMETIMES RIDICULOUS

ACKNOWLEDGMENTS

Thank you to RUBY FERRIS her invaluable copy editing
and proofreading.

Thanks to JOHN BLADES, Fiction Editor of *Chicago
Quarterly Review*, and *Chicago Tribune* Sunday book editor
emeritus, for his comments in the foreword to this book.
Thanks to Elizabeth McKenzie, author of the bestselling
novel, *The Portable Veblen*, and managing editor of *Chicago
Quarterly Review*, for providing the back-cover pull quote.
Thanks also to ELEANOR SPIESS-FERRIS for her cover
image. Some of the stories in this collection have appeared
previously in various literary journals and magazines.
Boryana Books serialized "Our Own Kind," in condensed
form. "From Cradle to Gravy" was published in the
Authors Electric anthology: *One More Flash in the Pen*.
"Some of Them Are Ice People" was published in AE's
horror anthology, *Ghosts Electric: Dark Sparks*. "Onion
Station" appeared in *Chicago Quarterly Review*'s 2015.
Twentieth Anniversary Special Issue. "The Flying
Dutchman of the Internet" was published by *Catamaran
Literary Review*.

FRONT COVER IMAGE:
Ark, gouache and colored pencil, 22"x30, 1988"
by
ELEANOR SPIESS-FERRIS
Cover photos: Umberto Tosi

SOMETIMES RIDICULOUS

FOREWORD BY JOHN BLADES

Reading Umberto Tosi's stories is like a vertiginous trip on a combination magic carpet and time machine, the passengers generously fueled with complimentary loco weed. He whisks readers nimbly from the light to the dark fantastic, with stopovers in the lotus fields of Los Angeles, where he spent a restless boyhood in the 1940s, and in San Francisco, for a tragicomic tale of love and death that centers on Golden Gate Bridge jumpers. There is also an affectionate maternal portrait of a ribald soprano, whose voice is as golden as her stage presence is disastrous. Always observant and audacious, Tosi's stories set off unearthly echoes of Ray Bradbury and Nathanael West, while displaying the Shakespearean gusto and mordant humor that marked his revisionist novel, Ophelia Rising, in which he resurrected the Hamlet heroine from her watery grave.

- John Blades is Fiction Editor of Chicago Quarterly Review, *and editor emeritus of the Sunday* Chicago Tribune's *Book World.*

1 THE KLUTZ SOPRANO

Theo half expected the theater to catch fire when his mother appeared, holding a lighted, silver candlestick in her trembling right hand, upstage left, at the head of a curved, prop-stairway, as a gaggle of singers and supernumeraries, costumed as post-Jacobite Scottish nobles, watched, horrified in the semi-darkness below. Donizetti *Lucia di Lammermoor* – issue of Sir Walter Scott - had lost it once again, and stabbed her family-foisted bridegroom to death in the nuptial chamber from whence she exited.

The candle-shtick had not been part of the dress rehearsal that Theo had seen the day before, only the bloody dagger she carried, upraised in her other hand, that was real, not a prop.

"Hey, ma, do you think that in the olden days," he had asked Alma after the rehearsal, "the bride would stab the groom, then toss her knife to the next wife? You know, like they do with the bouquet?"

He grinned, boyishly pleased at teasing, and

commenced a nasal mockery of Wagner's "Treulich
geführt," from *Lohengrin* – a wedding processional to the
scaffold in this case – drawing a finger across his throat.
"By the power vested in me, I now pronounce you …
dead! – Naw-naaa-na-na! Naw-naaaah-na-na...!"

"Theo!" His mother exclaimed before her dressing
room vanity as she creamed off her stage makeup. "That's
hoaaarrible! Stop that right now!"

Her son's macabre travesty amused and chilled her,
evoking her own wedding calamities, just as the little imp
had intended, subliminally. She longed for Giancarlo's
strong, reassuring embrace. He could chase her doubts
away, this solid, yet tender man, returning her passion, so
intensely focused on her that she came alive under his
touch and stare. He made the sun come out from behind
these clouds. Here, she thought – swooning with
infatuation – was a man who truly appreciated her, an
opera lover, a romantic from the old school and the old
country, yet a man of substance. And bello –he was
handsome,, sinewy, strong-jawed and slim in a leading-man
vulnerable way, with his gorgeous mane of wavy hair.

"Signor Wavy Poop," "Curly-Smell-Pants," as her son
Theo called him sotto voce just enough so his mother
could make it out, but never to his Greco-sculpted, poser
face.

Alma, however, shivered with the delight at the
thought of him in those early days.

She wasn't blind to her son's disdain, but felt it would
be best left unchallenged and would pass. The boy's
churlish jealousy was natural. She had spoiled him – and
Giancarlo volunteered in private. She'd given the boy too
much leeway. The boy needed a real man in the house, a

Clark Gable kind of man, except, Italian. She was confident that the boy would soon learn to see the suave and gentlemanly Giancarlo through her adoring eyes.

Theo noticed her suppress what he thought was a giggle with the scold, or he interpreted her tension that way. Good! If she laughed enough, she wasn't depressed and they wouldn't take her away to the hospital and shock her brains like last time when she sat staring like a potato for six weeks.

She was doing the show-stopping Mad Scene now. This was the scene the audience had been waiting for, there at the deco-Italian-Renaissance, Wilshire Ebell Theater. This was her big moment, as Lucia! All of this watched nervously by the current performance's impresario, the flamboyant, Spanish character actor and mustachioed man-about-town, Fabio Stellanova! Alma and Fabio had been lovers briefly, though never bride and groom – perhaps fortuitously, because he was already married at the time of their whirlwind affair.

"Did you know that Judy Garland was discovered as a child actor on this very stage at the Wilshire Ebell?" Theo's mother told anyone who would listen.

Theo pictured an abandoned baby in a basket lit up by stage lights as the Wilshire Ebell curtain rose and a conductor raised his baton. "Waaaaaah!!" the baby's cry echoed through the theater packed with aghast patrons expecting to see Verdi's Il Trovatore, in which a gypsy hag confesses to throwing a baby into burning pyre. (Theo knew his operas, back and forth, and loved to "conduct" them when his music-teacher grandmother back East used to put them on her drop-mechanism phonograph console.)

Just then a bald man stood up in his seat. He looked a

little like Elmer Fudd. "Why, that's Judy Gawlawned!" He shouted, pointing at the baby basket. "I'd know that voice anywheah!" The audience broke into wild applause, stomped their feet and began chanting, "Juu-dy! Juu-dy! Ju-dy!"

"And that's how Judy Garland – missing those long years – was discovered! Theo informed his imaginary fans, as he posed before an imaginary newsreel camera with self-congratulatory satisfaction, arms folded.

Theo got to see rehearsals even on school days because his mother had no one to pick him up or watch him.

His ma, Al-Mama— as he teased her, pronouncing it like the name of a Saudi Prince – descended the stairway in a lacy, full-length, white satin wedding gown, sans train or veil, her feet pale and bare as were her well-powdered, alabaster shoulders. A tangle of cascading copper-tinted tresses underscored her macabre dishabille. That, and the gobs burgundy stage blood smeared over the front of her gown, too copious to be post-virginal.

"Ecco la! - There she is!" A rotund baritone playing one of the wedding guests sang, pointing up the staircase. That was the cue for Theo's mother to begin her haunting, dulcet aria, "Il dolce suono," better known as the Mad Scene. Opera lovers consider it to be one of the most sublime arias in the bel canto repertory, perhaps too beautiful to denote insanity to modern audiences but for the eerie accompaniment of glass harmonica, an invention of Benjamin Franklin that Donizetti showed his trendy, 1830s chops to write into his masterpiece. That much, Theo, already a lover of oddities at 11 years old, knew.

By now a junior showbiz veteran, young Theo held

his breath while his mother descended the staircase singing like the demented angel she was playing. He had no fears about his mother's artistic prowess. It was her idiosyncratic, incongruous clumsiness and rotten luck on stage that made Theo apprehensive.

The exquisite agility of her voice never transferred to extremities. She was the Awkward Diva, the Queen of Clumsy, the Slip-n-Fall Soprano, the Klutz Madonna, accident-prone as the Three Stooges rolled into one soprano. She was such a bundle of anomalies – a Latin-dark, handsome woman, a svelte diva with a sumptuous voice who could sing the crystals off the chandeliers and make both men and women fall in love with her at first aria. One notice, quoted on her press releases and recital programs said: "A young, fine soprano, with a rich voice and a broad range. Her musicality is precise, lyrical and tasteful. And she is a compelling actress to boot. Still, she remained relatively unknown."

Also she was clumsy: who ever heard of a clumsy diva? Not many, given the lengths to which Alma and her handlers sought to keep this under their collective hats. Theo knew, however, and, in childish sadistic glee, had even enjoyed a few of her on-stage fiascos – for example the time when she slammed a prop door too hard and made a whole set wall collapse, scattering the players and bringing down the curtain of an Italian-language play performance, live at the LA's Embassy Hotel Theater a few months earlier.

The audience roared. "Well, at least I got laughs," she remarked at rehearsal the next day. "Why don't you tell those stage hands to get it together?" She complained to the director. Then sheepishly: "What can I do? Sometimes

I don't know my own strength. It's my nerves. I get nerves," she said and held out a hand, making it tremble while she batted her dreamy chestnut eyes. "I'm like Rosa Ponselle. She was a nervous wreck."

Ponselle, indeed was famous for extreme jitters in her heyday, and also as a great diva, with whom Alma shared other qualities praised by those few, but knowledgeable critics who had written her up during her less-than-famous career so far. "Her voice has an opulence rarely heard since the great Rosa Ponselle," said Barnaby Croft of the Boston Globe reviewing a debut recital. "Her range is breathtaking, with an evenness of scale, graceful legato, mastery of technique and above all, expressive warmth."

Her unintended pratfalls had gotten the most attention, however, since then. Her scenery-collapsing fiasco made the Hollywood Citizen News, which rarely covered Italian language theater.

"Diva Brings Down House – for Real!" The paper's "lighter-side-of-the-news" headline read.

This time could be more serious. There was this flaming candlestick. At any moment she would have to throw down the bloody dagger in horror as went soaring into her famous coloratura lament. What if she drops the lighted candle instead of the dagger?

No sooner did Theo think this, than, oops, she dropped the candlestick. Clang, bang, boink, boink, bonk, down the stairs it clattered, wick staying miraculously lit and igniting a bit of carpeting on the way down. The conductor dropped his baton, the music stopped and audience, singers, and stagehands let out a collective gasp. The conductor recovered his wits momentarily and urged the players onward.

They recapped the pre-aria bars over and over while stagehands rushed out with a fire extinguisher and sprayed the stairway and half the supernumeraries with white foam as the curtain came down. The waves of audience laughter subsided, the conductor got the green light from back stage, settled the orchestra with arms and baton outstretched, and started the scene da capo.

Theo's mother, got her cue, and began again... "Il dolce suono...".

Theo made his way backstage once the performance ended – with applause and bouquets of flowers thrown on stage as if the fiasco had never occurred.

"It was an accident, Fabio. Things happen!"

Theo could hear his mother shouting on the other side of her closed dressing room door. The boy knew his mother's whole routine. He put his ear to the door.

Signor Stellanova responded in a soothing, well modulated baritone. His continental accent mixed Italian with Spanish and a bit of British English, hard for Theo to follow. As always, he maintained a gentle, assertive and avuncular demeanor befitting his role as diva-whisperer.

Alma fumed. "It was your *caffoni imbecill* istagehands who put the candlestick in the wrong place." She declared. "My gown sleeve knocked it sideways as I was coming onto the landing. I had to reach out and grab it before it went over the railing onto the stage. Imagine!"

"I saved your theater, Fabio," she pleaded.

"*Ees* not my theater, *carissima*," he corrected calmly, "But yes, *ti comprendo, mio tesoro.*"

"Who knows what would have happened if I hadn't caught it? Right?" She pursed her deep red-rouged lips, batted her long lashes over wide chocolate eyes and raised her finely plucked eyebrows.... The whole set could have gone up. Mama mia!

She dipped into a jar of glistening white cold cream and rubbed it on her cheeks slowly, then wiping it off along with her stage makeup with fresh tissues, which she discarded with practiced motion into a trash bin at her feet. "Who put a burning candle on set like that? *Che catso pensavano?*" Now she was winding up.

Signor Stellanova, shook his head subtly and held out an open hand.

Theo opened the dressing room door slowly, just enough to slip inside sideways behind a costume manequin from where he could view the proceedings.

Alma went on: "I had to step up to my mark and sing, holding that heavy candelabra, my hair getting singed!..."

"It wasn't a candelabra," Fabio corrected her, always a mistake..

"No matter!" She snapped. "I had to carry that thing, even though it weighed a ton. What is it, solid silver? And me having to wave that butcher knife in my other hand. The thing was huge, like a meat cleaver! Did they get from a butcher shop?"

"It had to be, you know, *grosso – spaventoso*, you know, scary enough for people to notice," he explained, smiling through his black, neatly trimmed, Salvadore Dali mustache. "I'll talk to the stage director about the candlestick." He leaned towards her and added, more softly, almost in a whisper: "But *carissima, per piacere*, next time, if you see a candle or anything out of place out there, *no te preoccupe*, leave it. You just sing – *canta il tuo bel canto!* We've got plenty of people to watch the props."

"Never mind!" She sobbed a little now, milking the scene for all it was worth. "This is all very, very upsetting," she burst into tears, daubing her eyes with tissues from the vanity.

He shook his head. Mama always blames the stagehands, he said to himself, sotto voce.

"You can't blame the crew," he heard Fabio say as if reading Theo's mind.

Why couldn't mama marry Fabio instead of falling for that phony, Giancarlo?

Theo had cottoned to Fabio, even though he had seen the mustachioed man-about-town only sporadically since his mother and he broke up. He admired Stellanova Spanish swashbuckler dash, his Errol Flynn sunglasses, the snap-brimmed, white gaucho hat he sported, the silk scarves, the way he would drive his shiny, white Lincoln Continental convertible up to their Hollywood Hills bungalow. Fabio addressed Theo with easy grace and self-assurance – and above all, straight and free of the patronizing adult goo.

Stellanova, a one-time professional magician, had even taught Theo a few basic illusions and card tricks. And here was Fabio again, back in his mother's life bearing the precious gift of opportunity as he somehow had managed to organize this ad hoc, Stellanova Los Angeles Grand Opera Company and invited his mother to perform in it.

It was no small feat. Los Angeles, though it had expanded rapidly during the World War 2, had no opera company like other big cities. There were few cultural institutions. The city had only the fine, but not yet world famous Los Angeles Philharmonic, led by the redoubtable, refugee conductor Otto Klemperer, and patronized by

Pasadena old money that never thought much of grand opera. With his long list of movie credits, playing character roles, Stellanova claimed that he could compensate for the lack of old money by bringing in fresh support from opera-loving Hollywood celebrities, or so the pipe dream was spun.

Most tellingly, Fabio saw himself in the boy – and spark of the precocious, unpolished gem he had been as a boy growing up in Palma de Mallorca, as a Jewish Genovese, Italian boy named Saul Levi. This had been during the island's pre-fascist-Franco time of intellectual refugees and sun-seeking creative castaways, including Jorges Luis Borges, who had lived in Fabio's hometown briefly and let the boy run errands for him. That was until he ran away to Paris, London, and New York, became Fabio Stellanova – an opera singer briefly himself – and finally, to 1920s Hollywood, where he found his calling as a walking character on and off the screen.

"Your boy has genius," he told Alma more than once. "You should feed and water that rare flower with care, *mi querida*. Bring him to the best teachers that I can find you," he continued.

Alma nodded. "Oh, yes. He's very bright. Too bright for his own good, sometimes. I worry he will find trouble like my brother, Salvo," she added. Salvo had joined the Army to avoid jail and ended up killed on Iwo Jima.

All had been going well in the past year since Theo's mother had recovered from her nervous breakdown and split from his temper-ridden father. His mother seemed to be doing well for herself, performing jazz ballads at a local club, getting Italian dubbing jobs with the studios, and now this opera thing – a chance to be a star once more as she had been in Boston and New York before the war halted everything, it seemed.

Now this Giancarlo from Naples showed up in her life. What a phony, with his addictive flattery, his *sa-da-fare* (savior faire), his nonchalant, neorealist chiaroscuro posture. It didn't take much digging for Theo to discover – by overhearing bits of adult conversation – that Giancarlo was a poser, according to backstage gossip, among chorus members,

Giancarlo claimed to have been a tenor with the San Carlos Opera in Naples, an underground journalist in Rome, an anti-Fascist Bolognese partisan during the 1943-45 Nazi occupation and a three-star chef in New York. Gossip not withstanding, his cinematic. continental charms was like heroin to Alma's tragic operatic romance addiction. Theo wouldn't have been surprised if Giancarlo dyed his hair and had all those curls permed once a month.

Wily as a three-card-monte shill, Giancarlo spotted Theo's suspicions and preempted him with a show of benign, old-country patrician discipline, impressing his starry eyed diva, who hugged Theo, and acknowledged tearfully that "the boy needs a real father."

Theo thought of his real father, absent now for several years except for the occasional postcard from San Francisco, where he was supposed to have an office. The postcards were penned in a feminine script – probably by his father's girlfriend Carlita, whom young Theo had met once – and signed in darker pen by his father, actually.

But Fabio! Here, thought Theo, were possibilities. He sensed correctly that the impresario still carried a torch for Alma. Why not? They all fell in love with her to degrees, the tenors, the baritones, the conductors and even a few of the other sopranos.

As it happened, Fabio was available at the moment, unlike when Alma had her tryst with him. He was divorced over a year now. Romance seemed all about availability to Theo, like walking into a showroom and buying a new car.

Theo had been keeping his cousin Olive abreast of this. Olive, whom Theo had nicknamed "Pipistrella" - Italian for bat, because of her slightly over-long fangs — was five years younger than he, precocious like he, and hung on his every word. They were inseparable pranksters. She was Marcia's daughter.

Theo prided himself on his mother-diva-management skills. Somebody had to look out for his ma, even if she wasn't aware of it – especially her being oblivious to peril on all sides. She had to concentrate on her art, after all.

Theo rationalized that his mother needed a good manager. Once he had heard his mother reading her sister a New York Times Sunday feature asserting that famous opera divas always had to have an entourage of managers and guides because they were temperamental, emotionally vulnerable and needed to focus on the demands of their art without being impinged upon by quotidian demands. Theo didn't comprehend a lot of it, but got the message that his mother needed a protector – and that protector might as well be he. His mother laughed as she read the article, however. "What a stuffed shirt," she declared.

Marcia had chimed in. "I met that old ruè once at a tea. He tried to make a pass right there. Talked and talked, but couldn't tell a diva from a donut without somebody telling him. How do these old farts get to where they write these stupid things?"

He hadn't always had such savoir-faire.

12

When he was four-and-a-half, for example, his aunt Marcia took him to his first live opera performance – Verdi's *Rigoletto* at the venerable Aeolian Hall in Boston, with Alma Floria, his mother, then only 22 in her first starring role, as Gilda.

He and his aunt had a complementary box to themselves. Marcia, who was pregnant with her own daughter, Olive, at the time, kept slipping him biscotti, as if he were still teething. As he chewed, scattering yellow crumbs all over the red velvet upholstered box seats, she told him the story of the opera in segments between the acts. She was big on child education and on Theo. "Such a bright little *cioccolino* (little chocolate)," she would say. "He knows so much, reads already. You'd think he was born old. He even plays the piano," Marcia would add, referencing the player piano in her flat on which he loved to run rolls and pretend to be tickling the ivories.

During the final intermission, before Act III, Marcia explained how Gilda's hunchback father, *Rigoletto*, hires an assassin, Sparafucile, to stab the womanizing Duke of Mantua to death for having taken advantage of his daughter, Gilda. But Gilda, still in love with the feckless Duke, overhears the plot and sneaks into an inn to prevent the murder, or offer herself in the Duke's place like any self-sacrificing 19th century Italian opera heroine would do in a snap.

"Does the bad man really stab Gilda?" Theo asked his aunt.

"Oh, yes," she answered. "It's very tragic."

That was that. Soon as the curtain rose on the final scene and Gilda entered, little Theo shouted at the top of his screechy, panicky child voice: "Look out, Ma! He's going to stab you. He's got a knife! Get out of there! Don't go in there!"

Theo kept yelling as his aunt dragged him out of the theater to the titters of the audience and stares from a bewildered conductor. What laughter they all enjoyed over this incident later. It became an instant family legend. No hot water for dramatics in Alma's family, not when it provided laughs.

Back to the Wilshire Ebell: "You must-a realize what is at stake here, Alma," Theo heard Stellanova beginning to hector his diva. "Edna Buff and her circle will be attending the second Lucia tomorrow night! She could finance a whole season for this opera company with a snap-a of de fingers!"

"Don't worry, Fabio," Theo's mother responded.

"Any shenanigans and we're go down the tank," he said. "Dis is your-*colpo!* Lightning strike, *querida!* Don't forget that."

Theo's throat tightened. "You shouldn't have told her that," he whispered like a stage prompter from behind the manikin. "She'll choke for sure! She'll fall off the stage or something" – though he knew that even breaking her neck, she would never would miss a note, being too conscientious an artist for that.

Time to make an entrance. Theo stepped from behind the manequin and presented himself, with an exaggerated, Cherubino-esque bow.

Alma turned in her seat, rag in hand, having rubbed off her makeup to reveal the bruise on her left cheekbone before she had a chance to cover it up. "Theo! Have you been spying on us?

"No, ma," he said. "I was just playing hide-and-seek

with..."

She dismissed the explanation. "What do you want?"

"You have a phone call – on the pay phone down the hall, Ma!" He made this up. He bit his tongue. He hadn't wanted to drive Stellanova off. Quite the opposite.

She waved Theo away. "Go take a message," she told him. "Fabio, can you give him a pencil or something, a piece of paper.

Fabio fumbled in his pocket and produced a small notebook, from which he tore a blank page, then handed Theo a pen from another pocket. "Bring de pen back, please, Theo," he smiled at the boy.

Theo backed slowly from the room, bowing every few feet, opera buff-style. He stared at his mother's bruise, however, just to make to show that he was not going to ignore it. He'd seen these before. She turned away from him to her vanity mirror, and swiftly dabbed over the discoloration with some face power, too late.

She pointed to the discoloration, shrugged and smiled wanly, first at Theo, then over to Fabio. "I tripped and fell against a door this morning. I'm such a klutz. I should look where I'm going."

Giancarlo, Theo whispered to himself. He had seen him slap Alma once, as he had come back into their bungalow from its tiny backyard unannounced. "The Duke of Staring Daggers,: he had nicknamed Giancarlo to his little cousin Olive.

Little Olive loved to hear every detail of Theo's espionage missions and other misadventures. He did not tell her about the bruise, however, when he saw her the next day after Alma dropped him at her sister Marcia's house for the weekend.

Instead, he made up a guessing game about all the ways characters were murdered in opera, especially tenors. "The Duke of Mantua," he said. "That one should be easy."

"Daggers and swords," Pipistrella squealed. That was what she called the game. She loved the way her cousin told her opera stories – all fractured and cartoony.

"Mmm... possibly, little lamb," he responded with mock seriousness. "But that's a trick question. He doesn't get stabbed at all. I know that one all too well," he smirked.
"Anyway, stabbing is messy, and you'd have to wear rubber gloves, nowadays anyway."

"Gloves?"

"Don't want to leave fingerprints," he said.

"Radames and Aida get sealed up in a tomb and suffocate!" Pipistrella squealed again, then grabbed her throat, stuck out her tongue and made gagging noises. She loved her cousin's opera tales, the gory ones and the romantic ones.

"Impractical," he said, musing, distracted.

"Give me another one!" She said.

"Mmm.. Tosca?"

"I don't remember." Pipistrella made a big-eyed, sad-puppy face and stuck out her lower lip.

"Here's a hint." Theo pantomimed firing a rifle. "Bang! Bang! Bang."

"She gets shot!"

"No, but Mario, the painter, gets the firing squad! Floria Tosca leaps off a castle wall. Pssseeuuw, SPLAT!" He thought a moment. "I wouldn't want ma to do that. She falls down enough."

Pipistrella piped up: "What about the one you told me yesterday, the opera Zia Alma sang in last summer at that outdoors thing? The naughty one, she said you're not supposed to know the story of, but you do?"

"Ah! Don Giovanni!" He tilted his head, remembering his mother rehearsing for Zerlina. "The Commendatore's ghost returns as a monster statue and drags Don Giovanni straight down to hell!" Theo acted out bum's rushing the hapless Don.

Pipistrella clapped and squealed. "You could do that!"

"Yes. Well, not quite, but we could make Giancarlo's life a hell on earth." He smiled.

"That would be such fun, cousin Theo. Could we do that? Can we? I don't like him either. He's a meanie."

-------------------- -

17

The telegram read:

"TO MR GIANCARLO GIANINNI=STOP=
REPORT TO FEDERAL BUILDING=STOP=
300 NORTH LOS ANGELES STREET=STOP=
RM. 1011=STOP=
MONDAY 4 NOV=STOP=
9AM-4:40PM=STOP=
OR ELSE =STOP=
SIGNED THE JUDGE=STOP="

"Porca Madonna! Lunedi! Monday is today," growled Giancarlo as he tossed the yellow telegram down on the dining table, half crumpled after reading it aloud for the second time, quizzically.

Theo had used the little tin, Maxie Junior Litho DialWriter that he got last Christmas to type the "telegram" in purple ink, all caps, on a blank, yellow message form that he had filched – along with an official-looking envelope – from a Western Union office a block from his school. Theo had overheard Giancarlo talking to a lawyer on the phone about the federal building, and forms to fill out regarding his immigration status – about getting his "green card" once he married Theo's mother.

Quick-tempered Giancarlo, who had never received an actual paper telegram, didn't examine it very closely after he found it slipped under the front door. Neither did he stop to consider how such a telegram would have been delivered to him there, at Alma's bungalow where he had only moved in "temporarily" a week earlier.

"Better get going," said Theo.

Giancarlo gave Theo the death stare. "You don't tell grownups what to do!" He said. "And Monday you speak Italian, and use the formal form addressing your elders."

"'*Scusa, signore, altissimo, commendatore*!'" Theo piped, and bowed with a flourish, then jumped away from Giancarlo's grab. His long fingers pinched and left marks whenever he caught the boy's arm, painfully, just about the elbow, shaking it. Theo twisted loose and jumped out of range. Giancarlo could be bolder with Theo's mother out of range having her bath. He never hit the boy, but his semi-surreptitious pinches seemed worse.

Giancarlo re-read the "telegram" and this time put it, crumpled, in his shirt pocket just behind his red pack of Pall Mall Filters and gold-plated Ronson Imperial cigarette lighter. He picked up his car keys from the fake fireplace mantle, and tapped on the bathroom door.

"Tesoro," he said unctuously, "I have got to go on an errand. Be back in a few hours." She called him into the bathroom where Theo could hear them chatting a few minutes before he emerged and headed out the front door.

Theo smiled to himself. He had already let varying amounts of air out of Giancarlo's tires – just enough to make steering difficult, he figured.

He heard Giancarlo's Pontiac Silver Streak sedan start up and pull away. Maybe he'll smash up his car, maybe go off one of those new Hollywood Freeway bridges, he thought. Theo pictured Giancarlo scurrying around the federal offices trying to find his "appointment," and losing his cool, getting arrested and maybe deported to Naples. Theo wasn't clear about his aims and that is always a mistake.

Theo didn't see Giancarlo until three days later when he returned from his aunt Marcia's where his mother had parked him after the accident. Giancarlo shot dagger eyes at him from under the white bandage still wrapped around his forehead and brow where his head had banged into the steering wheel as the Pontiac spun out into a guardrail.

"My poor Giancarlo," Alma sat, nylon-ed legs crossed, one high-heel dangling, balanced on an arm of the easy chair in the living room where Giancarlo sat like a king on his throne, stem glass of Chianti in hand. She kissed the bare skin of his forehead just about the bandage, then briefly on the lips before running a hand through his dark, curly hair. "You were so brave! Thank God you're okay and nobody else was hurt."

"The car," Giancarlo growled, "though, is-a *tottalmente distrutto!*" He stared accusingly at Theo in a way that his mother could not notice.

"Don't worry about that, deah." Alma smiled as winningly as in her recital announcement photos. "Remember what Zeffy told us yesterday." Zeff Ginsberg was a studio attorney and an investor at the increasingly popular gourmet Italian Opera café – Alma's – where Giancarlo was chef, and a founding partner.

"Zeffy said the restaurant could buy us a brand new car with money from what he called "investors." A briefcase full of cash, he showed us. Always flirting, that one." She rubbed Giancarlo's curly hair again. "Don't worry, *carissima!* I'm true to you always."

She turned to Theo, Marcia and little Olive, eyes aflutter. "And good news! I forgot the best part! The lawyer also says no problems with my darling Giancarlo's visa! He said the telegram must have been some mix-up.

20

Zeffy says the sooner Giancarlo and I get married, the better it will be!" She rested her cheek on his head for a moment, then rose from the chair to pour herself a glass of wine.

Theo tasted vomit.

Alma bent to hug Theo's on her way to the kitchen. "And my precious Theo is back home too... And dear Marcia and little Olive. Time to celebrate!" She hugged them too, then turned toward the kitchen door.

She caught a toe on the edge of the carpet and nearly took a fall on her way to their small kitchen. Her sister caught her just in time. "Oh my!" said Alma, recovering her balance.

Little Olive edged closer to Theo and tugged on his sleeve while peeking around him at Auntie Alma's latest lover as if he were a scorpion brought home for a pet.

"What now?" Pipistrella whispered to her cousin.

"Plan B," he whispered back.

"What's that?"

"Don't know," he answered.

"Do you know what's the most powerful word in the English language, Pipistrella?"

"Gumdrops!" She giggled, and kept transferring shiny stainless steel ball bearings from a Murphy's Hardware bag into an old mayonnaise jar half filled with olive oil. Plop, plop, plop, plop, plop...

"Why!" Theo said, without interrupting his task of prying white thumbtacks from their original rectangular backing and depositing them in the mayonnaise jar as well. He looked out from behind the bungalow's backyard trash incinerator every so often to make sure they weren't being seen.

"Why what?" Little Olive, aka Pipistrella, cocked her adorable head, cutely showing off the red satin bows at the ends of her chestnut pigtails. Her hair was pulled back tightly, and parted in the middle. When she furrowed her little brow with worry, she reminded Theo of Margaret O'Brien in Meet Me in St. Louis. Zia Marcia had taken the two of them to see a special reprise showing of the Judy Garland musical just a week earlier at the Pantages Theater on Hollywood Boulevard. Margaret O'Brien with fangs! She had lost her two front baby teeth. The gap accentuated little Dracula's pointy, over-sized incisors even more than before.

"If you keep asking why, adults will tell you everything they know, even bare their deepest secrets just to get rid of you," he said.

"That so?" Pipistrella plopped the last ball bearing into the jar. "Is that how you figure this out?"

"Absolutely! The physics of friction and slippage, for example, I learned from a gas station mechanic. The electrician who came to fix the wiring told me all about AC-DC currents, resistors, fuses, switches, wires and insulation. Mama's friend, Verrico the bookbinder told me all about history politics and World War 2 -- and snipers. He was a POW back then." He noticed that Pipistrella's eyes had glazed over. "And so forth," he wrapped up.

He screwed the cap back onto the mayonnaise jar, then concealed it in the hardware store bag. Pipistrella ran back into the little house to check if the coast was clear. Soon her little Margaret O'Brien face appeared behind the screen of the open bathroom window at the back. She grinned and waved. Marcia was still down the street at the Laundromat and Alma was napping. Giancarlo was at his restaurant already, preparing that evening's fare. He would return late, and take a shower.

"Mr. Ginsberg, esquire, told me all about the law," Theo continued as he finished his task.

Theo had given Ginsberg a why-why-why grilling on several occasions at the Alma bistro whenever the opportunity presented itself.

"Why does Giancarlo need a passport?" Theo had asked, feigning ignorance.

"Well, he's got a passport – from Italy. He needs, well, did your mother tell you?"

"Why?"

"Because he needs what we call a 'permanent resident' card, not a passport.

"Why?"

"So he can stay in the United States."

"Why can't he stay here anyway?"

"It's complicated. Lots of red tape. Then we have this quota."

"Why? What's a quota?"

"Because they don't like swarthy people coming here."

"Swarthy?"

"Well. You dagos, and Greeks, Chinese, and Mexicans and Jews. They want to keep us to a minimum."

"But we are here. Are they going to send us back to Italy or wherever."

"Would if they could..."

"Is that why he has to marry my mother?" Theo switched gears..

"You'd make a fine lawyer, kid. You know that? Anyway, you'll have to ask your mom about that one. People get married for all kinds of reasons. We lawyers are just here to help them get what they want – legally, that is – not tell them what they should need. I rest my case."

Theo stuck out his chest. "Ladies and gentlemen of

24

the jury..." He started.

Theo carefully hid the bag containing the jar-full of ball bearings and tacks in a cabinet under the bathroom sink. Then, he stood atop the commode and loosened the overhead light bulb, leaving only the dim lamp over the mirror to illuminate the space that night.

His father, Victor – suddenly taking an interest at the urging of his own mother – would be picking Theo up after dinner for a long-awaited weekend together – out of the blue, but welcomed in this case. Victor had rented a beach house in Pacific Palisades for the weekend. Just before leaving, he would feign using the bathroom and while inside, pour the contents of the jar evenly over the shower's tile floor, closing the frosted glass door. Aunt Marcia would have taken cousin Pipistrella home by then, and his mother would be on her way out to a rehearsal.

Perfect!

--------------------- ---

Theo stayed with Victor and his new girlfriend longer than expected. A full two weeks in fact. After closing the beach house, his father drove them north to his father's flat in the Central Valley town of Stockton, where his father's business was centered at the time. He even let Theo take the wheel on a quiet stretch of the Highway 99.

It was summer and he had no school. Theo really liked Rosita, who fed him homemade cornhusk wrapped tamales and frozen strawberry and lemon paletas, and mainly baby-sat him while his father seemed continually out on business. His father and Rosita conversed in Spanish – his first language from a childhood in Buenos Aires. She taught Theo a lot of Spanish words – trabajo, juego, baile, besos, dinero y amor, manzanas y naranjas y galletas...

Theo talked to his mother by phone at the end of the week and got all the bad news, which made him smile, at first. Giancarlo had suffered a series of mishaps, starting with the baited rattrap someone had slipped into one of his jacket pockets going off and breaking three fingers on his right hand. Then there was the fall in the shower, followed by the health department raid on the restaurant. The list went on.

"Too bad," said Theo, going all goose flesh from *schadenfreude*. Victor couldn't suppress a laugh when Theo relayed the news to him. Victor and Giancarlo had been golfing friends for a while in L.A. before the divorce. Victor, in fact, had taught Giancarlo the game, assuring him it would help him connect with important people. Mr. Curly-Slick-Bluebeard just wanted to get close to Alma.

After the split, when Victor learned that Giancarlo was seeing Alma, he spotted Giancarlo in the lobby of the Hollywood Roosevelt Hotel having a drink one afternoon. He dragged a surprised Giancarlo off his barstool, out onto the sidewalk, where he pummeled him and bloodied his nose.

Theo almost giggled when he overheard Giancarlo relating the incident to Alma in Italian. Now he pictured a decimated Giancarlo, with broken fingers, his arm in a cast from the fall, his feet still bandaged, along with a Band-Aid still on his brow from the car accident.

It wasn't funny, however, because with the news, Theo's mother had announced that she and Giancarlo were on their way to Las Vegas to be wed. "When you come home, sweetie, you'll have a new stepfather," she said. "Marcia will be my maid of honor. It's that wonderful."

Theo razzed into the receiver and hung up.

"I don't want to go back," he told his father at the end of that August. "I want to stay here with you."

"Can't do it, Theo," his father said. "It's not in the agreement. Plus, I've got to go east on business and Rosita has a job in Fresno. There won't be anyone here to take care of you."

"I can take care of myself."

"I don't doubt that," said Victor, sipping his morning cup of drip coffee and reading the paper. "You can come back for Christmas, maybe. Or next summer. Then we'll see."

It was from that moment that Theo began to doubt that he was master of his fate, that magic powers did not extend beyond fairy tales, and that knowledge, cunning and will could only get one so far in life – that fate makes travelers of us all. Just an inkling. He did have more tricks up his sleeve, however, and assessed them as he packed. He'd have to think this through and be more clever, he thought, and ask why, why, why about love and power and why the world seems run by fools more often than not.

Alma and Giancarlo were Mr. & Mrs. Giannini and had AG-monogrammed terrycloth towels – a wedding gift – when Theo got back to Los Angeles. She even asked if Theo wanted to be known now as "Theo Giannini. It has a nice ring to it. Anyway, so there won't be any confusion at school when I have to sign notes."

He bristled at the suggestion, and felt torn about disappointing his mother, yet realizing that allowing his name to be changed would send a hurtful, passive-aggressive message to his father.

Alma backed off. She also kept her stage name professionally. They had moved up to more commodious digs – a three-bedroom, rented, Mission Style house with view, a small, kidney-shaped swimming pool, and tile patio tucked into a Laurel Canyon Drive, side-road above Sunset on the L.A. side.

Patronage had picked up at the restaurant – now open for lunch as well as dinner – including a cadre of impeccably dressed mustache Petes from the New York and Naples who always sat at the same round table near the low-rise dining room stage where the singers performed each evening.

Theo's new junior high school was near the restaurant now and he often walked there after classes and did his homework in the upstairs office at the back of the building. That's when Theo kept noticing a regular who Giancarlo called "Sullie." The man – who looked to be in his thirties, was one of the New York mustache Petes. He usually sat at a back table reserved for Giancarlo's cronies. But he did more than order pasta and wine. He delivered a black leather briefcase to Giancarlo's office every other afternoon precisely at 4. Theo tried in vain to get one of these cases open. He couldn't peek inside, but he did notice that it was heavy.

Customers filled the place Thursday through Sunday to catch the opera dinners featuring Alma herself and a pair of younger singers performing opera and show tunes favorites accompanied by a piano player, and sometimes an accordionist.

Giancarlo put Theo to work part time, busing dishes after school. This was over his father's futile, long-distance objections. One night, Theo thought he overheard one the mustache-Pete regulars talking about "*Alma 'na canaria così 'bele, ma che meglio stare attenta a ciò che canta.*"

He had some difficulty with their Neapolitan dialect, but he interpreted that as meaning his mother was a "a canary who better watch out what she sings."

The second season of Stellanova's Los Angeles Opera Company would open soon. Fabio had secured more funding somehow, though not from the San Marino-Pasadena old money set.

Stellanova would open with an ambitious, full production of Georges Bizet's surefire Carmen. He asked Theo's mother to perform the part of Michaela, the virtuous country girl whom Don Jose jilts for his femme fatale, Carmen.

Alma cried and threw a small fit when she saw him. She wanted to the starring role, Carmen.

"But that's for a mezzo, my dear," said Fabio, "You haven't the range."

Alma begged to differ. "I debuted as Michaela. I don't do supporting roles anymore. My tessitura goes lower now," she said. "I know Carmen backwards and forwards. Please, Fabio! It's my dream!" Alma pleaded. "Claudia Muzzio, Geraldine Farrar and Ponselle all sang Carmen – dramatic sopranos, not mezzos, as you well know, Fabio!"

"Let me think about it," said Fabio, mollifying her. Fabio, however, had his latest diva-in-waiting, Maria Solis, lined up for the role, from Barcelona by way of New Zealand, and favored by Deena Chesney, of the Pasadena Chesneys.

Theo eavesdropped on this dust-up, as was his habit. On this particular occasion, he listened for opportunities for catastrophe could abound if Giancarlo showed up backstage.

Giancarlo was all into his mother's operatic doings lately as he became more and more consumed by jealousy. Their spats had grown into full-blown arguments in which Giancarlo used intimations of Alma's unfaithfulness as a controlling device.

She argued back, having become more assertive of late, Theo noticed. Perhaps her chats with Arnie Fisher had helped. He was the columnist from the L.A. Times who had taken an interest in Stellanova's opera company crew. Theo could tell that Fisher was crushing subtly on Alma, though he was married.

This got by Giancarlo, who fixated on Alma's vocal coach, Martin Wallace, a fine accompanist who was, by the way, as openly homosexual as one dared be in 1950s L.A., even among fellow bohemians.

Theo, thinking ahead to the grand opening, would volunteer to be a supernumerary, better yet, one of Carmen's ragtag boys marching along behind the soldiers in the first act.

Theo saw in the Hollywood Citizen News entertainment section that a local group would be giving J.M. Barrie's Peter and Wendy at the Wilshire Ebell just prior to Stellanova's Carmen. The play that inspired Disney's new animated Peter Pan that Marcia had taken he and Pipistrella to see on Hollywood Boulevard.

Marcia had promised to take them to see that as well, telling them they would get to see Tinkerbelle and Peter Pan" fly" – live right on stage.

Theo already knew that stage flight – as opposed to stage fright – involved hidden harnesses and wires. He opposed fooling children with fairytale nonsense. When he got Pipistrella alone, he explained the stagecraft that went into creating illusions of Peter Pan "flying," drawing details of pulleys, harnesses and wires on a piece of notebook paper for her. She nodded, but didn't seem all that interested in the mechanics.

"Last night I dreamed of dropping a sack-full of sand on Signor Curly-Que-Poop-Face-Giancarlo who was Porky Pig, but skinny." Pipistrella giggled after his explanation.

"Never mind about that," he continued. "We're going to be performers ourselves!" He told her that he would get them both into Carmen as supers. Then he got a pencil and piece of stationery from a box in his mother's closet and sketched Little Olive a picture how things work behind the scenes. "You'll be seeing a lot of this," he said. He sketched a boxy, theater interior, with back stage scaffolding and catwalks.

"See? This is how it all works," he lectured, explaining how fairies could fly and scenes could change in minutes. "The world of make-believe – just like my magic tricks," he grinned proudly. "Watch for it in Peter Pan. Then, when we get to be on the stage practicing for Carmen with your auntie Alma, look up and you'll see it all from the magicians' point of view."

Pipistrella looked over Theo's sketch, and pointed here and there for more details, which he filled in.

"Think of what we can do with all those ropes and pulleys, my dear cousin, Baby Bat," he told her, and filled in roughs, including circles for the giant klieg lamps and ovals for the sandbag-counterweights hanging from catwalks in the rafters high above the stage.

"Who knows what could happen?" He told her and pictured a fixture hurtling downward at Signor Curlylocks Poop-Face as he spied on his mother from the wings all green with jealousy – just as he looked at everyone from his creepy place inside.

To quote Bugs Bunny, he said: "Dis means wah!"

Theo had climbed to a catwalk before the curtain rose on the fourth and final act of *Carmen*. As luck would have it, La Chesney had literally broken a leg in rehearsal and Alma got to play Carmen after all.

Theo and Pipistrella appeared in costume as street village urchins who mimicked soldiers of Don Jose's regiment. After the first act, their parts done, Marcia let them get soft drinks from the backstage vending machine and took the two of them to see the rest of the opera from a reserved, second balcony box.

Towards the end of the last intermission, however, Theo told his aunt that, as a reward, Fabio Stellanova had arranged for them to watch the rest from a special spot backstage if they hurried. "He wants us to deliver bouquets of flowers to Mama and the other singers during final curtain calls at the end of the opera," he told his aunt Marcia. This part actually was true.

Marcia hesitated. "How come he didn't tell me this?"

"He's been really, really busy, but it's all arranged. Don't worry," Theo told her, "You sit back and enjoy the opera" Marcia, who was a little tipsy from a between-the-acts glass of wine, and exhausted from the stress of opera preparations over the past week, looked relieved and sat back in her cushy, red velvet box seat. Theo, after all, was nearly 12 now and old enough to have baby-sat Pipistrella on several occasions. They knew their way around the theater. What could go wrong?

Just as he had predicted, Theo had glimpsed Giancarlo in the wings during the performance, keeping a squinted eye on Alma and her Latin tenor, all the more handsome singing his heart and soul out as Don Josè. The tenor, Alonzo Ruiz Martinez from Mexico City, charmed Alma in the weeks leading up to the performance — an impeccable professional who – unlike typical tenors – was generous onstage and not full of himself.

There was chemistry. By Act 4, the star soprano and tenor had already garnered wild applause for their arias and duets, bravos and, prolonged curtain calls at the ends of the first three acts. The tingle of a big hit already was palpable backstage, but no one dared mention it for fear of bad luck.

Fabio Stellanova strutted about, beaming. The delighted impressario didn't notice when Theo had slipped away from the chorus and boys who had appeared in the first act marching scene and was not nowhere to be seen backstage.

Theo had a dizzying bird's eye view of the chorus milling about the Seville-town-square set far below him on the catwalk, as a crowd awaited the arrival of the bullfighter, Escamillo by the entrance to the arena with Carmen. "Les voici! Voici la quadrille!" They sang. Carmen looked stunning, in her Spanish gypsy costume, and black silken scarf, embroidered with blood-red roses. Don Jose, waiting to approach her, had his broken heart and stage-dagger at the ready to proffer one, then the other for the opera's tragic ending.

Giancarlo had a knife too – a mother-of-pearl, five-inch switchblade. Theo had seen it many times.

Theo's believed that his newest plan would be the most diabolical yet -- but also the most challenging to pull off.

He spelled and paced it all out in secret with little

Olive over and over, leading up to the opera, drawing diagrams on sheets of paper, working with toy figures and her doll house standing in for the theater. The daring duo would climb the spiral iron service staircase backstage leading up to the catwalks just as the act was beginning, while the stagehands remained engrossed in performance cues.

He planned a two-stage (as it were) attack.

Step One: Pipistrella would hide on the first-level catwalk and be a lookout, while Theo would climb two more levels to where the rows of fat, cylindrical klieg lights were bolted. He would choose the spotlights he could aim precisely downward onto the wing of the stage where Giancarlo stood. From the lower catwalk, Pipistrella would make hand signals to help Theo adjust his aim exactly.

From there, Theo would point one of the spotlights right down at Giancarlo. Then he would shake and pour a bottle of Coca Cola – which he had concealed under his costume peasant jacket, straight down on Mr. Curly-Poop-Face's Victor-Mature-curly mane. Then he would drop the bottle for good measure. Bombs away!

When the liquid hit his head, Giancarlo would look up, and be blinded by the light. People below would assume the bottle had been dropped accidentally, probably by a passing stagehand. Pipistrella would signal "coast-clear" once the Coke spill, as intended, scattered anyone who might have been standing near Giancarlo. This would set up:

Step Two: Theo would use an adjustable crescent wrench that he had also hidden in his jacket to loosen two main anchor bolts that secured the klieg lamp to its mooring on the catwalk. A quick kick would send the lamp plummeting down on Poop-Face-Wavy, crushing him like a cockroach.

With the commotion for cover, Theo and Pipistrella would be able to climb back down to the stage unnoticed. They would grab the bouquets that Stellanova had assigned them to deliver to the singers during curtain calls at the end of the opera.

Things began to go south, however, as Theo positioned himself to the stage left side of the third landing over where he figured Mr. Wavy would be standing. He leaned over the catwalk's thin-pipe guardrail but saw no one at the spot where he had left Pipistrella standing two catwalks below him. Neither did he see any sign of Giancarlo below that in the wings. Maybe little Olive had moved. He leaned further and scanned the first landing below. Nothing.

Where had she gone? He pulled the coke bottle out from inside his peasant jacket and flipped off the already loosened cap. He called for Pipistrella in a hissing, high-pitched stage whisper. The Act 4 music soared upwards, filling his space now and drowning out his clandestine cries. Now he began to worry. He made his way hurriedly back and forth along the catwalk, knocking into klieg lamp clamps, pulleys, knots of massive guide ropes and electrical cables.

No sign of Pipistrella. He climbed down to the second level catwalk. There was still no sign of his little cousin. Why had he taken her on this foolish misadventure? Zia Marcia will kill me if anything happened to Olive! Poor little Pipistrella. Tears welled up and ran down his cheeks now, blurring his vision as he ran back and forth.

The music of the final scene filled the space around him, strangely distorted by the baffles of scene screens and raised curtains. "You are mine," the maddened Don Jose sang in French as the orchestra poured out Bizet's luscious, poignant and tragic themes. "Now you think you can run away and laugh at me while in his arms!" Sang the tenor in a rich, sobbing voice. Words that Giancarlo could well say to Alma. No. No. No. Carmen refused. "Kill me or let me be free," she responds.

Theo suddenly flashed on his mother quoting that a few days earlier. "This is why I love Carmen. She dies a true heroine, refusing to be enslaved by any man, keeping her independence to the end!" Theo had never heard his mother, ever the romantic, speak with such surety, much less express such views.

Four acts now and she had not knocked over a vase, or a candlestick, or walked into a wall or broken a glass that she wasn't supposed to. A small miracle!

Theo came to an abrupt halt as he ran towards the spiral stairway connecting the second catwalk from the first where he had left little Olive. The figure of a man seemed to levitate out of the stairwell and block his way. Even through his tear-blurred vision, he recognized Giancarlo, his switchblade drawn.

Theo backed away, looking for something with which to defend himself. He heard a little scream above the music – more of a chirp. He realized then that Giancarlo held Pipistrella by the neck in his other long-fingered hand. She looked up at Theo in terror.

"Let her go, you bastard," he tried to shout above the orchestra. "*C'est toi! – C'est moi*! You will come with me." Strangely detached now, Theo could hear the tenor's anguished pleading, and his mother's voice soaring, triumphant refusals while a crowd cheered Escamillo from the bullring. Atta way, Theo thought. He could tell this was one of those nights when everything comes together in an opera and it transcends all the arts it conjoins and reality itself. It was there that Theo decided – perhaps offering himself to a god he hardly knew in one final prayer: If I can save Pipistrella and I survive this, I am going to be a great conductor.

Suddenly, he felt the giant bolo knot of a fat rope tied to a load-bearing girder in a sailor's hitch. He pulled it loose, desperate for something to hurl towards Giancarlo. The end of the rope was tipped in metal, making it a lethal projectile. Giancarlo raised his hands defensively as the rope struck him. The force of it toppled him off the catwalk.

It distracted him just enough to allow Pipistrella to free herself and run past Theo, who turned in pursuit, Giancarlo now closing in behind them. She made to another spiral stairway and headed down to the first level, followed by Theo, then Giancarlo, knife in hand.

This stairway, however, dead-ended onto a short, mezzanine catwalk, not the main first landing and freedom as Theo had hoped. The mezzanine landing was cluttered with gear of some sort. Theo managed to grab a long, hooked pole that he used to poke at Giancarlo to keep him from coming all the way down the staircase to get them.

The crashing of chords and rolling timpani, the shouts of the chorus and sobbing lament of the tenor told him that the opera had come to its inevitable, tragic – and in this case, boffo ending. The audience was shouting, clapping, stomping, cheering incessantly as the curtain rang down, and the singers came out of curtain call after curtain call.

Pipistrella screamed, but no one could hear her.

Theo realized what the mezzanine rigging was for. He poked Giancarlo extra hard, breaking his nose with the pole's tip and nearly toppling him over the staircase railing. "Pipistrella!" He yelled, taking advantage of a lull between curtain calls. "Strap on that harness over there!" He pointed to a canvas and leather harness secured by rope and pulley at the end of the platform. She ran to the harness while Giancarlo fought to regain his balance. Theo jumped to help little Pipistrella buckle on the harness and climb over the railing.

"You're going to fly! Just like Peter Pan!" He spoke loudly into her ear. "Don't be afraid. I have a hold on you. You'll be safe. Here you go."

With that, he pushed her off the edge of the mezzanine landing through a gap in the railings. He grabbed a massive electrical cable with set of button switches and prayed it would work. If not, there was a geared, hand-cranked wheel, presumably a manual backup. But it proved unnecessary, as he saw Pipistrella, holding her peasant jacket out wide like bat wings, glide gracefully along a wire trolley towards a prop-wall window, where, thankfully the guide cable remained anchored a beam.

Theo heard the crowd break into oohs and ahhs, then cheers and applause. Camera flashbulbs popped as Pipistrella make a graceful, three-point landing upstaging all the singers in the middle of their final bows, with the main curtain fully raised to allow the conductor, all of the chorus and supers to take their bows as well. Pipistrella, Theo's dear little Cousin Bat, had stolen the entire show!

Pure luck and cheapness saved her. Stellanova's designer had left a stage wall there from Peter Pan to save costs, and simply touched it up to look resemble old Seville instead of Neverland. Theo turned just as Giancarlo stumbled off the stairway and lunged at him. Theo dodged him, and Giancarlo tumbled over the railing himself.

Again, luck was with the Stellanova Opera company because the outer curtain had just come down for the last time just as the luckless Signor Curly Poop-Face toppled and landed, flat on his back, his fall broken by a peasant cart loaded with straw, pulled by a donkey, which startled and pulled the cart wildly around dumping Giancarlo painfully on the floor. Alma turned to see the commotion and berserk donkey. "Dear God," she said, "Did I drop something again and panic the animals?"

Alonzo Ruiz took her hand and kissed it. "Nothing to worry about, *querida*. You were a triumph tonight, absolutely fantastic. Let the stage hand worry about jackasses." She smiled, kissed his cheek and patted his hand. "All thanks to you my dearest.

Just then, two plainclothes FBI agents arrived, along with ambulance attendants. They had warrants, and cuffed the battered Giancarlo to the gurney as the emergency team wheeled him outside. "We got an anonymous tip," one of the agents told Fabio as they accompanied Giancarlo's gurney.

"I wonder who," said Fabio.

It seems Giancarlo was wanted under his real name, Luigi Bagani, in New Jersey on racketeering-related charges.

There was no reward, except that Theo never saw Curly Poop-Face again except in the newspaper, below the rave notice for Stellanova's Carmen and its principles.

The Hollywood Citizen News featured a front-page, three-column photo of little Pipistrella, grinning, arms outstretched in mid-flight over a star-studded opera stage.

The story-caption read:

"Carmen meets *Der Fledermaus* at Ebell!"

With a read-out:

"Bat Girl Finale Surprises Fans of Hit-Opera Performance."

Followed by: "L.A. Opera Company Director Stellanova says the stunt was "to promote upcoming all-Strauss fund-raiser." Obviously, Fabio was thinking on his feet as always.

2 FROM CRADLE TO GRAVY

Kate had lost control of her gravy. Ida's unerring nose picked up the scent of possible calamity all the way from the dining room, where she sat listening with half an ear to small talk from the nice man that Kate, and Ida's son John, had seated next to her – another eligible homme-du-jour.

Had her loving daughter-in-law consulted her, Ida would have said: 'That's all right. If I want a date, dear, I'll bring one.' Truth be known, Ida loved nothing better than the luxury of solitude on those rare evenings she had free from running Maison Oseille. But this was Kate and John's tenth anniversary party. She hadn't thought they would last this long, but now they seemed a rock. Kate, whose mother had died young, had become like a daughter, phoning about the kids, and asking her cooking advice. Their traditional old-timey marriage seemed alien to Ida, as did having grandchildren.

She turned her attention back to Frank Ywan; an improvement over Ida's previous table mates. He didn't ask "what were the Obamas like" - Barack and Michelle had dined quietly at Maison back in 2014 - or inquire as to what the various celebrities who frequented Maison liked to order.

She hated to be badgered into name-dropping. Celebrities, per se, were a nuisance anyway. She preferred her regular local customers; well-heeled to be sure, but low profile – Berkeley professors, a novelist or two, patrons of the arts. Ida could always anticipate just what they wanted. She had the touch, and a flawless instinct for mixing piquancy with elegance: or so said the food critics.

Ida hadn't know that Frank would be Asian. She wondered if the classic black-and-white Jason Wu silk slacks and blouse she had chosen to wear would come off as somehow patronizing, or if he would even notice, or care. Anyway, she liked the weightless, slinking feel of them on her slender, ageing body.

Frank was silver-haired, slender himself, and tawny, with chiseled features and wire-rimmed glasses, nonchalant, but distinguished in dark slacks and a purple shirt worn open over a black tee. He gave the impression of a musician at rehearsal – and, indeed, he turned out to be a bassoonist for the San Francisco Symphony, not the usual lawyer or dentist that Kate and John had tried to fix her up with on previous occasions.

He flirted just enough to be playful, but without pressing, and talked just enough – and not about himself. Nevertheless she held herself primly aloof. If I want a date, I'll get one.

'Do you like foodie movies – you know, like Big Night, or Eat, Drink, Man, Woman – or hate them for getting it all wrong, the way Hollywood does with musicians.'

'I never saw Big Night. I liked Mostly Martha – the German film, not so much the American remake with Catherine Zeta Jones … I think … can't remember the title – but that was about the woman – don't remember her name either – not about cuisine, though that was tolerable...' Ida winced at her rambling. 'I don't mean to sound like a snob.'

'Not at all.' He offered a basket of sliced sour dough.

She smiled and passed it on. The bread, she noted, hadn't been warmed enough to give off its characteristically enticing aroma. Oh God. Why am I doing this? Why can't I just relax and enjoy the evening? She tried a demure smile on him. 'I don't see many movies...'

'I know how that is... Barely time to sleep.'

Ida imagined John and Kate telling him too much about her. 'How do you know my son?'

'He did our contract. I'm the orchestra's music union rep.'

'Were you really going to strike last season?'

'We had a series of sidewalk concerts planned in front of Davies Hall, just in case.'

'That would have been fun.'

Her mind shifted back to the gravy – that trace of burnt odor again. She wondered where Kate was. Why did sweet little Kate insist on cooking their anniversary dinner in the first place? Why not have it catered; or go out?

Ida drained the last of her wine. It was a Napa Chardonnay from the Cakebread Cellars case she had given Kate and John last Christmas. To her annoyance, they apparently had not opened it until now despite her admonition about letting white wines sit about. To Ida's relief, it seemed to have weathered its incarceration.

Kate was roasting a turkey of all things; mainly because she knew how, but also because John had always loved it from when he was little and Ida – a single mom working two jobs at the time – used to order it already cooked from Frank's Market on Chestnut Street in San Francisco.

And of course, it wouldn't have to withstand comparison: Kate and John always steered clear of cooking dishes that might appear on Ida's chic, California cuisine menus.

Still, the gravy! The edgy burnt scent sharpened as

Kate and John's guests nibbled appetizers off earth-hued Southwestern plates set around the large table, which was tastefully adorned with a generous, red-orange amaryllis bouquet centerpiece and pungent dried eucalyptus from Kate and John's Berkeley Hills water-saver-eco-garden. The children played a video game intently off in the den, acting-out in place, silently to earphone music. Where was John? Where was Kate? Why weren't the kids at the table? Was she expected to entertain this bunch of semi-strangers – Kate's ceramics classmates, John's law partners, Kate's cousin Wilma from Willamette?

Ida's impromptu companion refilled her wine glass, and they clinked a friendly toast, as he went on, relating some anecdote about the orchestra. His charm was wearing thin, their conversation dissolving into mere chit-chat. Ida got enough of that at her restaurant.

Her attention strayed again, focusing instead on those hints of a scorched pan bottom mingling with the voluptuous, comforting aroma of roasting turkey seeping through the closed door to the kitchen.

Ida didn't mind so much about what Kate and John served, for her own sake. On her travels and many humanitarian fund-raisers, Ida had learned to tolerate culinary mediocrity, just so long as it never raised its ugly head near her bistro. But failed gravy was a zero-tolerance event!

Ida knew sauces. She knew glazes. She knew gravies. She revealed all their secrets every holiday season on her weekly, syndicated cooking vlog. She nearly waxed poetic as she demonstrated how to make the ideal gravies for turkey, chicken and goose.

'Gravy should be like a gorgeous blond diva that makes your dishes get up and dance,' she would say, stirring vigorously on camera, 'translucent, buttery, aromatic, distinctively flavorful – just viscous enough to cling and coat slices of turkey breast and nestle in mashed potatoes, but nevertheless, graceful, light and fluid. Good gravy is the sine qua non of the great American turkey dinner, even more so than cranberries.'

Ida's son John's law practice success had never translated into social graces. He still needed adult supervision. In that - letting go of her initial doubts about their pairing - Ida had passed her maternal baton to Kate, a sensible young woman adept at managing the household, John, the two children, little Sammy and Adele, while keeping the books of both house and business balanced.

Kate had no family of her own to speak of after her mother had perished - of drink they said - during Kate's pre-teen years; an absent father was reputed to have been killed in the first Iraq war, but more likely, Ida surmised, had been unknown in the first place.

Ida liked her daughter-in-law. When John had first brought his new fiancée to the Maison Oseille, Kate had lapped up Ida's perfunctorily gracious words, mistaking them as sincere affection - something Ida rationed out cautiously - and making her feel guilty. Kate wasn't perfect: a little mousy, never svelte, but with a pert smile and doe eyes which she cast warmly on Ida's son, no model of charm or affection himself. Better Kate, Ida had concluded, than see her son, heady with newfound success, take some narcissistic trophy wife or girlfriend.

The subtle – but to Ida, acrid scent intensified. It galvanized her at last to overcome her misgivings about meddling. Ida rose, picked up her wine glass, excused herself to her suddenly dumbfounded, but amiable dinner companion, and made for the kitchen forthwith.

She entered. Let the door swing closed and stopped in her tracks. The kitchen was empty. As swiftly as army nurse Diana Prince morphing into Wonder Woman, she grabbed an incongruously patriotic red-white-and-blue striped apron from a linen drawer and slipped it over her designer ensemble.

She sized up the situation instantly. One sip from a tablespoon told her the gravy was past saving. The situation called for radical action. Ida pulled the heavy black cast iron pan containing the offending sauce off the front burner of Kate's gas stove. She deposited it quickly in the sink, turned on the water and switched on the disposer to send the offending gravy into oblivion.

She pulled another black pan from a rack above the stove and set about her work with the concentration of a prima ballerina. She opened the oven. Without even having to look at the meat thermometer protruding from the roasting turkey breast, she could tell that the bird was done. She turned off the oven. She put on oven mitts, rescued the turkey and put it atop the stove to cool and shape up for carving. Not a moment too soon, she thought. Just enough time to reconfigure the gravy while the white meat sets and reabsorbs its aromatic juices, the dark congealing well and richly flavorful.

She whirled out the potatoes au gratin and yams from a second oven and started fresh cranberry sauce to simmer, adding sugar and a touch of brandy. Wonder Woman couldn't have done better with her magic lariat. She thanked the good lord that a fresh salad already stood prepared in the refrigerator.

Back to the gravy. Ida siphoned up drippings from the roasting pan with a turkey baster, transferred them into the black frying pan and turned on the gas burner under it.

She followed this with fresh garlic chopped fine, walnut pieces, fresh herbs and butter, a drizzle of olive oil, a squeeze of lemon; ah yes, and the rest of her Chardonnay together with a splash of golden Madeira from the cupboard. She moved without hesitation, accustomed to improvising from whatever she found at hand in a kitchen.

'Watching you cook is like ballet,' came a male voice. Her blind date had followed her into the kitchen.

'Thank you,' she said, 'but I'd call this resuscitation.'

She grabbed a yellow box of corn starch from the cupboard, spooned some into a cup, added some cold water and briskly stirred it into a fine slurry.

'Can I help?'

'You can keep me company.' She went on without a breath, as if doing her cookery show. 'Doing the gravy this way,' she explained, reflexively dropping into her best TV voice, 'ensures that the thickener won't lump up when you mix it into the hot drippings.'

'I prefer corn starch over flour as a thickener because it's lighter,' she continued. 'The starch holds the gravy together, and allows all the flavors to come out, but should remain minimal and discreet at all times, undetected by the palate. Call me a guardian angel,' she said.

'Or a good mother-in-law,' he said, causing her to stare at him a moment.

'... but don't tell my John or Kate.'

'... a stealth fairy godmother?'

'You seem to know a lot,' she said sardonically.

'Really... Can I help you?' he said, deflecting. 'Or should I say, may I please help you. I want to tell my granddaughter that I cooked with the famous Ida Poli.' He laughed.

'Not all that famous,' she said, then relenting, '... okay, yes, as a matter of fact, you can help. There,' she motioned to the heavy wooden block in the centre of the kitchen, 'chop me some more garlic. The gravy needs it,' she said, tasting it. 'There's another apron in the drawer below the counter.' She pointed with a wooden spoon.

He stepped to the sink, washed his hands quickly, and donned an apron bearing the words "Call me Cookie" in bright lipstick-red letters against a white background. Then he set about swiftly peeling and chopping garlic cloves.

'I'm impressed,' she said. 'You chop like a sous-chef.'

'I once fantasized about being a chef. I even took a class at California Culinary Academy, but another Escoffier I was not. I did learn to make a mean paella, and to appreciate cooking as an art.'

He finished his task in short order and whisked a handful of sharply sweet, well minced garlic onto a small plate that he brought to her. 'Here you are, my lady,' he said, with a mock bow. 'Smells delicious!'

'Let's see if you like the "grand" result first,' she teased. She dumped the additional minced cloves into the pan and continued stirring it into a gentle, fragrant boil, turning the heat down the instant pinprick bubbles appeared.

'Perfect! Thank you,' she said. She smiled. She kept stirring and soon the intoxicating aromas of drippings, herbs, wines and butter married into the distinctive fragrance that told her the mixture now had transformed into the creation she wanted.

'God! Yum!' he said, drawing a deep breath. 'What a delicious smell! You're making me very hungry,' he said, making double-entendre Groucho eyebrows at her.

She laughed. 'That's the point of gravy. Okay,' she said, and took another spoonful to taste. 'Want to try it?'

'Absolutely.' He stepped closer and opened his mouth wide, eyes closed like a baby bird. She gave him a generous taste, and laughed at his reaction. He held the gravy in his mouth a moment, swallowed, opened his eyes wide and jumped. 'Wow!' he exclaimed. 'That is great! That's the best I've ever tasted, no kidding!'

'Thank you,' she said. She handed him a wooden spoon. She turned the heat as low as it would go. 'Here,' she said. 'Your next assignment. Keep stirring the gravy so it cools a little and blends, while I wash the other pan in the sink. I hate to leave a mess.'

'Sure thing,' he said, and took up stirring as instructed. 'We should set this to music.'

Ida squinted. Was he coming on to her or just making more small talk? 'Thanks,' she said. 'Now, if you'll excuse me. Keep an eye on the gravy, while I look for that daughter-in-law of mine.'

'Kate? I saw her right out there on the patio,' he said, nodding towards a drape-covered sliding glass door on the opposite wall.

Ida walked to the door, pulled the drape aside, slid back the glass and stepped outside. She saw Kate sitting on a lawn chair by a trellis staring blankly at its wilted climbing roses. Her eyes were puffy and red.

'The turkey's ready to be served, honey,' Ida said as she approached. 'Are you okay?'

Kate looked up at her mother-in-law and burst into sobs. 'John's leaving,' she said. 'We're getting a divorce. You might as well know. Sorry to tell you like this.' She turned a tearful face away.

'Oh... poor baby,' Ida said. 'I don't know what to say... I'm so sorry, Kate.' She stepped close, crouched down and took one of Kate's hands. 'Oh,' she said again, sharply this time, and put one knee down to balance herself. 'Shouldn't have done that. These old knees.'

Kate took her hand, then helped her up. They hugged for a moment. Ida looked around over Kate's shoulder, eyes searching for any sign of her son.

'What happened?' Ida asked. 'What can I do to help?'

'Nothing,' Kate said. 'There's nothing you can do. You should talk to John.' Abruptly, making an effort, she said tightly, 'I think you're right. It's time to serve the turkey. Thank you.' Kate disengaged herself from their embrace.

'I will,' said Ida, 'but I think – I hope – you two will talk about it more. You should, really, before you call in the lawyers,' Ida said, and went silent just holding Kate until the younger woman's sobs subsided. Then Ida touched Joan's shoulder. 'Kate, honey, could you please tell me what's going on?'

'This seems so sudden. I didn't even know you two were having problems... other than, well, I know how John can be... maddening sometimes. But you love each other. You have the kids.'

Kate started crying again, this time tinged with anger. 'Tell him that! I think that jar has been emptied. 'I'm sorry," she said. 'This isn't how I wanted to tell you ...'

'Dinner is served ladies!' John popped his head out of the kitchen door momentarily and waved a hand at them, smiling as if nothing had happened, then disappeared.

'John?' Ida walked to the door and peered in just in time to see her son heading out the other door into the dining room carrying the golden brown, steaming turkey on a platter. Her table-mate Frank, still wearing the "Call-me-Cookie" apron, held the door open for John, then fetched a filled-up gravy boat from the counter and followed.

Ida went back to Kate. 'Come on, honey. Let's join your guests and eat before it gets cold. We'll go over everything after everyone's left.' Ida handed her a soft, clean napkin from a drawer. 'Here, darling. Wipe away the runny nose and tears. Remember. The drama may run high, but the dinner must go on.' That got a brave smirk from Joan. Ida put an arm around her daughter-in-law and guided her inside.

John carved the turkey. Kate passed side dishes and wine bottles around the table and made cheerful conversation as bravely as she could. The kids finally joined the adults at the table, sitting across from their grandmother.

Ida filled their plates and, to her annoyance, fought off tears herself, confused, and with a growing sense of loss that she could not yet define clearly. Stay out of it. John and Kate are adults. They'll work things out, one way or another. I can't do anything but make things worse if I meddle, she kept saying to herself, unconvinced. Not my life, not my business.

Neither Kate nor John, however, looked at each other all through the meal and the lively table chatter – though both stole guilty glances at Ida. Determined that the show must go on, Ida sipped, ate with her usual delicacy, and gave her compliments to Kate and John, as did the others.

'Good gravy, or, should I say, great gravy!' said Frank on Ida's other side, going for thirds while flashing cheer-up smiles at her. 'Here's to Kate and John for cooking a great meal.' He raised his glass, and everyone followed suit heartily. Ida smiled through clenched teeth and lifted her own glass in salute.

Later, she had to fight off drowsiness as the guests left, one by one. Ordinarily, she would have left by now herself. There was work to do, getting ready for tomorrow at her restaurant. Frank stayed until just a few guests remained, and unexpectedly, she found herself glad of his company. Low-key, solicitous and charming, he talked only enough for it to seem supportive.

'Well,' he said, after a decent interval, 'I suppose I ought to be going now, too. Can I offer you a ride?'

'Thank you, I have my car,' she said pensively.

He leaned forward and in a lower, more discreet voice murmured, 'Can we pretend that John and Kate didn't introduce us, so we can meet somewhere else and start over again?'

Startled, she laughed despite her growing melancholy. 'Sure,' she said after a few moments. 'Why not? Nowhere to go but up, after today.'

Not wasting any time, he said, 'Okay, for starters we could, you know "run into each other" say, in North Beach. I've been known to frequent Mario's Bohemian Café on the square at all hours.' He paused. 'Actually, I remember spotting you there, once or twice, you know. I could try to pick you up. See if I get to first base." He grinned.

She smiled back. 'Your timing is so, so wrong,' she said. 'But...' But something is cooking, she wanted to say.

'It's the only timing we happen to have right now,' he answered. 'I don't want to stick my nose in anyone's business, but -' He glanced to where Kate was now saying goodbye to the last of the guests in the living room, 'I've been through a lot with my own kid. Somehow things do work themselves out.'

'I suppose,' she sighed, her eyes on Kate too. 'But I'm

from the old school. Deep down I'm an old Sicilian nonna in a black dress and kerchief, trying to keep the ragout together in a world that tears us all apart.'

'Too many cooks spoil the ragout.' He smiled and paused. 'You know what to do, I'm sure,' he added, holding up a hand, trying to back off from seeming pushy. 'Here's my card.' He pointed at it, awkwardly, as if she wouldn't recognize what it was. 'There's my number. Thanks for talking – and please give my thanks to your son and daughter-in-law for inviting me.' He drew closer again and whispered, 'Your gravy was to die for.'

After Frank and the other guest had departed, Ida hovered just outside the front door before taking her own leave. She searched for the right words, and then, finding none, finally said, 'I don't want to talk in front of the children, but maybe one of you can call me later and tell me what's been going on here, please. This is new to me. I thought you two...'

Kate teared up again. "Not now, but, I don't know, in time..." she paused and shook her head. "John will have to tell you."

John said nothing.

Ida hugged each of them. 'Whatever happens, the best gift you two can give me is to try your best to work things out in some way that's good for these kids, as well as yourselves.'

'Okay. Okay. Thanks, mom,' said John sheepishly.

'Thanks, mama,' said Kate.

Ida turned up the stereo on the drive home in an attempt to drown out her gnawing curiosity and a sense of helplessness stretching down the road beyond her headlamps. She felt she was mourning her own life, and the transitory nature of existence along with the illusion of her son's happy marriage.

She rolled onto her brief driveway and clicked open the automatic garage door of her Russian Hills flat. She sat in her without going inside. Ordinarily, she would have phoned Kate soon as she got home. But the impulse choked her up now. Going inside seemed inappropriate. She shuddered at the thought of confronting her brightly hued, Joan Brown self-portraits, her Diebenkorns and the sunny wit of her Wayne Thiebeau San Francisco street scenes. They might distract her from this grief, but that wasn't what Ida wanted at the moment. Instead, she drove back down the hill and around to North Beach; by some small miracle and a prayer to the parking goddess, she found a space right off Washington Square.

It cheered her just to see people still crowding the sidewalks along the rows of cafés on a Sunday night. She walked over to Mario's, sat at the bar, and ordered a glass of Sangiovese.

She thought of phoning Frank. He had slipped her his number. She dismissed the impulse. If he walks in now, we have something special started, she said to herself, then shook her head at the silly romanticism of it.

'Have we met someplace?' came Frank's voice right behind her, making her jump. He sat next to her, laughed, and ordered a Birra Moretti.

'That's a terrible line,' she said.

'I wouldn't even call it a line,' he said. 'You come here often? What's your sign? Nice shoes.'

'My sign is "Do not disturb." But I'll make an exception, if you behave yourself,' she said.

'I promise to be bad,' he said, 'in a good way, of course.'

'I'm going to bend your ear, now,' she said. 'How good a listener are you? I need to talk.'

'Let's get a table.' He picked up her glass of Sangiovese and his beer, and together they stepped across to a vacant table.

3 MY DOG'S NAME

"Guess what I'm going to name my dog?"

"I give up, Winslow. What? " Harry Zucco searches the cabinets for sugar to stir into his coffee. He needs warming. Gobs of rain splatter the kitchen windows for the fourth straight day. Hates California, it's cold and its damp. The Pineapple Express they call it on the news. He might well have stayed in Chicago for Thanksgiving, but this is the only family he has, if he can call it that. He shuffles in red fuzzy slippers and a floral cotton bathroom borrowed from cousin Elizabeth. Why do kids have to be so damn perky in the morning?

"I'm going to name him..." Winslow pauses for suspense: "Kitty!"

"Kitty? You can't call him that!"

"Why?"

"The other dogs will tease him. They'll meow at him and yell 'here-kitty-kitty' when he comes by, and try to chase him up trees!" Harry arches his eyebrows and makes dog-and-cat sounds.

"But what if my dog can run really, really fast?" Winslow makes like a dog running in place.

"With a name like 'Kitty,' he'd better learn how to fight." Harry puts up his dukes and growls.

"Oh yeah? Woof! Woof! My dog can beat up anybody. I just give him the signal!" Winslow punches the air, snaps and snarls back.

Harry keeps looking. "Right here." Winslow stops and hands Harry the sugar bowl off the small, kitchen table. "Right in front of your nose." Meester. My dog would have found it like that!" Winslow tries to snap his fingers but makes no sound.

"Thanks, kid. I was just testing your powers of observation to see if you qualify for secret agent."

Harry stirs in two spoonfuls and takes his coffee mug into the living room.

Winslow grabs a power bar off the counter and follows, mocking Harry's swaying gait. "Okay Uncle Harry, What's the real name I'm giving my dog?"

Harry sits on the edge of Elizabeth's black leather sofa where he spent the night, and tries his coffee. Just right. "Okay... ah … Wolfgang? Or Lady Gargoyle? Maybe its a girl dog."

"Wrong again. My dog's name is Anubis."

"Ah ha! Now that's a cool name. Anubis – the jackal-headed Egyptian god of the dead, guardian of the lost souls and orphans!" Harry makes woo-woo sounds.

"I know, except about the orphan part."

"How do you know about Anubis?"

"Nickelodeon."

"Now you're going to name the dog Nickelodeon?"

"No. silly. House of Anubis is on Nickelodeon. It's about stupid teenagers living in a haunted house or something."

"Glad that's settled."

"Anyway, I'm an orphan – from Brazil. So, Anubis can guard me too."

"An orphan with privileges – and a mom." Elizabeth and Dr. Marcus adopted Winslow while they still were married. That was before Elizabeth took up with Jimbo, who used to play in Harry's band.

"Mama says your name means pumpkin in Italian."

"Yeah. You're up on everything, kid. Languages, Egyptian deities, the works."

"You're not orange, but you're the right shape."

"Everybody's a comedian."

"How come your name is different from ours, if your family?"

"Your mama took your daddy's name."

"You mean from Brazil?"

"No I mean from here. You know, when they adopted you."

"I don't remember him either. I remember somebody called me João." Winslow peels the wrapper off the power bar and bites off a chunk. "My dog's is black. He's a part German Shepherd with wolf mixed in."

"You've picked him out already?"

"I can see him."

"Where?"

"He's right here."

"You mean when you close your eyes."

"He's here when I close my eyes, or open them. Doesn't matter."

"I had a dog like that once when I was about your age." Harry sips more of his coffee. He moves a stack of sheet music and some magazines to set his mug down on the coffee table.

Elizabeth glides into the living room, coffee cup in hand. She's barefooted, looking good without makeup, in faded jeans and her red, Stanford University sweatshirt, her silky golden hair down and all over the place, as tall and lithe a woman as Harry is rotund. Seeing her, he grins, sits straighter and tries to pull in his gut. "Hey! Morning Liz. I see you found the coffee."

"Thanks for making it. How are you, Harry?"

"Okay." Harry raises his mug to her.

She hugs Winslow and kisses the top of his black mop. "Morning sweetie. Glad you got your power bar. I'll make you some eggs in a bit."

"It's okay, mom. I want a pop-up, in the toaster."

"Just for now, but don't fill up on it."

Elizabeth plops on a chrome and burgundy leather chair opposite Harry, tucking her feet up under her. She stares through the living room's sliding glass doors at the downpour wetting down the deck and obscuring the usual canyon view. She looks back at her son. "Winslow. Have you been pestering Harry about that dog again?" .

Harry intercedes. "Not a problem."

Winslow trots off to the kitchen for his pop tart. play-barking.

"Not so much noise, Winslow." Elizabeth puts her coffee mug on the coffee table. "Be careful with that toaster. No sticking forks in it."

Harry laughs.

She doesn't. "Drives me crazy, Harry. Every day its the same thing about dogs. I told him a million times we can't have a dog. We both work. Who would take care of it?"

Winslow yells from the kitchen: "I'll walk him twice a day and feed him and teach him tricks."

"Big ears." Elizabeth throws her voice back at him. "Maybe when you're older, Winslow. You're too young to go walking around this neighborhood yourself. They don't even have sidewalks on this road."

"Anubis will guide me. And he'll be protection. I'll teach him to attack on command. He's a police dog."

"Got an answer for everything."

Harry straightens the robe around him, a girlish gesture. "Smart kid. Like his mother."

"He comes up with a new name practically every day. And he knows all the breeds. He watches dog shows on TV. He's forever asking people about their dogs."

"I think he has an imaginary dog, same as I did as a kid."

"Winslow is a very literal child – and single-minded."

Winslow pipes in from the kitchen again. He's a real live dog!"

"I think your son can hear as well as any dog."

Elizabeth nods. "Anyway, whatever! No pets now, especially how things have been going. Plus Jimbo is allergic."

"What's happening with you and Jimbo?"

"I don't know, Harry. Can we not talk about that right now?"

"I just meant: Is it Jimbo versus a dog? Maybe I shouldn't meddle."

"Don't. Let's stick to dogs."

"Dog-no-dog." Harry puts his hands together prayerfully, then raises them palm out, guru-fashion. "The dog will appear when its true name is evoked."

Winslow runs halfway down the hallway, arms outspread. "Anubis has spoken!"

"God forbid! Winslow. Go back and put your dish away if you're finished."

"Didn't use a dish."

"Now I'll probably have to sweep."

"If we had a dog, he would eat the crumbs off the floor, and lick the dishes clean. You wouldn't need a dishwasher."

Winslow scampers back to the kitchen.

Elizabeth falls back against the couch and looks up at the ceiling.

Harry reaches over the pats her hand. "How about a hypoallergenic dog? Remember when President Obama and Michelle got Portuguese Water Dogs for their daughters?"

"No way. Jimbo read that's a myth about them not causing allergies. They're just easier to keep clean, and groom or something. Anyway, they cost a fortune."

Winslow reappears in the doorway again. "I know. I'll call him Barak!"

Harry smirks. "Bark?"

"Barak, Barak" Winslow imitates a dog again.

Harry joins in, "Bark, bark, barak, barak, woof, woof."

"God, Harry don't encourage him! Winslow! That's enough now! Stop it."

Winslow pauses and pants, holding his hands limp in front like paws.

"I'm muzzling you both." Elizabeth can't help but laughs. She drains her mug and takes it back to the kitchen. "All right, let's get going here. I ..."

A key in the front door, and Jimbo walks in, no umbrella, water dripping off his Levi jacket and black jeans, his running shoes tracking mud, his coppery hair flat against his skull, soaked from his brief climb upstairs. He had parked in the driveway that winds up to the house from the canyon road, their garage being filled with his sound equipment.

"Hey, hon." He slides a black, dripping overnight case off his shoulder.

Elizabeth glares at him.

"Did you get my text message? I tried to phone. Flight delayed. What a night!" Elizabeth shakes her head. "Please don't," she says. He notices Harry, and looks relieved. "Hey, guy. What are you doing here? Good to see you. Nice robe. You look so sexy in yellow and pink, and those slippers!"

"I came for the meeting, remember?"

"Oh yeah. Sure thing." Jimbo doesn't acknowledge the way his old friend Harry looks down and away.

Winslow runs in and goes to his mother's side. He doesn't say hello.

"Hey guy!"

Elizabeth prods the boy.

Winslow looks at Elizabeth then back at Jimbo.

"Hello, Jimbo. Uncle Harry is going to take me the shelter to pick out my dog."

"Jesus!" Elizabeth fumes.

Harry furrows his brow and hunches down a little.

Jimbo forces a smile. "Hey, Winslow. It's okay with me if it's okay with your mother. She's running for boss of everything around here."

"Don't play games, Jimbo and especially not with Winslow, goddamnit."

"Hey, sweetie. We' can discuss this later." He looks at the boy. "Hey, Winslow. You got that we were just gabbing – tossing ideas around, for someday, if you're a good boy and learn to behave."

"I'll decide that." Elizabeth fumes. Winslow's face pales and he disappears down the hallway, our of their sphere.

Gotta take a shower now and get some Zzzz's, Elizabeth. We can hash all this out. I have good news, believe me. But now I'm wiped." He takes the bag and retreats down a hall to a bedroom.

After a minute, Elizabeth follows Jimbo into the master bedroom. "We have to talk." Harry hears her say before shutting the door.

Harry carries his mug back to the kitchen.

My cousin Elizabeth. She sure knows how to pick them. Harry looks around. No Winslow. He shrugs. Must have gone to his room. He hears the TV. Worse thing, putting a TV set in a kids room. Still worse, what am I doing here? Why did I come out to L.A.? Whole place makes me sad.

------- -

Winslow pulls up the hood of his raincoat and walks around the back of the garage, careful to keep his footing on the muddy path between it and the chaparral. It's getting towards evening and the rain has let up a bit.

He carries a take-out bag from Burger King, snugly under his coat. He finds where the path splits off and follows it uphill, squeezing between tall sticky-branches of

Coyote Brush, up and up, slanting left from the house. The high brush gives way briefly to black stubble where a tongue of last summer's fire reached. He knows the pathway well enough not to lose it through the stubble and back into high brush. Winslow reaches a small, natural, domed clearing sheltered under a cluster of dark, evergreen California live oak.

The red flat, sandy floor of the chamber remains dry, even in the heavy rain. A wooden salad bowl he filled with leftovers yesterday stands empty. He takes a cheeseburger from the bag and places it in the bowl, along with several hot dogs pilfered from his mother's refrigerator. "Wooooo! Here, Anubis!" He steps back and sees a pair of yellow eyes staring at him from the brush.

"Anubis! Good boy!"

The eyes move closer. Winslow moves several paces back from the bowl and feels the twisting black trunk of the evergreen oak against his back. He checks for handholds to climb the tree in case of trouble. The creature slinks slowly out of the brush towards the bowl, glancing warily in Winslow's direction. It's face is open, playful-mischievous, large eyes knowing, curved fangs peeking but not drawn, alert pointed ears, long, over-large paws – long-nailed toes with talons, lanky legs giving it an adolescent gait, its rangy body rich with gray-brown and black fur and busy tail, tucked low at first, then relaxing out to its full magnificence as he secures the meaty contents of the bowl in his mighty jaws, keeping eyes on Winslow.

"Anubis." Winslow whispers it this time. The rain resumes, harder again, pelting the canopy of leaves above him and drizzling down here and there.

The stately beast stops, as if deciding not to run off after all, but simply stare back at this small boy. Winslow thinks he sees mirth in Anubis eyes.

The creature chomps and downs all the victuals in a few gulps, then eyes Winslow, head lowered, one paw out as if in polite introduction. Winslow steps closer and extends a hand. The creature sniffs it and seems to nod and okay, allowing it closer until Winslow rests his palm on the animal's wide massive head. The fur feels velvety as he strokes it softly, then steps back, hands at his side.

Flashes light up the chamber, followed by rolling thunder drawing closer and closer. Winslow hears the rain pounding against the thick tree branches above him. Streams of water fall through gaps here and there, harder and harder.

"Here, Anubis." Winslow reaches into the paper bag and pulls out some remaining french fries. The animal raises its head and sniffs them haughtily, then takes a few, downing them tentatively, leaving the rest. Winslow dumps the rest of the fries in the bowl, which Anubis ignores now, perhaps disdainfully leaving the rest for raccoons.

---- -----------

Harry goes to the sliding glass doors overlooking the deck, glistening wet, on its stilts jutting out from the hillside. He watches the panorama lit successively by anonymous flashes. The thunder rattles the windows now. It reminds Harry more of prairie thunderstorms rolling towards the lake back home in Chicago, except it hangs there over them, slowed by the coastal mountains as it blows in from the Pacific.

At home, he always felt that he could stand on solid ground, come what may, but not in this city of slippery slopes, shaky ground, Apocalyptic fires, mudslides and slick hustlers, of maybes and wannabes, of crossing fault lines no matter where you stand, of freeways of people rushing nowhere.

"What the hell is that?" The rumbling changes. It seems to come from below now, getting louder. He feels the house shaking. Is it an earthquake? Can't be a tornado in the Santa Monica Mountains. Then he sees it. "Elizabeth! Get over here and take a look at this!"

Jimbo and Elizabeth come out of the bedroom where

they have been yelling at each other. They get to the glass doors just in time to see their hillside seem to give way suddenly, collapsing like a tent with the pole removed. The house sways and jolts violently, forward, knocking them to the floor. Everything speeds up. "What the fuck? Oh shit!"

--------------- -----

Winslow follows Anubis higher up along the narrow path through the dense hillside brush. The footing is slippery. Rain cascades over the top of his hood obscuring his vision, but he navigates keeping eyes on the tip of the coyote's tail, raised high. Finally, they find shelter under a rocky outcropping. Winslow turns and looks back just in time to see the hillside below them give way – as if a giant scooped out a huge semicircle of earth, and become a viscous mass enveloping houses and streets below. Somewhere down there, his house, his mother, Harry, Jimbo, but that cannot be.

He looks hard. What's left: a few unattached roofs,? They all look alike. Suddenly, it didn't happen. He cannot comprehend it. He turns to Anubis, who moves closer and sits. He puts one arm around the creature and rests against the dry rocks, rain pouring down on all sides.

He hears words unspoken but clearly in his mind. "The end of the world." It keeps repeating. Then: "Worlds end and come into existence all the time. You are in one now. Our world. It is your world now too. Anubis will protect you." Winslow feels the warmth of this creature spreading within himself.

"Here near ground zero, Dave, we see emergency personnel from all over the region moving in. They've moved heavy digging equipment forward in this driving rain, in the hope of finding survivors of the mudslide that all but buried this hillside neighborhood just a few hours ago.

"No sense of relief yet, Dave... Authorities have counted twelve dead, fifteen injured, with a score more residents missing so far and some say as many as a double that with fifty homes destroyed. We hope to know more when Fire Rescue Captain Bill Zonga makes a statement to the press expected soon. This is Shirley Wu, in Malibu Canyon for KCBS."

Shirley Wu, in her familiar yellow rain slicker - the TV news second stringer familiar to viewers whenever there is a storm or local disaster, weaves among the emergency workers and knots of stunned, silent onlookers who have come out from their houses along the canyon road, talking to people here and there, then sets up again with her cameraman. He pans past red-blinking emergency vehicles and shows the road blocked by a mountain of mud and rocks, with water still streaming down the roadway seemingly from beneath it.

"Shirley Wu, back here at this scene of this incredible disaster, Dave, still waiting for word from our fire captain. What you see is only a portion of the gigantic slide from the collapse of water-logged mountainside here only hours ago. We still don't have a count, but the casualties may run high, one official told me. Meanwhile, in just one of many tragedies, I'm told that one woman survived when part of the house where she and a cousin were standing was sheared off by the massive slide, pushing them down the canyon ahead of it as if they were riding a surfboard. Her husband and son, however, apparently were in another part of their house that was completely engulfed and buried, probably under millions of tons of earth and rocks."

"I have at least one name for you Dave. Apparently, former child star Elizabeth Parker, of the popular family TV sitcom, The Peppers, is among the injured. Rescue workers pulled her and her cousin, identified as Harry Zucco, from the wreckage. They both suffered serious injuries, including broken bones, and were rushed to a nearby hospital, but not before Ms. Parker made a impassioned plea to find her son, who apparently also was in their house when the slide hit. Let's take a look."

Wu cues those in the TV truck as the camera cuts away for the segment. "Please.. My son, Winslow... if anyone here can locate him..." Elizabeth, pale, her eyes sunken, hair spattered with mud, neck wrapped in a brace speaks as she's been taken to an ambulance on gurney.

"Shirley Wu, again. A few minutes ago, I talked to one of the engineers on the scene, who unfortunately held out little hope that the woman's son or her husband, in the house as well, could be found alive, or even if remains could be identified if they were buried. But workers haven't given up hope for them and the many others up this road, which unfortunately at this moment is blocked by a wall of mud and rock. They intend to keep digging. The engineer I spoke to said that the force of such a mountainside collapse could pulverize nearly everything under its direct path. We'll be following up soon as we hear more. This is Shirley Wu, KCBS News, Los Angeles,. Back to you Dave."

----------- -----

A book about the disaster, written several years later by Shirley Wu, starts out: "What followed the Malibu Hills-Paradise Canyon tragedy has been the subject of many accounts, some of them fantastic, meant only metaphorically perhaps. No one will know for sure. All versions could well be true, in superposition. For what are we in any moment but how we perceive ourselves and allow ourselves to be perceived?"

----------- -----

I liked this boy. I liked that he called me by my ancient name, or one of the names of ancients passed down. Then they called me jackal. Here they call us all coyote, though some of us are more than others. Blanca took to him, as well, or the others might have seen him as a good hearty meal or two. She let him suckle with the other cubs, big as he was, like in the stories told by long ago humans. Not the humans here now, fools, oblivious, half blind, gobbling up the earth with their smoke belching, farting, roaring monster-chuggers everywhere. They make messes and foul the air. We tolerate these interlopers for various dubious reasons, most of all because they leave a lot of food around for us in their heedless fouling - all free and easy to take, or catch with little trouble like their fat cats and lapdogs.

The others scoffed, but I saw the immediate advantage of having a member of our family with opposable thumbs – convenient for getting us into things – and able, under certain conditions, to speak to bumbling bipeds in their own tongue and still be on our side. He thereby increases our potential for guile exponentially, or will, once trained to our purposes, this boy. Of course he cried for his mother at first, and, he will always lack the strength and agility of other cubs, but we do not ask him to hunt rabbit.

Some of my brothers look askance at Blanca and I for adopting this bipedal pup. They it threatens our independence and ancient ways, what separates us from dogs. But the boy is more one of us than of the house dwellers. This will become evident as he draws strength and inner guidance as from the milk of Blanca, her wisdom. He shows talent for our coyote arts -- creating illusions and shape shifting. I am teaching him how to stow his all his vital aspects and his mortality in the tip of his finger, just as we coyotes can do in the tip of our tails. I say this advisedly, for lapses could prove be dangerous.

------------------ –

It was first time Winslow felt at one with them – and felt the tearful cloud of homesickness lift from him. All this came with the pizza, extra-large, double-cheese, with sausage, olives and pepperoni, steaming with herbal redolence in its leatherette warmer. Winslow remembered that this same, gawky delivery boy, with the vacant blue eyes, head-bobbing, with ear-phonic hip-hop, had come to his house once during the time before the world ended.

Now he recognized the battered red-and-yellow minivan with the Angelo's sign on top.

The delivery boy had driven up a long dark driveway of a large house high up in Malibu canyon, just one on his route that night. The boy got out of his car, carrying two pizzas boxes and a bag of sides, and rang the doorbell. They let him in, possibly while figuring the bill - good luck for Winslow and Anubis. The car, engine running, steamy in the cool night, lights on, beckoned.

Winslow trembled. Dim memories propelled him, as from a dream one tries to remember - hunger gnawing, a constant of *favela* life, toddling after his sister Tica, climbing a mound of garbage. The smells. Better smells now, deliciously seeping from the car as he pulled the door handle.

Anubis could not have opened such a door, but Winslow did it with ease. He took the wide pizza - bigger than a full rising moon at sunset - off the passenger seat, proud as they ran off with it into the high chaparral. By now Winslow could see in moonlit darkness almost as well as his dog-coyote.

The aroma of cheese, cooked meat and red sauce filled his nostrils and made his mouth water. But Winslow showed worthy self-discipline and followed Anubis to their den burrowed under the outcropping. Blanca looked up and the cubs dropped their mouse jerky soon as they saw Winslow. From then on, they gave the cub human a name of his own, *"Chaka'Tek'Poha"* – "Bringer of Great Bounty." "Chaka" for short. The cubs would tell their children and grandchildren one day of how he tricked the giant four-pawed rumble-beast and stole its cheesy treasure. After the feast, Anubis and Blanca climbed to the top of the hill behind the den and howled for a long while, letting the others know of their good fortune to which answers came echoing through the canyon, putting chill in the bones of humans in their yellow-lit houses.

-------------- -----

This isn't the way Harry dreamed about being with Elizabeth as they were growing up together around Chicago. Second cousins could marry. Or was it cousins twice removed? He could never get that straight. Genetics would have been moot, anyway, because Elizabeth could not have children. They were not really cousins anyway. Elizabeth was his grandfather's daughter, a late child with the old man's Ukrainian trophy wife, Elena, therefore, technically, his great aunt, even though a year his junior. It was easier to say they were cousins.

After his mother fell ill, when he was 11, he spent summers at his grandfather's big house in Evanston facing the lake, and eventually stayed through the school year through high school. Grandpa and Elena had servants and an au pair who was supposed to shepherd the two kids, which meant they pretty much had the run of the place.

With or without her leg, he found Elizabeth attractive, not only for her severe beauty, but her ways, even of being troublesome at times. An apartment in Santa Monica, subsidized by FEMA, accommodated well enough for convalescence, shared with Harry, achy on the mend himself. Harry worked on his patience. She could be difficult, mercurial, blowing up at little things, Harry knew, to relieve all the regrets and anger at Jimbo and mostly herself. "We never would have moved into that place but for him. Why didn't I get Winslow that dog? Tell me that, Harry!"

"Hey, Liz, I know. But you can't be God. You can't move mountains or stop rain, or hold back a mudslide. You would have worked all the rest out. It's just the stuff that happens..."

"Like 'shit happens?' I don't get that and I don't get that 'act of God' shit either."

"I don't get anything, myself, Liz.'

"Who's going to want a one-legged actress?"

"Me.... Anyway, you're more than that."

Elizabeth picks up the remote and clicks on a reality

show. She can't stand them. Fitting punishment.

Harry hobbles to the kitchen. "I'll make us some lunch."

------- -----------

Detective Sergeant Agnes Cranberry drives up a ravine road in the Santa Monica Mountains. Almost two years since the big slide and they still have only one lane open. Several miles in, she reaches a paved driveway with a tall iron gate, announces her name and flashes her ID at the Web cam monitor. Then a steep drive up through a canopy of date palms to the house.

Agnes has only seen photos of the place - a faux Moorish affair, but with odd angles and a lots glass to accommodate the panorama. You might say, Frank Lloyd Wright on hashish. It squats on a shelf carved from a hillside facing the Pacific, shimmering silver, blue and green in the distance on this already warm morning, as the coastal mist burns off.

A maid opens the wide, carved oak front door for Agnes and her rookie partner, Javier – aka Dave – Saldana. The maid shows them to a flagstone patio – wide as a ballroom floor – where Indira Bhatt-Macht is having tea in a chaise lounge after swimming her morning laps in their mosaic-tiled pool. She invites them to sit at a glass-topped table facing the sea.

"Will bagels do?" Ms. Bhatt-Macht's buttery tease befits a Bollywood beauty, though she's getting a little old for those extravaganzas, having settled down with billionaire developer Warren Macht now. She's playful, but in her manner reminds these two working stiffs that neither will of them will ever be her neighbors here atop the hills of Paradise Canyon Estates - Mr. Macht's crown jewels, second to her, of course.

"Can't get enough, Ma'am." Agnes plays along. "With cream cheese? Lox, maybe?"

"Please call me Indira. With a latte of course, I would expect nothing less of Malibu's finest." She claps lightly and sends the maid off to fetch the order.

Dave flashes his badge. "We're with the sheriff's department, Ma'am. This strip is unincorporated. I'll take just coffee black please."

"Whatever, my darlings. Let us get down to business. I had my secretary write a list of what was taken. You'll find a copy in the folder on the table. She also should have e-mailed it to you."

Agnes slides over the folder and opens it. "The Malibu police forwarded it to us, too, Ma'am. We just want to ask about a few items and inspect the door where the perpetrators broke in, then have a look around, if you don't mind."

"Of course. We went over that with the police that came when we called, but I'll be glad to cooperate if you think that will help."

"Thank you." Agnes directs this to the maid who arrives with the bagels and coffees. Then to Indira: "What do you estimate the paintings were worth? I don't see that here."

"You'll have to ask, my husband. He's in Mumbai now on business.

"A similar Klimt fetched $20 million at Sothebys recently."

"Well, then, officer. You certainly do your homework."

"We just want to find out how much you had it insured for. It might help in tracking it, if someone tries to unload." Agnes helps herself to a bagel which she laces generously with lox and schemer.

Saldana refrains. "Ms. Roscoe: what about these other items – a strange assortment: you've listed a half-wheel of Parmigiano-Reggiano. Is that right?"

"Concetta, our cook, noticed it missing, along with a Parma ham."

"I read that you were a vegetarian."

"Fan gossip. I am, mostly, but Warren loves Italian."

"I hear that you own a castle in northern Italy? Any trouble there."

"That's where we were when the break in happened. What are you driving at, detective?"

Agnes ignores the prod. "Wasn't this place guarded? The report says your alarm system went off."

"Useless. The groundskeeper fell off a ladder the week earlier and was in the hospital, unfortunately, and the alarm company sent a patrol, but, as you may guess, it was too late. Absolutely useless, those people. Let me tell you."

Agnes took her time finishing the bagel. Then went back to the list. "If that's the case, how do you think the intruders, whoever they were, would have had time to take so many oddball things – for example, your son's running shoes, a pair of designer jeans and two sweat shirts, plus silverware and carving knives. Why would jewel and art thieves mess with that stuff?"

"That's your job, to figure out these things." Indira sits forward. "Never mind all of that, officers. What about my little Binko? I wouldn't give cow poop about the rest if you can just just find my Binko." Her eyes shine with tears as she turns sideways to the light as if for a close up.

"Your yorky?"Agnes reaches to pat her arm. "Sorry for your loss." Agnes didn't mean for the automatic sarcasm of too many police calls. "We're checking. Could be the dog just ran away when the burglars broke in. Or, it could be they took the dog for ransom. These things happen."

"But what about the dog droppings on my carpet – not little Binko's, but very large, like from a big dog?" Indira squints and wrinkles her nose.

Agnes looks at Dave, then down at the report, then back to Indira. "I'm sorry to have to tell you this, but our lab report said that was coyote scat. One or two might have come into the house through a broken door after the burglary, and ... "

"Oh my God! Do you think? Oh, my poor Binko.

This has been going on, all this trouble in the canyon with coyotes. The homeowner's association wants to hire a bounty hunter."

Dave raises an eyebrow. "I believe that's illegal without a special permit, Ma'am."

"Don't get me wrong. I don't believe in harming any animals. But poor Binko!"

Agnes stands. "We believe it's purely coincidental. The burglars left your sliding doors open and those critters waltzed in. May we take a look inside at those doors and the rest of the crime scene, please."

"The other police went over all that, but if you insist."

"Again, sorry for the inconvenience, Ma'am."

Agnes drives them down to Pacific Coast Highway after the interview, silent all the way until they park in a public lot off Pacific Palisades beach. They can see the Ferris wheel turning on Santa Monica Pier to the south of them. The sun is high overhead now, the water a deeper blue green. The tide is coming in. Big breakers today after a few days of storm. "I find this a good place to think." She gets out of the sheriff department sedan. Dave seats himself on the hood, his feet on the front bumper looking out to sea.

Agnes muses. She stands, hands on hip, as if meeting the waves. She is a tall, straight-backed woman with a long face. Her wide, dark, inquisitive eyes peer from under an assertive brow. Her aquiline nose seems to be constantly testing the air. She wears her hair pulled back, with a jet black braid spiraled atop her head. When let down, her hair reaches the small of her back, straight and thick, a gift from the Dakota Nation half of her heritage

"Consider these facts together, my friend – the third burglary up there in as many weeks, each with the same M.O. Each time we find scat and other evidence of animal intrusions. Then we have the locals up in arms about a so-called coyotes, a nice red herring to distract us. Now we have random shootings in the canyon, and the a jogger who was winged but turned out to be on anti-coagulants and bled to death in the ER. So now that's murder."

"That's in LAPD's hands, and they have a drug dealer they like for that."

"It's no drug killing, and they know it. They just want to keep caseload down, and they probably wanted that gangsta for something else they couldn't make stick."

Dave lights a cigarette and puffs. "Okay, you got a bunch of puzzle pieces that might just fit together, but you won't close anything unless you have the right ones. Then again, you know these canyons. Shit always happens, lots of it random. Some of it spooky – all kinds of critters and creatures lurk in the shadows, some human, some animal, some neither."

"Trust me, we're on to something, Saldana."

"What do you mean, me, kimosabe?" Dave stuffs his cigarette out in the ashtray. "Gotta clean that tray out before we turn this car back in."

"Don't look at me. I don't smoke. You're lucky I put up with you doing it."

Dave takes a long breath. "Okay. I see it coming. You got one of your hunches, again. Right? Doesn't matter what the official line is."

"*Verdad!*"

"Go on. Spit it out. You suspect the husband."

"Bingo. It's always the husband."

"What about motive? The guy's filthy rich. He's a developer and an investment banker. He doesn't need to be a burglar when he has a license to rob us all blind and without ever getting shit on his Guccis."

"Rich on paper. Do the words, real estate crash and great recession mean anything to you?"

"Warren Roscoe has enough heft to throw you, me and this car right over those hills into the drink, boss. Half the mayors and Board of Supervisors are in his pocket, not to mention our esteemed boss, Sheriff Hazlett."

"But a fatal flaw, as well, Saldana, like them all, hubris. Greed, my friend, greed. They gotta make more and more, slice and dice assets, leverage and squeeze profit out of every rock and pebble in these mountains if they can until it all crashes down."

"Your forgetting one thing, Agnes."

"What's that?"

"Ever since Shirley Wu did that dopey segment on Channel 2, the media has gone ape shit over this 'Coyote Canyon Marauder' angle. You know very well that Sheriff Hazlitt, Supervisor Tepet and the developers around here will be in our faces unless we show some results on that instead of wool gathering the way you're doing now."

Agnes puts a fist near her mouth and mimics static. "Attention passengers: The captain has turned on the seat belt sign. Turbulence ahead."

"First thing is, we're going to talk to this Roscoe guy, just routine at his office, but lean on him and see what we shake loose."

------------- ----------

Pete Smark rests against a scrub oak obscured by prickly tangles of buckthorn, toyon, greasewood and assorted chaparral. He still itches from last week's stumble into poison oak. This is as good a blind as he can find in the patchy, uneven cover, looking at an angle down to the fire trail from where scrambled up unreliable sand, adobe and rock. Everything smells of dust, sage and pungent, oily branches with their hard berries and myriad, waxy, dwarfed leaves.

The stored heat of a summer scorcher radiates from the ground, as he waits for darkness in a dry sweat. He chases down his chronic apprehension and resentment with a hit of vodka-spiked lime Gatorade. Tastes like piss. Won't help his aim. But hey, this AK-47 that he picked up in Yuma beats that .22 peashooter from before. He can lay down enough fire so that accuracy won't matter much.

He's taking a big chance bringing any rifle out here

again after accidentally winging that jogger – damn fool, out on this trail after dark. That's why he got rid of the .22. But, damn, two weeks of laying out poison and traps have got him nothing but rodents, couple of possums, a raccoon, a feral cats, and somebody's runaway Yorkshire terrier, poor little bastard. No coyotes.

But there's a good bet now, with a full moon rising, that the yellow-eyed devils will be loping along the fire trail below him once the sun sets. It's the quickest way to easy pickings back of the gated abodes of Paradise Canyon Estates. Bang, bang, bang, by dawn he'll have cut him off some tails to show Warren Roscoe to pay up, like he promised, the tight sonofabitch. The real estate market is crappy enough without wild rumors of coyotes marauding around the properties he developed. Paradise, my ass.

---------------- ---- -------

Chaka has overcome my reservations. He learns ways of Trickster with surprising ease. He is still too eager, though, to play in the realm of magic - always risky - and to hunt, likewise too risky, and unreliable as well. I prefer prestidigitation.

The boy developed his powers well on his own, having natural talent. After all, he summoned me in the first place as a mere cub. As he had become part of our little family, I took on the task of teaching him the artful dodges of our kind, along with the cubs, growing up and ready now themselves, almost.

He takes to his tasks quickly. "It's all in the eyes, Chaka'Tek'Poha. Hold your adversary's eyes with yours, and you can direct or misdirect their attention at will. In that moment, I make my move – creating illusions, sowing confusion, striking or transforming to our ends – for we never hunt alone. Now a full moon rises, giving good light tonight. Time to go forth."

---------------------- -

"I dreamed about Winslow again last night."

Harry waited, not pressing Elizabeth, out on the Santa Monica Freeway doing 70. He watched the endless, wide river of traffic in which they moved, packed just shy of clumping into a jam. Then he checked Elizabeth's Levi-clad, prosthetic right leg working the pedals of his leased Prius. She seems to be handling matters just fine on this, her maiden voyage since the end of everything. She's had the prosthetic leg a good while now, and months of therapy. It's a high-tech, lightweight, wonder of its kind. She looked to have mastered it – moving almost naturally. Nevertheless, Harry had continued to chauffeur – not so much because of her disability, but out of habit, and, to be honest, as a guy thing. Then, the other day, she called him on it and took the wheel - another healthy sign.

With Harry about to go on tour, opening for The Duchess de Dada, Elizabeth would have to fend for herself. She had reached a point of nearly overcoming her physical injuries. The psychic damage, not so much. Her bouts of depression persisted. He picked up her prescriptions for this regularly – another good sign. To his relief, she curbed her drinking. Her appetite returned somewhat. Weed, meditation and time coaxed her back to something akin to being the Elizabeth he once knew, though never fully.

She had started to write. Best of all, she had work again – voice acting. She had always been great with voices, a natural mimic as a kid. Helen, her agent, from the old days, came through with several commercials. "They love you, Elizabeth. You voice comes across as reassuring, young, yet maternal, upbeat with a just enough sex appeal."

"Thanks, Helen. I guess that's why I'm so perfect for candy coating horrendous lists of horrendous side effects in drug commercials, or telling viewers that their oil company really cares about them."

"Don't knock it, Liz. It's a living. I'm working on better." True to her word, Helen soon had Elizabeth up for a supporting role in an HBO series about Leon Trotsky. At the moment, meanwhile, she landed a character voice role in an animated feature scheduled by Dreamworks.

Lance Crowley, the director from London, called for a read-through this morning at the lavish hilltop house he is renting in Malibu Canyon. The prospect put Elizabeth in a cold sweat. She had become phobic about driving into any canyons since the disaster and panicky even at the sight of the open sea on television. She had to take tranquilizers when it rained, and wore ear plugs during storms. She was working on all of this. Fortunately – for her in any event – a drought year followed that of the mudslide.

She wanted Harry to accompany her to the meeting. He talked her out of it, promising he would get her to the door and pick her up afterward. He suggested that she drive as well. Better that she feel a sense of control. He'd be there if it got scary.

They continued in silence for a ways. Harry noted her knuckles whitening on the steering wheel. "Ah... so, what about this dream? Do you mind? What do you recall?"

"I woke up and walked into the kitchen. You know: one of those dreams where you think you woke up but you're really still in bed asleep? It was dim, just first morning light. Half in shadow, I see a boy. I know it's Winslow. My heart skips. But he's taller than Winslow, and then the boy has the head of a dog, or a jackal, or a coyote – like one those Egyptian gods. He's taking stuff out of the refrigerator, then putting it out on the kitchen table where three other coyote boys sit playing cards - like that goofy dogs-playing-poker painting. Then the first coyote boy hands me a drawing. It's of me. Very strange."

"Maybe you're picking up a memory about Winslow naming his imaginary dog after the Egyptian god, Anubis, who had a jackal head."

"Well, now I remember, this Winslow-coyote-boy spoke to me in some odd language that sounded maybe Native American, or could have been ancient Egyptian … I don't know. But I just knew from his voice and eyes that it was Winslow. I cried his name and tried to put my arms around him. They they he and the others suddenly ran out through the back door. I tried to run after him,but my legs sunk into mud just outside. Then I woke up. Damn it." She wiped her with one hand. "Damn it. Damn it!"

"Hey, it's going to be all right, Liz. Look, there's an exit. Let's get off here and grab a quick coffee. I can drive us the rest of the way."

Elizabeth straightened up and drew a deep breath. "It's all right, Harry. I can do this." She wiped away the tear with the back of her right hand, then reached to Harry's hand where it rested on his leg, giving it a gentle squeeze. He lifted it gently to his lips, before letting her return it to the steering wheel. "Thank you, Harry. Thank you for everything, you dear, funny man."

------------------ ----------

Detective Cranberry knew these back roads and fire trails well from her patrol days. But her partner still gripped the side of the door hard around precarious hairpins and over impossible gullies. She took out one of the department's all-wheel, Jeep Grand Cherokees for the afternoon, she said, "for Coyote Burglar investigation," officially anyway.

"Saldana teased her about it. "Hey, cop a plea, boss lady. You just want an excuse to play cowboy with this big machine."

Agnes made a fist. "Watch out there, esse. Yo soy muy macha!"

"You don't really expect to find clues up here. It's too rough a for a perp with all that stuff."

"Think about the Roscoe house. The Klimt painting alone, wouldn't fit in a car." Agnes spoke straight ahead, as if to herself. "Nobody saw any vans or trucks around that time, and that includes the gate guards - at least when they weren't getting stoned. The remote cams were of no use. Half of them don't work or point the wrong direction, the rest showed no unusual vehicles."

"Maybe the perp took the canvas off the frame and rolled it up."

"Not enough time." Agnes hit the brakes as they came out of a curve. Wind gusts rocked the jeep, high up now on this narrow dirt road, with hardly a shoulder and a rocky drop-off on the passenger side. The later it got the harder the hot, dry Santa Ana blew. "Whatsa matter, Javier? You look a little 'chile verde' there."

"Screw you, Ags..."

"Dream on, Saldana. You know I like pussy."

"Me too."

"We have so much in common."

"Made for each other. Shit, why stop here?" Saldana didn't relish the idea of having to drive back out on these treacherous roads after dark, even with Agnes at the wheel.

"Look!" Agnes pointed up the steep hillside to their left.

----- ---------------- -

"And now over to Shirley Wu in SkyCam One. What's the latest on this fire, Shirley?"

Lots of noise from the chopper. Shirley, wearing a headset, looks pertly into a shaky camera. "The news is not good, Dave. As long as this wind keeps up, fireman can't predict when they might have it under control. All they can do is try to isolate the houses that they're able to protect down along the road. What with the fire so big, they can't do much for homes higher up this road. They've already evacuated a thousand homes and plan more. The fire already has burned up and over the top of the range and covers a large area now, along the ridges from the ocean into Malibu Canyon almost as far as Thousand Oaks. As you can see, aerial bombers are dropping water and chemicals."

The TV wobbles as the helicopter tilts for a better view of the cargo plane releasing it's load on a burning slope, orange flames licking upwards, curtains of of gray black smoke catching the sunset colors as the rising ominously to the stratosphere.

"Any casualties?"

"So far, fire command reports six firefighters with minor injuries, Dave, but at least two deaths, they believe, caused by an accident during evacuation."

"Any idea how the fire started?"

"Unknown at this point, Dave. But probably man made, whether deliberate or not. Investigators will have to wait for now."

Indira Bhatt-Macht clicked off the TV and took one last look around. Concetta the maid waited out in the Benz with as much as they could pack in a hurry, with priority to Indira's shoes and originals. She held Cèsar - her recently adopted Chihuahua - in one arm, yapping and licking her face. No word from Warren, and nothing more to say, anyway.

Jimmy, the pool boy who happened by, had been recruited to hose down the roof of the house. Time to evacuate - in fact, not just to the local YMCA shelter, but as far away as she could get with the bricks of cash and a first class ticket back to Mumbai in her black snakeskin Hermés Birkin handbag.

---------- --------------- -

It's so easy to slip over the line when you run a hot start-up enterprise like mine. The way Warren looks at it, the faster you take off, the quicker you can fly straight into trouble, with everyone - investors, confidantes and competitors alike - looking to shoot you down in flames. Trust no one, especially your friends, especially your wife.

All the big boys know to take no prisoners, and that sooner or later, corners have to be cut, rules have to be broken, heads broken if it comes to that. Survival of the fittest. Let the devil take the hindmost. The unseen hand guides the market, but if you don't watch your back, the unseen fist will be up your ass faster than you can check your stock quotes.

Warren sits on a lawn chair in the grand formal dining room of an unsold hillside McMansion, one of his best, he thought, but never occupied. Bad timing. He swigs Cognac des Borderies XO straight from the bottle, his second of the day - might as well - and the sun - merciless today - has yet to dip into the Pacific, which he could see beyond the hills if he had not drawn all the blinds. He prefers to stare at the magnificent Gustav Klimt mounted on the wall opposite him - to forget everything in this Sapphic allegory of three women - as they say, who look naked in lothes and clothed in their nakedness.

What does all the rest matter.? If only he had pursued his artistic dreams and not the god-almighty dollar. Where would he be now? Not headed for ruin or worse. If he were poor, he might not be happy, but perhaps he would have captured and developed something more in himself, so lost now. But he's not poor, only precarious in ill-gained his affluence. It comes with the territory, he muses. Now he seeks only the numbness and sense of well being provided by fine French Cognac to wash down the pills.

He forgot the gun out in the car – perhaps subconsciously on purpose. Maybe he wasn't ready to cash in. He had a plan, and it still could work. That lady sheriff doesn't have anything but a lot of speculation.

Father warned you'd amount to nothing. He said, 'straighten up, be a man.'

But I showed him. I've got more than he ever had at my age.

A billion? A striver like Warren can never have enough to stave off his fear of losing it all? Markets dive. Competitors eat your lunch and insiders stab you in the back. Schemes unravel- even the legal ones constructed by lizard lawyers and greedy bankers. Their best laid plans crash. They bail out in time, usually, but leave fools like Warren holding the bag. They would never let him in their club. They would take their fees and drank his cognac and ate his steaks before it was over. *I'll not give up my Klimt, though. I won't lose that.*

Warren picks a large, open tin of Russian Beluga Caviar Malossol off the floor by his chair, scoops out a mouthful with three fingers and washes it down with more well-aged cognac. It's all turning to shit, he knows it – with that dyke sheriff sniffing around. She's got nothing, but she'll keep on it. He knows the type. And the feds are closing in, looking at his books. He didn't plan an escape. It was all legal, he reasoned, his God-given American right to take what he wanted and let the suckers worry about the rest. Fuck grandma and her pension, fuck Mr. & Mrs. Wannabe Yuppie buying up what they couldn't afford, screw those Muppets buying up overpriced, phonied-up shares. They're no better than him.. Caveat emptor! What happen to that?

Something seems to move in his peripheral vision as he sets down the bottle. Gray fur, yellow eyes. He turns, scooting his chair around, not bothering to stand up.

Out of nowhere, a pair of lanky coyotes regard him from the kitchen area. Or is it a wild boy covered in dust, and with a coyote? No. Can't be. One clutches a long, French baguette in its mouth, still in its wrapping. The other munches the remaining slices of a pizza that Warren brought with him last night. When it's done, it eyes his tin of caviar.

"Deja vu. Just in time for the festivities, you hairy bastards. I figured you'd get here sooner or later. You followed me into all those other houses, didn't you?"

The smaller one, half-boy, seems to speak. "*Você tem mal tudo que você tocar, mas você não pode derrotar-nos...*"

"*Buenos noches to you too, little fucker. Come to get your treats?* I'll give them too you, all right..."

"... for the last time. But first I'll say thank you, boys! You gave me cover. Your marauding proved a perfect distraction for the cops and all the upstanding citizens in the canyon. Sorry to say, your services are no longer needed. You give Paradise Canyon Estates a bad name. So, to give the story credibility, management – that's me – will have to put an end to you."

Warren takes another swig, then laughs. "Never no mind. Fuck it! You're lucky, for now." Warren remembers his gun is in the Mercedes outside.

Pete could show up. He was supposed to get coyote tails to prove Warren was on top of the problem. He must have missed these coyotes. Surprise if he hit any of them. It was a mistake to tell him to kill that sheriff lady. He'll botch it up for sure and make matters worse, the worthless shit.

The jogger he hit already died. Now we've got a murder. Time to erase Pete too. He knows too much. There's a back-hoe outside the unfinished house to bury Pete deep along with these two intruders.

Warren waves at the coyotes. "Come, join me. There's plenty of caviar left. I have a case of the stuff. I think you'll like it, though it's an acquired taste." Warren stands slowly, weaving, waves a hand and bows his head. "You have come to take me to the next world, I trust, but there is always time for caviar. I don't suppose either of you drink cognac, but I have some Bailey's Irish Cream and a couple of bowls in the cabinet."

Warren feels woozy. The air thickens and tastes of ash. The boy-coyote keeps fading out, vanishing and reappearing in different parts of the room. Instead of a boy, Warren sees a scrawny warrior wearing a coyote skin rope with an animal's head. Fear grips him. He wants to vomit. He's seeing with coyote eyes – back through thousands of years. A native Tongva shaman has come to claim his spirit - like the Anubis of Pharaoh's tombs, come to weigh the soul.

Warren smirks and backs away. One of the pair comes forward, keeping baleful, yellow eyes on him, sniffs and starts licking at the caviar. Warren slips out a side door and makes his way out to his Mercedes. His eyes burn. Wow. Lots of smog today. Thick. He coughs. He opens the passenger side door, reaches inside and takes his Walther 9 mm., semiautomatic from the glove box, loaded as always. He flips the safety off.

As he turns back towards the house, he sees yellow flecks through the smoke. Fucking coyotes. He pulls the trigger. One down. Warren steps over the fallen beast to go inside. Man, boy or beast, this creature will not take Warren Roscoe without a fight, damn it.

--------------------- ----

Detectives Cranberry and Saldana get out of the Jeep and walk a few feet forward on the yellow gravel fire road for a better look up the steep hillside ahead. Saldana raises his sunglasses and points. "Shit, you're right Agnes, fire!" He puts the glasses back. They glint in the setting sun.

"Looks like it's from the next ridge over, not this one." Agnes squints, and steps back to the Jeep to call it in. She can smell it now, the unmistakable, acrid, pungent incense-like odor of burning chaparral, wind gusts whip fine bits of ash and glowing cinder around them and start to coat the hood and windshield of the vehicle.

A shot rings out, then another. Then rapid, heavy fire -- crack, crack, crack. "Fuck." Saldana drops and belly crawls back behind the Jeep, service revolver drawn.

"Officer down. Need assistance, about six miles west of checkpoint 12 on fire road 822-A." Agnes takes a rifle from its holder and positions herself behind the open door of the Jeep. "Hey, Davey. You all right?"

"I'm okay." Saldana's voice rasps, high-pitched. "Oh fuck! Blood."

"Where?"

"My leg. I'm hit."

"Stay there, I'm coming." Agnes gets off four rounds in the direction of the incoming fire. She grabs a first aide kit from inside the cab, then scoots around the back of the Jeep to her partner, who sits, half propped up against the car door. Agnes scrambles, almost losing her footing along the narrow shoulder, kicking rocks down the precipice. She checks out Saldana, pulls away the pant-leg gingerly, applies a tourniquet, and dabs at the wound. "Looks like it's superficial, but we got to get you down to a hospital.

Several more shots echo through the canyon, a couple making a thwack against the hood or roof of the jeep. "Son of a bitch!" Agnes half crouches behind the Jeep fender, takes out her revolver again, aims and fires one shot at the spot where she saw muzzle flashes.

A shadow blacks out half the sky, tips of advancing flames come at them. Then a giant bird seems to come fast out of the setting sun with a roar, mixed with a high-pitched whine. Suddenly the sky pours greenish gravy over them and the world. "Fuck! Fire retardant." Saldana curls against the Jeep and covers his leg with both hands.

As the roaring passes, Agnes rises slowly and pulls her splattered sunglasses up on her head. Something is crashing downward through the thick underbrush of the hillside up ahead. She hears it scream - branches crackle. It cartwheels and a body, covered in goo like a flour-battered fish ready to fry, tumbles onto the road ahead of the Jeep, then lies still. Detective Cranberry, gun at the ready, approaches cautiously. "Hands behind your head. Stay where you are!" She slips her handcuffs from their holder.

--------------- ------------

The bad man stood in the doorway, silhouetted in a smoky sun. "Hey, mister. Watch this!" A cognac bottle flies at the man and stops, suspended in front of his face. He jumps sideways, but it smacks into the side of his head anyway. The boy hears loud popping. The man is on the move. The boy is behind the kitchen counter, then on top of it - a coyote. The man shoots at it repeatedly.

Bottles fly. A fusillade of beer cans and plastic utensils hits the man. He trips, falls and cuts the side of his face against the fireplace mantle. More shooting. The boy is in front of the big picture on the wall. "Don't touch my Klimt, you little shit!" The man fires at the boy's shifting shape. Holes appear in the canvas. "Oh shit!" The boy is nowhere in sight. The man fingers a canvas flap, trying to cover one of the holes. "Fuck." He turns, squinting, hatred in his eyes, starting to burn with the smoky air from the still-open front door.

He sees a blur behind the marble archway to the living room and advances, firing again. Something lands on his back and bites into his neck. He screams and reaches behind him and grabs at the boy creature, clutching him and biting again, deeper this time. The man grasps a leg and twists the boy off him violently, slamming him to the floor. The boy-creature lays face up, eyes glazed, blinking. The man points the gun downward at the boy's head.

The man screams. Something sharp clamps onto his leg like a bear trap just above the ankle. He hears a muffled crack of bone breaking. He sees fierce yellow eyes as he falls sideways and slams his head against the side of the archway. Another cracking sound and the man is still.

The boy draws to his feet. "Anubis!" The coyote limps towards the boy and lies at his feet.

The boy sees the blood darkening the side of his mentor's haunches. He crouches down and hugs his friend, stroking his head.

You see, Chaka, magic can be unreliable. Coyote God survives by hiding his spirit and vital parts in the tip of his tail when in danger. But mortal ones like we cannot always act that quickly. We must resort to other schemes sometimes.

"Anubis! Don't worry. I'll get you out to a vet. You'll be okay. Please, be okay!" The boy says this neither in English, nor his Portuguese mother tongue, in the scent and mind language of the Coyote, not translatable precisely. He puts his arms around the massive animal and tries vainly to lift him.

Chaka-Winslow runs outside to the driveway and looks around. Thickening smoke begins to sting his eyes. The dry, ash-laden wind whips hotly around the house, sparks darting like fireflies through it. Powerful gust parch his mouth and nearly topple him as he moves about frantically. He spots idle construction gear near the unfinished portion of the house. Quickly, he comes back through the front door, pulling a large, rubber-wheeled handcart.

Soon as he arrives, he helps his coyote companion, shakily on all fours. "Can you climb in there for me Anubis? I'll give you a boost." He removes a slat from the cart and points.

"Shirley Wu here, back on the ground. We're watching firefighters rushing to reinforce a perimeter around a cluster of expensive homes being evacuated along this Santa Monica Mountain road. The wind has subsided somewhat, stalling the fire. Workers here had set up floodlights and are using bulldozers to clear a break between the houses and the fire-front, hoping to keep the fire at bay when and if it flares up again. It's grueling job, for these exhausted firefighters, Dave, in searing heat that continues unabated even now, two hours after the sunset."

"Thanks for that great report, Shirley. You stay safe now."

"Dave."

"Yes."

"I have film director Lance Crowley, here, among the evacuees."

"Go ahead."

"Quite a welcome to Los Angeles, Lance. How do you feel?" Shirley points her hand mike towards a tall, gangly, sandy haired man with a hawk nose and piercing blue eyes staring out distractedly from his large-boned long face.

"How would I feel? Same as anybody, I'm looking for the others in my crew."

"Were you all evacuated?"

"Yes, from that house over there." He points.

"You must be worried about your home too."

"It's not mine."

"You're here to work on a new animation blockbuster for DreamWorks, I understand."

"That's right. But it's not a concern right now. I just hope everyone is safe. I want to thank these brave firefighters." A gust stirs ash around them. "That's not a good sign."

Shirley glances worriedly up the road toward a ridge.

"Looks like we may have to pull back. Are you going to an evacuation center, Lance?"

"No, I have my car. But I want to make sure all of us who were in the house have a way out before I go."

"What were you doing?"

"Having a read-through for the actors. Ah, there's one now." He waves. "Elizabeth." A tall woman walks toward them with a limp. "She's no stranger to disaster in this canyon. Maybe you want to talk to her."

Shirley turns and the cameraman gets a shot of Elizabeth as she steps into the TV truck lights. The reporter's eyes widen. She tilts her head. "Well, Dave, we have something extraordinary here. Ms. Parker! Over here." Shirley looks into the camera. "This is Elizabeth Parker, former child star, who was involved in the tragic canyon mud slide near this spot some two years ago. "Ms Parker! What do you think of the situaiton?"

Elizabeth limps past Shirley, the crew and truck to the middle of the road. She stares into the gloom just beyond the glow of construction lights. A small figure advances out of the darkness. A boy emerges pulling what looks like a wagon with a dog lying in it.

The boy's clothes are ragged, his black hair waist-length and tangled with twigs and dried leaves. A fine layer of ash makes him and the dog look ghostly. Elizabeth walks trance-like, her own face drawn. I'm in my dream again...

Shirley Wu and her cameraman follow Elizabeth, with Lance looking stunned, just behind. "

The boy howls, eerily in strained, choked voice that nevertheless can be heard above the din of the firefighting scene. Then he wails: "Ajudem o meu cão! Por favor, ajudem o meu cão, que está ferido! Ajudem o meu cão!"

"Stand by, Dave. I think we have a new development here on the ground. It appears that the boy is trying to say something, but we can't understand it."

The wild boy keeps howling and wailing: "Ajudem o

meu cão! Ajudem o meu cão!"

Shirley Wu moves deftly to the fore, microphone in hand. "This boy – perhaps homeless, seems to have appeared virtually from the direction of the fire, Dave ... and with his.... what looks like a dog, perhaps injured."

The boy howls again. Shirley Wu takes a step back.

Elizabeth goes down on her knees, awkwardly, nearly falling, grimacing in pain, and puts her arms around the "apparition," trying to comfort him. She gets ash all over her bare arms and face.

The boy keeps howling.

"What's he saying?" Shirley Wu bends to look at them. "Is he speaking Spanish?"

"No. It's Portuguese. I know it from when I was in Brazil." Elizabeth's eyes light up. She gazes close at the boy and wipes ash from his brow. "Oh, my God! Winslow? My little Winslow," she sobs. She kisses him furiously all over his face.

The boy says nothing.

She tries again. "Meu Jôao, Meu filho precioso Jôao."

"Mama! A minha querida mãe. Eu amo você." The boy kisses her back, tears making rivulets down his ash-covered face. Finally he says: "My dog! Mama!" He points the coyote in the wagon, then bends and hugs the stricken animal."

Shirley motions her camera crew in closer. "The boy has just been reunited with his mother, apparently separated by the onrushing fire and evacuations, Dave. Now he's hugging, my goodness, what he says is his dog."

"That's a coyote." Lance has come over, cell phone in hand, waving at an ambulance rolling towards them from the fire line. "Be careful!"

The boy tells the coyote softly. "Don't worry, Anubis. We're getting you a doctor. You're going to be okay. You want to come live with me?"

"Winslow!" Elizabeth starts to say, then stops herself. "It's okay. Sure." She addresses the animal. "Yes. We'll take good care of you. Get you well. And if you want to stay with us, you are welcome." She smiles and the coyote moves its head for the first time and catches her eye.

"Do you know my dog's name, mama?"

"Anubis?"

"O-let'-te!"

Elizabeth hears a voice in her head. It is calming, powerful, and almost palpable. That is what the native people called me. Your boy is very brave. He does you honor."

4 SOME OF THEM ARE ICE PEOPLE

I stared into the frozen stillness of my favorite boreal meadow, as is my nocturnal wont. A figure emerged from a line of larches and shuffled towards me through knee-deep, crusted snow. I judged it to be that of a young woman, probably a chiikago, as Alaskans call a greenhorn from the lower forty eight. No Yup'ik, Koyukon or white villager in his or her right mind would venture out here alone on foot at this hour.

The blue-green pulses of Aurora Borealis turned her struggle into a strobe-lighted dance. It reminded me of Ashleigh, a disco queen from Seattle who worked the Prudhoe Bay camps and was murdered by a drunken pipe fitter in '78. But this snow dancer was alive – for the present. I saw the glint of unhappy rabbit eyes and noted the smart red piping on her steel gray Gor-Tex parka. (I keep up on snow fashions thanks to social media, where phantoms mingle with mortals as freely as in dreams.)

Like most mortals, she wouldn't see me until she crossed the threshold into the realm of death she apparently sought – on purpose or not – with this heedless foray. How odd, I thought. If she sought an icy end, why

95

stay zipped up, scarfed and fur-hatted? Wouldn't it be quicker to strip and let go to shock? Being incorporeal, I discounted how the flesh seeks comfort, no matter how hopeless the circumstances.

Soon my chimerical, jade-green, straw-haired, blue-taloned, amphibian nemesis Qalupalik would appear – humming like a high-voltage line – and drag her down to the icy sea where he keeps lost children. So the indigenous folk tell their offspring to keep them close.

The First People sang of Qalupalik eons before the snowmobiles and pipelines. Tribes shared spirits. But successive interlopers and migrants have released their own gods, phantoms and demons into the mix.

By dint of seniority, Qalupalik sees himself as king of our roiling phantom kingdom. I see him as first among equals at best. To me, all of us – ghosts, gods, goddesses, sprites, demons, angels, fairies, elves, gnomes and trolls – are inventions manifested by human imagination, derivative, though no less real for it.

Qalupalik, is for separation of church and state. He is forever telling us to keep our noses out of human tents. All the while he appears in frosted windows, scares children and delirious drunks. Separation is noisome for preternaturally meddlesome beings like myself. It's a fiction. Spirits and mortals are inseparable. We permeate people's myths and visions, riding sky horses into their minds.

I am a Tuatha Dè Danann, once a warrior of Goddess Danu's Celtic spirit tribe. I was transplanted here in the human year of 1897 by a red-bearded opium-smoking poet from County Kerry by way of California digging for Klondike gold. Like every immigrant, he brought his own demons and released them into the modern melange – Gnomes of Anglia, Navajo coyotes, Black Forest moss people, Hassid dybbuks, ghosts, faeries, golems and assorted unclassifiable apparitions walk perpetually past chalky Ba jiao gui, with her wailing baby under a hangman's tree.

"Infidel! Denier!" Qalupalik hummed from beneath the mush ice of a nearby stream. My green friend always wanders up the Yukon and Tanana rivers from his ocean lair with the first melt of May. "We are not mere human inventions. We are real. They are the aberrations."

"I was wondering when you'd show up." He had been keeping watch on me since I diverted that team of pasty-faced surveyors into hallucinatory woods. I explained to Qalupalik that I had been compelled by a village shaman's spell who wanted a pipeline detoured, but he didn't believe me.

"Don't even think of toying with the fate of that foolish snow damsel," he hummed at me now. "One more affront and I'll tear out your liver."

"I don't have a liver."

He sputtered and sprayed brine. "Figure of speech... You know what I mean. You'll be in a world of pain."

Ejection. He and the holy host had the power to cast me out. I could wake up as a worm. Even worse, a squalling baby with no memories, only discomfort and terrifying inklings. Threats told around fall harvest bonfires to scare children and spirits: I'd heard them all before.

Qalupalik droned into one of his standard sermons. I rolled my imaginary eyes. Long before two-legs appeared on the earth, he rode white fogs and mountain winds across tundra basins with caribou, moose, wolves, hares, badgers, geese and grizzlies, through valleys of river spirits – the Kuskokwim, Yukon, Klondike and Tanana descending from the mountains of fire and ice.

He never acknowledges that he's mouthing tales of First People. I don't believe them anyway. Humans shape us, but they don't explain us. No one does, because no one can. We come from the same place as their magical stories in spiraling strange loops.

Qalupalik's preaching always inspires me to perversity. Now it made me want to keep Gor-Tex girl out of his green clutches, fate or no fate.

It's a generational thing. The new gods always defy and ancient ones. The myths tell of new destroying old, or vice versa, sooner or later. But perhaps I just enjoy vexing Qalupalik because I'm a trickster, like Crow and Coyote. I can't help pulling his chain.

I mounted Chollima – the ancient Chinese flying steed I acquired a few months ago at darkest solstice from an itinerant, undead jiangshi off a Shanghai tanker down in Anchorage. I materialized as a medieval Hungarian iron war helmet and clanked down the visor to shut out Qalupalik's hectoring, and glided across the meadow into Gor-Tex girl's hallucinatory amphitheater.

She didn't notice me at first. She just leaned on the trunk of a giant larch, wan from her gyrations, shivering and glassy-eyed. Giving up.

I raised my visor and dismounted, an unlikely ghost in shining armor, except she wasn't buying it. She gazed through me, then blinked.

I saw through her too, in a different way – through transient psychic lenses of rage, despair, hope, terror, each its own hue. I back-tracked through memories she had left with the zigzag snow tracks that led back into the woods, along an embankment and scrambling from the shoulder of an old forest road. I saw the wavering image of a gunmetal gray pickup pulling away. Her eyes had followed the disheveled sandy-haired driver's head through the rear-window gun rack with loathing and grief as it receded around a curve.

What's wrong with me?

You're asking the wrong question.

Who? What...are you? Her mouth didn't move when she talked. Am I dead?

Maybe, but I don't think so.

Are you going to suck my blood?

I'm a vegetarian.

That got half a laugh out of her. I heard humming,

rising in tone, drawing close. Qalupalik. I summoned gusts of wind to envelope Gor-Tex girl in white out. Qalupalik had poor vision. His hummed right by us and receded towards the half-frozen lake from where he had come.

I can't feel for mortals, being disembodied and all. But I can imagine, a practice that, as you know, can get one in trouble.

I conjured a vivid vision for Gor-Tex girl – a first-class hallucination from her dreams and the vapor of her breath. She saw a dark-eyed little boy rise from the snow and run away from her, looking back and giggling every few paces. I didn't mean to be cruel, but I could see that it was.

Gor-Tex girl shrieked and spun toward the child, reaching out with both hands. "Donnie! Donnie!" Her voice cracked with hope and apprehension as she ran after the boy. I realized that I had sprung her little lost half-Yup'ik boy from Qalupalik's underwater limbo. He'd be back after us now with a vengeance.

I led Gor-Tex girl across the meadow on the diagonal away from the lake and Qalupalik. I teased her through a thick copse of white-barked birch, then over a knoll and down an embankment, picking up the frozen stream and out into another clearing. I heard Qalupalik's humming coming towards us again.

I lured little Donnie across the creek on the felled trunk of giant pine. Gor-Tex almost slipped off in pursuit. We scrambled up to the old road. I wasn't sure where I was taking her and little Donnie. We crossed a wooden bridge over an ice-covered gulch.

The bridge troll growled and came out spoiling for a fight, just as I intended. I heard him tangle with Qalupalik behind us as we sped ahead. It would be a long brawl. I realized now that this was the troll who had overturned a school bus that carried little Donnie two earth years ago. The troll and Qalupalik had been fighting over the children from that bus ever since.

Gor-Tex girl would be out of Qalupalik's reach once the first light of Arctic spring sun rose feebly over the southern horizon. But her vision of little Donnie would fade as well. If she were lucky, and determined, perhaps her habitual state of inchoate grief would diminish to background noise someday.

Out here on this road, the young woman still risked ending up as half-frozen carrion for bears hungry from months of hibernation. She didn't have much reserve left. I could see her skin paling to blue-gray from hypothermia.

I'd taken my game as far as it could go. The sun wouldn't melt me, but I'd have to keep out of sight. I'd have to think of a good story by nightfall when Qalupalik would surely call me on the carpet before the spirit council.

I was feeling so sorry for myself I didn't hear the dogs barking at first. They caught me with their wolf eyes and had picked up Gor-Tex girl's scent.

I heard a human shouting and whistling trying to keep his team going along a snowy path that paralleled the road. He looked left and right for what had spooked them and struggled to keep his sled from overturning.

"Damn." I heard the man swear as he braked the sled. Gor-Tex girl had stumbled and collapsed across the dog-sled trail that paralleled the roadway. His lead dogs were on top of her, licking her face, the others braying and barking as she struggled to get up.

The man ran over to her..."damn," he cursed silently, over and over.

He pulled the dogs off and half-carried her to his sled... he found a blanket to wrap around her and looked back and forth. He gave her brandy. Light showed in the sky now. He strapped her to his sled, untangled his dog leads and prepared to push off again. Gor-Tex girl gazed at him as if he were another hallucination. He turned the team and his sled around to head back towards the village where he had stopped over for the night.

"You're gonna make me lose this race, girl!" The man groused at her. "Lucky for you. Not so much for me." He mushed his team back up to full speed.

She craned her head back at him standing on the sled runners. She smiled wanly and whispeedr a thank you. Their eyes met and I saw a spark there.

Now I had done it. A simple prank had turned cascades of unintended consequences. I had ripped the curtain that separates the worlds of spirit and stuff. This young woman's life would have ended. Now it resumed. The outcome of a dog-sled race may have been altered. Money would flow differently. There would be a fuss back at the human settlement about the rescue. The sheriff would investigate. Gor-Tex and her dog hero would fall in love and have a baby. I could be in big trouble, and it was not going to be easy to hide Qalupalik and his minions.

I turned myself into a predawn meteor shower, hiding in plain sight, keeping fingers crossed, as if I had them. But meteor showers don't last long. Qalupalik might cast me out of the spirit world altogether and make me human. I could well be that baby. That's what he does with those lost children and elfin miscreants, if we're not quick enough. I like humans, but not that much. Yuck! I smiled to myself in falling stars. Lucky for me, I'm quick.

5 ANGELA'S ETNA

The fruit vendor smiled at the girl through sightless eyes, tasting the warm salty breeze. He bantered with customers and seemed able to recall the smallest details about them, even ones they couldn't remember sharing with him. The girl had been coming to his stand for as long as she could remember. He told her things she could take away, savor and puzzle in her head, sometimes things that came true.

Studiously, the girl selected a basket of the dark cherries her mother wanted and bagged them. She weighed them on the hanging scale and the vendor called a price. He seemed able to determine weights accurately, perhaps from the sound of his spring scale. No one knew. The girl counted out and put the asked amount into an open cigar box next to him.

Nobody in the town ever tried to cheat the blind vendor. They were honest townsfolk. What's more, elders said the blind vendor was a seer, a shape-shifter who had always been there, as long as anyone remembered, as long as their parents remembered, and their parents' parents, probably for as long as the very ancient stones of the piazza itself.

As she turned to leave, the girl patted the old vendor's hand and said, "I'll see you tomorrow morning, friend."

Still smiling, he replied, "No, you won't..."

A week in Santaliu hadn't gotten Angela Vanni used to the tremors. This wasn't upstate New York, though it did feel like home in so many little ways. She didn't remember flagstones doing little tarantellas under her sandals the last time she had been here, but she was a little girl then, long ago, clowning with her cousin Carmela.

The locals went right on browsing the fruit and vegetable stands, haggling with the vendors and chattering amongst themselves, seemingly oblivious to minor earthquakes, just as they had on other such spring mornings for thousands of years amid these wind-worn marble columns.

Neither did anyone but Angela bother to look up at Mt. Etna, rising snowcapped as an Alp, spewing ominous ashy smoke in the near distance from their white stone houses, Grecian temple ruins, Moorish-Gothic-Roman marble churches and winding cobblestone streets. This was home, nestled safely between a bright Ionian Sea and the verdant orchards of a brief coastal plain. Etna had watched over it, rumbling from time-to-time to keep order as invader-after-invaders came, conquered and were captivated.

Kids bawled, laughed and yelled, and mothers ordered them them to behave while they haggled the price of blood oranges in their Sicilian dialect laced with metaphors and ironies that Angela barely comprehended, but found as delicious as the aroma of her grandmother's long-ago ragú.

Well shaken by one jolt, Angela stopped to stare up at the summit of Etna, as if expecting a tsunami of lava or a pyroclastic cloud to bury them all like the sybaritic citizens of Pompeii. *"Non ti preoccupi, mia Angelina, bella Americana che sei diventuto* " said her cousin Carmela, considerately in the standard Italian that Angela could understand well. With a gentle poke Carmela, leaner, more angular and more olive-skinned than her cousin added, in English: "Don't let the shaking scare you, cara mia. The tremors are nothing but Etna waking up in the morning, when she is always a little grumpy. We know which kind of... *terramodo* ... deeper earthquake tells us to watch out," she laughed again. "The Romans said the kind of shaking you feel now was simply Vulcan inside the mountain forging armor for Mars."

Angela looked back at her cousin, "Yes, I suppose - while Mars made love to his wife – Venus."

"Trouble at home," said Carmela.

"I know about *that* kind of earthquake, too" Angela said.

"*Prova questo*! Try this!" said her cousin Carmela, changing the subject and handing Angela a glistening sample slice of apricot on a toothpick.

"First of the season," said the blind fruit vendor, in heavily-accented English, startling Angela. She remembered this old vendor, wizened and swarthy as as a sun-dried tomato. Somehow he looked no different than she recalled him from her childhood summers. She didn't remember the vendor speaking any English then.

"*Paradiso...,*" Carmela chimed in, taking a morsel for herself. True, nodded Angela. The apricot dissolved into a dulcet jam in her mouth. Nothing quite equaled the aromatic, honeyed fruits of this place, grown in a soil rich and thick with Etna's volcanic ash. Like Kali, Mother Etna continually created, nurtured, destroyed and resurrected the life around her in all its incarnations. Angela had soaked up such wonders of faraway worlds, through a lifetime of reading and teaching back home, but had taken few bites of this fruit since her childhood summers in Santaliù – and now.

Angela felt a rush – away from the tremors and the

coldness of her recent life and back into sunlit days on which Angela's great aunt Iolanda, used to take the girls with her to shop in the square. Whenever they went there, Carmela would beg her "zia" for coins to have the old vendor tell the girls' fortunes.

Unlike many of her black shawled local contemporaries, Iolanda was a woman of science trucked neither with what she called superstition or with the teachings of the church, for that matter. She held degrees in biochemistry and enology. Ever since her husband had been killed fighting with the Partisans in World War II, she had applied modern methods to her management of the family vineyards and winery on the edge of town.

Nevertheless she would indulge Carmela, who had always been her favorite. What was the harm? The vendor told "fortunes" in the form of riddles and tales the children liked, but adults found cryptic, and to which, conveniently, they could project meanings that they had already in their own heads.

Carmela giggled and nodded and gave the old vendor's pronouncements rapt attention. Angela made nice for her cousin's sake, but didn't like the stories. They scared her. She shivered, despite the warm summer breezes, at the blur of images that rushed through her mind – volcanic eruptions, demons, strange armored warriors, fantastically garbed, beatific pagan gods and goddesses, and the faces, some painted with strange symbols, of all colors and in all moods appearing out of these odd stories in an old Sicilian language that Angela strangely remembered understanding then, but not now.

But today, Carmela did not ask for any fortunes to be told when they stopped at the vendor's stand. She simply bought lemons and apricots and sun-dried tomatoes and chatted about the nice weather – without mentioning Etna either. And, out of the blue, the vendor, also addressed Angela, in that same reedy voice she remembered from long ago, but now in a near perfect English, as if his grasp of the language had been improving minute-by-minute this strange morning. "What a pleasure to sense your presence here again, Angelina. You have grown up now into a fine woman."

"Thank you, and it is good to see you too," Angela answered, having no more luck suppressing the quavering of her voice than she had controlling the vibrations of the ground beneath her feet. Her face reddened. She regretted immediately using the verb, "see" to a blind person, as if to rub in that she was sighted.

"It is good that you do," said the vendor, "and that you come with my dear Carmela after all these years. Do not be fear or be self-conscious in my presence, for I see all that need be seen, always." He paused, and everything in the piazza seemed to fall silent for a long moment. Then he continued. "Do you remember that last day you came here to see me as a little girl, Angela?"

"You said we'd never see you again!" Angela blurted, inquisitorially trying vainly to fight back the memory of that other morning.

"Poor child," said the vendor, his voice now soothing as fine wine pouring into a crystal glass. "I said we would not see each other that next morning. That is different. And, we did not."

"Not until now," said Angela. "And I feel like something terrible is about to happen again," she said choking back sobs.

Carmela stepped close and put an arm around her cousin. "Go ahead, cry now, my beloved cousin," she said reassuringly. "You need to let it out. Believe it or not, this is why I brought you here today."

Angela broke down, her shoulders wracking, tears pouring, angry and embarrassed at not being able to control herself but oblivious to all else in the piazza. Her tears seemed to freeze everything. "I'm sorry," she managed finally, through choking sobs.

"You need to let it out, cousin," said Carmela, once

again. "If keep trying to keep your American 'cool,' you you will explode with the sorrow and the rage that I can sense inside of you, seeking to surface like molten basalt."

The vendor joined in, his words seeming to flow seamlessly from those of Carmela, like they were performing a piece of music. "Etna gives us life as long as she breathes, fumes and flows with hot lava high up there. We fear her not when she rumbles softly, but when she goes silent. Then we are the ones who shake and look to her and say our prayers."

Angela took a tissue from her purse and dabbed her swollen eyes as her sobs subsided. "I don't know what came over me," she said.

"Grief – espeically long held grief - comes in waves once it starts to flow. Don't fight it," aid Carmela. "I remember that day, seeming so long ago when we left here. You did not cry then, and you did not cry afterwards... not even at your father's funeral. I thought you were so brave then, keeping your solemn face. I wanted to be like you, courageous, I thought. But now I realize that can be poison."

"You are courageous," responded Angela, "very much so, cousin. I am the one who has been a coward." Angela was thinking that in a few days, Carmela would hike back up the side of smoldering Etna in her heavy hiking boots, packing her vulcanologist gear, including breathing mask, ever eager to observe and discover what she could, as close as she dared to the fires. Carmela had always been the more adventuresome of the two, in play, later in loves, and most of all realizing her ambitions.

The day she arrived back in Santaliu, Angela had listened in amazement to Carmela telling of her latest, harrowing, observation trip high up the mountain, "not a commonplace one, I assure you,"

Carmela added, laughing. "You would find most of my work detailed and dull – a lot of time reading instruments and working in front of computer screens. But not yesterday," she went on. "We had gone up to an observation post – a small house high up near the northeast crater – to re-calibrate instruments and take some samples. We stayed overnight and early the next morning the crater began a series of Strombolian eruptions, spewing fountains that kept intensifying. I went to the windows with my field glasses for a better look. Being present close up to eruptions is our holy grail," she said. "In a while, though, we began to feel the heat rising inside the house and I noticed the window panes vibrating and bending. We grabbed as much as we could carry to get out of there at that point, but foolishly I took a few extra moments to stuff instruments and disks into my backpack instead of just running like the devil as I should have since the eruption was peaking fast.

"By the time we scrambled away down a fire trail, we could feel the heat burning our skin and making our eyes tear. Running hard, we made no headway as a powerful wind began blowing back towards the crater, the effect of a sudden burst of vapor and white hot particulates that shot nearly two kilometers high.

"Then spent – *o mio* Dio, my God – it showered hot dust and rock in all directions – a volcanic bombardment from which we could only cower terrified on the spot. Stones rained down around us, several as big as a small car, and one barely missing us, I thought we were done for, but by a miracle – or simply fine luck – I stand here, my dear cousin Angela, to bid you welcome from America!" With that Carmela hugged her cousin and kissed her on both cheeks.

Angela wondered if she'd ever see her cousin again, after this next sortie up the side of that spewing volcano.. Angela herself would have to take ferry and train back to Rome, just as she had to get to her family town, and then a transatlantic flight home, given that Etna's latest ash and fire fit had caused the closing of Sicilian airports.

But now there was this... unfinished business

entangled with the new. Carmela took Angela's arm once the crying subsided and the two walked over the smooth-worn flagstones of the ancient piazza that had witnessed so many tears of sorrow and joy, triumphs and defeats, invasions, wars, peace, hard times and good, and always, the sweet nectars of fruit and life flowing over them like brook water endless.

"You should stay longer, *cara cougina* Angela," said Carmela, "until all the crying is done for your father - and for the loss of Jeremy such a short time ago, *quel bastardo*, that bluebeard, running off like that con quella troya, putana..." she laughed. "You're too good for him to break your heart, after so many years you worked and stood by him and raised his children, not even your own, thankless little monsters," Carmela added. "*Via!* Good riddance."

"That's just it," said Angela, her crying gone as suddenly as it had descended upon her. "He didn't break my heart!. After he walked out, I realized that I didn't love him. I confess to you , cousin, that I never loved him, and that is far worse than a broken heart."

"Worse?" Carmela tilted her head.

"Worse, I buried my own heart long ago, right here. I wasted 25 years with a man I didn't love, living a good life, but a dead one. My heart stayed safe. Better I should have had it broken," she added.

"Well, cara Angelina," said Carmela, "it's never too late as long as you draw breath, dig up that heart of yourself.. You can be the archeologist you wanted to be and start by unearthing what is most dear to you under our Sicilian sun that shines on all of us, mafiosi, and priests, scoundrels and saints, artists and clowns, children and mamas ... and we are the mamas now..."

The ground rumbled once more beneath Angela's feet, this time in undulations that nearly made her lose her balance. But this time she only smiled and continued walking with her cousin out of the square and up a narrow street headed back towards home.

.

6 ONION STATION

"Is that where pop went?" Theo pointed out the window to the tower that rose above the cluster of nearby, South Loop buildings. His mother glanced up from where she sat on the edge the unmade hotel bed. She lowered the receiver, put a Chen Yu crimson-nailed, index finger to her glamour lips — morning faded — and gave the boy an indulgent smile, dark lashes fanning admonishment. Theo read the slight toss of her Rita Hayworth hair as annoyance. Movie star mom, he called her — always in character even though she only played bit parts on screen.

Alma adjusted her satin robe, took a drag of Pall Mall from a pearled cigarette holder and continued in her long-distance voice. She exhaled words in steam nicotine curlicues "...You tell me, Maasha. I'm out of ansahs. ... No. I khan't say when we'll be theah... We missed the goddamn train connection yestahday. Awful stoahms! Snow, snow snow all the way heah." Two-thirds home and already her tongue was in Boston — her "r's" lost as luggage.

"He's off to God-knows-*wheah!* And he has the goddamn tickets... Some big Chicago deal, he says. Now it's onions! You know Victor" She never called Theo's

112

father Vic. "He's always with some deal. No goddamn considahration for me or his son or anyone. I just want to take Theo and come home..." Three years now in California, and Boston was still "home."

Theo pointed out the window, down at the streets. "I want to play in the snow first!" You could never be sure of snow by Christmas in Boston or anywhere, but there it was, new, velvety as meringue piled along the icy Chicago sidewalks – only an elevator ride away, if it didn't rain and melt everything.

"Quiet, Theo!" Theo's mother waved her cigarette holder but didn't look at him this time. "I hate to ask you to wire the cash, Maasha deah, but you know Victor."

Alma never made a move without consulting Aunt Marcie, her costume designer and the family matriarch in Boston, where they would be by now if their City of Los Angeles streamliner had not pulled into Chicago twenty-three hours late from having to crawl through a Midwest blizzard. He would press his face against a window whenever the train negotiated a laborious curve, hoping to catch sight of the snowplow engine that sprayed crystal plumes in magnificent rainbow arcs out its sides in each direction.

Their accommodations – two compartments that his parent occupied separately– were an upgrade from last year's trip home. The war – its shortages, rationing and government buys, we don't mention the blood – had been good to his father, 4F due to scarred lungs from having the Spanish flu as a boy, though he always appeared in combative health.

Except maybe for sledding and making snowballs, Theo loved train riding better than anything – the cozy encapsulated freedom of rolling through landscapes and towns, free of it all - home, school, chores, strictures. Free of the miasma of domestic strife that hung over this little family triad. On the train, his mother and father would suspend the worst of their bickering - neutralized by convention. They would exchange "looks" but keep their jaws tight through a three-day traveling truce of convenience. This state of affairs gave Theo maximum leeway. He loved delays along the tracks. The slower the train, the more time he would have for running free as a wild bear cub through the holiday-crowded railcars with half-dozen other, temporarily feral. traveling kids. They had found each other the first day out – each one liberated from disoriented parents riffling through old copies of Life, sipping highballs, playing gin rummy a penny a point, smoking, smoking, smoking. It didn't take much pestering to get Theo's mother to tell him: "Okay! Go play. Just be good ... and get back here when you hear the dinner chimes!"

Two men in dark overcoats and snap-brims had approached his father in Union Station as they came up the ramp into the echoing marble lobby, from where they would have grabbed a cab to La Salle station to catch the Boston train. His father seemed to recognize one of the men – the shorter of the two, a squat man who had to be bald under his greenish fedora. His father shook both men's hands and stepped out of earshot, but Theo could still distinguish his father's gritty, nasal tenor, sharp with feigned irritation, cutting through the crowd buzz.

Theo's father stood taller than both men. He moved loose-jointed, deceptive as a pitcher – he had played triple-A ball – looking in for his signal. He edged close enough to the men to make them look up at him. Tallness was his superpower, growing up as the third tallest of four brawling brothers, in a fair-haired family originally from the mountainous, alt'Italia Piedmont.

"It's all business, everything - war, politics, religious, movies, even love, and especially marriage!" Theo's father was a wellspring of dismissive cynicism. "Right on the money," as he would say. Tallness gave Victor a dashing look that his unruly, wavy hair, narrow, hazel eyes and hawk nose might have ruled out.

His northern Italian family's above-average height made he and his brothers stand out. It had also got his younger brother Vincent picked off while by a Waffen-SS sharpshooter in the Ardennes forest in 1944.

While Theo's father parleyed, his mother sat with her small son and their suitcases, She made sure Victor noticed her fuming in her usual, stagey way, staring daggers, blowing Pall Mall smoke, legs crossed, high heel pump kicking. The men didn't back off. One of them put a hand inside his jacket for an envelope that he gave to Theo's father, who took it, turned away and strode back to wife and child, gray faced. "Change of plans" Theo's dad said. "I need to do some business. It's urgent."

"It's always money with you."

"You think it grows on trees."

"You've got plenty. You and your whole stingy family. You and your big deals."

"If I don't take care of this, I'll be finished."

"Big shot." Theo's mother adjusted and threw the muzzle end of her fox fur stole over one shoulder. It stared accusingly down at Theo with amber glass eyes.

"Six boxcars of onions probably stuck in the snow somewhere in the Nebraska. If they freeze it's all over. We go belly up."

"What did you expect?"

"It's a freak storm this early."

Red torpedo onions from Washington – just like the bulbous magical one in Theo's coat pocket that he filched from a bag in his father's sample case.

Just before they left California, his father had handed him a fat wad of gray green hundred dollar bills. "Feel that, Theo? That's power. It's what makes you somebody." Then his father took back the money and handed him one of the sleek magenta onions from a sample case. His father took glee giving these kinds of object lessons to his son.

Theo half listened and pocketed the onion – a Flash Gordon rocket, elliptical, fat, ends tapered gracefully, with its fuchsia skin that felt silky but fell away papery. He could pilot it between the towers of this Oz and see open-mouthed, blanched faces of people staring from office windows.

Yesterday's storm had given way to cobalt skies and dunes of glistening snow. He wanted to take a churning elevator ride back down to the streets and run out of the hotel into the powder, crunching it with his galoshes. He could roll in it piled high along the curbs by snowplows, unnoticed by the wool-bundled shoppers already crowding the streets, puffing cold vapor under the strings of Santa Claus lights, determined to be jolly for their first real Christmastime since Pearl Harbor, exhausted, more thankful than puffed with victory, smiling wearily into the dawning Atomic Age.

Being, "short for his age," as his mother put it. Theo had to move the little desk chair over to the window and stand on it to get a good view. "Be keaw-full theah!" His mother had waved the cigarette holder at him.

He could see his button-eyed reflection, faint and translucent, in the window pane, mop of chestnut hair needing a cut, cowlick waving, long lashes, pretty and girlish. "He looks so much like you, Alma! Honestly," His aunt Marcie would clap his face in both hands. "Little cioccolino della zia!" She would plant a wet kiss on the forehead of her little chocolate drop.

Theo leaned against the pane; hissing out is reflection with hot breath. When he closed his eyes he could feel the building itself swaying subtly. Or maybe he was still feeling the roll of the of the train under his feet from their two-day journey, getting his "land legs," his dad had called it.

Everything is in motion, even the ground in California with its mini-quakes and that bigger one that woke him up one morning, seeing the ceiling lamp swinging, feeling his bed pitch and roll, hearing his room rumble like a freight train. The earth itself flew like a rocket ship through space, the whole solar system that his father demonstrated to him with oranges, lemons and grapes on the kitchen table. Change, change, change, and it's all relative, his father, who knew all, had told him. Einstein said it, and that's how they made the Bomb. And what if they dropped one on us?

He schemed and hoped his mother wouldn't drag him shopping and to another interminable movie matinée. They had no sooner checked into the hotel yesterday than Theo's mother dragged him down the street to her favorite escape, in this case, the grand, French baroque New Palace Theater on a glittering Randolph Street.

They took the plush theater's rococo, faux French palatial decor for granted. Theo's mother appeared briefly in the second feature – playing a nightclub singer in a noir detective caper.

The caper was on the bill with "*And Then There Were None*," an adaptation of an Agatha Christie whodunit with Louie Jordan. The lead actor then was being divorced by Ida Lupino during the filming, Theo heard his mother say. Ida found out Louis was "that way." His mother raisee an eyebrow and let her wrist go limp of the wrist. "She should have figured that out at the start, but maybe the studio arranged the whole marriage as a cover."

Theo's mother plowed on in full-Hollywood-gossip mode. "Ida isn't Italian, like everyone thinks, she's English and a real troupah" A year earlier, his mother did a walk-on in a Ida Lupino movie. "She directed. Imagine! A woman!" Theo had to squirm through the entire double bill, just as he did her movie stories – plus a stupid, live dancing girl number, a stentorious newsreel, a novelty short, and – finally, the only blessed relief: Bugs Bunny in "*Herr Meets Hare*," only slightly dated now that the toon's villain "fatso" Göring had gone the way of the Third Reich.

Theo leaned on the window harder and calculated that he could fly straight over the Christmas streets below and land atop that other tall building without having to gain much altitude. He wanted to touch the serene, silvery robed female figure that crowned it – see if she was real, and maybe she could tell him her name and why she was there, and why they were staying so long in Chicago.

He'd just have to say, Shazam! – Like the lame newsboy in his Whiz Comics, Billy Batson – to be Captain Marvel. But he would have to be alone, so no one would discover his secret or be singed by the lightening bolt. He could try, maybe when mama took her shower. Still, he'd never flown from this height, only off the motherly branches of the California black oak behind their bungalows off Santa Monica where the big red trolleys ran.

Then there were wind currents and navigation to manage. Theo concerned himself with names, locations and the why of things a lot. He read all signs and memorized addresses and slogans. He noted every detail about the hotel where they stayed -- "the Morrison, Clark and Madison: tallest hotel in the world," the cursive legend on a postcard read – he filched them as they traveled: "In the Heart of the Loop, 46 stories high and standing 506 feet above the sidewalk. Home of the Terrace Casino and the historic Boston Oyster House" – where Alma took Theo with her to dinner last night and thought the saw Barbara Stanwyck having martinis with Robert Taylor, denizens of the kind of talkie flicks Theo's mother dragged him to all the time. "... Every room with bath and circulating ice water! The postcard bore a colorized image of the hotel's square block base and fluted tower with its red brick facade. Decades later, attending a Chicago publishing conference, Theo walked by the massive bank building where the hotel once stood on Clark and remembered how the Morrison's elevators churned his stomach.

He overheard his mother telling aunt Marcie that she was meeting some movie person – a man – downstairs later for lunch at the Boston Oyster House. Theo squashed his nose against the window and silently mouthed: "Please, Mystic Lady, keep me safe from boring lunches and another hideous double feature with mom!"

"... As close to Boston as I'm getting for now, Maasha... I miss you."

Theo interjected. "I want to stay here and color, ma!" Alma shushed him again.

Theo's mother braced the phone receiver with one shoulder, adjusted her satin dressing gown.

Theo stayed pressed against the window. He traced his flight, between the buildings, under bridges, along the river, over the train running along a section of elevated tracks – The Loop – looking from above like the Lionel set he had made known that he wanted from "Santa" – catching his father in a grimace. As he flew overhead, he imagined Christmas shoppers craning their necks in amazement, dropping their bundles, letting go of leashes as their dogs chased the hats that flew off from his wake.

The mystic lady atop the building could be the Virgin Mary or Wonder Woman, aglow from the pale winter sun. He imagined her beaming golden rays directly at him, conveying powers, perhaps, sending secret messages. In a fantasy, believable to him in this Emerald City of towers with its giant icy lake scattering light. He could ask the Mystic Lady to make him tall – even normal sized so people wouldn't think him so much younger than his eleven years or call him a shrimp, and so the disappointment in his father's eyes would fade away. But then would he still be able to fly?

The nanny from the concierge would be easy to outwit. Theo's mother hung up the receiver and stared across the room at nothing for a while, letting the Pall Mall in its holder burn out on the night table ashtray. Her tears, held back, did not spill over. Her lower lip trembled. Theo pretended he wasn't catching every nuance in his keen peripheral vision – one of his known superpowers. Another was his ability to distinguish between his mother's real and stage tears, the ones that flowed freely for close-ups, not held back. He tried to resist an awkward compulsion to give her some comfort. A hug in such circumstances could bring on sobbing that would overwhelm him.

"It's okay, ma." He let his voice bounce off the windowpane at her faint reflection. "It's going to be fun here." He let his voice go high and babyish.

"Finish your cereal, Theo." She sniffed, dabbed her eyes with Kleenex and nodded to a half-consumed bowl of Rice Krispies that had long lost their *snap, crackle and pop* on the room service table. "Children are starving in Europe. Mama has to change and get ready now. A nice lady will come stay with you for a little bit until I'm back."

Alma picked a velvety green, classic two-piece suit. It was an Elsa Schiaparelli knockoff that her sister Marcie, a design-copy virtuoso, had made for her. Alma removed it from the closet. Its travel wrinkles had been brushed and ironed out the night before. She never wore slacks. "They make me look like a shrimp. I'm too petite – ha ha, my legs are too short." She fished out some peach, satin undies, bra, girdle and precious nylons from a suitcase and took everything into the bathroom, her full-length robe trailing behind her.

Theo jumped off the chair and changed out of his Red Ryder pajamas into street clothes as soon as his mother closed the bathroom door behind her. Quickly, playing master detective, he rummaged the hotel room desk. He thumbed through the guidebook, brochures, postcards and maps for clues.

Ah ha! For one thing, he learned that the name "Chicago" came from the French version of a local Indian word shikaakwa, for a wild, "stinky onion" found by the Chicago River. His red torpedo onion didn't stink. It smelled faintly sweet and sharp, promising good things to eat. Torpedo onions must have special powers.

The center spread of the guidebook showed a cityscape with the hotel and the mystic lady tower. "The

Chicago Board of Trade ... tallest building in Chicago," said the legend.

He flipped a page and saw the lady close up – gray-white metallic, dwarfing tiny figures on an observation deck, austere in fluted robes, a spiky crown of metallic laurel, and her face, blank, like in a dream. "... Ceres, the Roman Goddess of grain ... thirty feet tall ... aluminum ... She is to Chicago what Lady Liberty is to New York..." and something about cereal. Snap, Crackle and Pop's mom? Mystic Cereal Woman makes things grow. Why not me?

Romans believed she rises from the Underworld every spring – like Lena does all the time. Theo's little sister died as a newborn when he was two. His mother mentioned Lena to him only once – "something was wrong with her heart" – and ignored the many questions that followed. Theo doesn't tell anyone about Lena's visits – in a blue dress, looking about the age she would be had she survived, not saying much, just tagging along, though he hasn't see her since they got off the train in Union Station.

Theo's mother was in the bathroom getting ready when the hotel nanny arrived with a timid, single knock. The skinny pale blond with aqueous eyes already looked tired in her ill-fitting maid uniform. Standing in the door without letting her, Theo told her that his mother's appointment had been canceled – nanny services no longer needed.

Theo heard his mother's muffled voice through the bathroom door. "Who was that, Theo?"

"It was Pop. He's back." Theo stepped close to the bathroom door and spoke loudly. "Pop said to tell you that he's going to his room to do some paperwork and that I should come and stay there while you're out shopping."

There was a pause. "Is that all he said? Nothing about train tickets?"

"Yeah, ma. That's all."

Theo heard an irritated sign. "Okay, Theo. Go on over to your father. Tell him I'll come get you in about two hours, okay?"

"Okay, ma."

Theo pulled his navy blue, woolen pea coat, leggings, hat and gloves from a suitcase, closed it and ran with them out the door. He had already torn a city map from the guidebook and shoved it into the lining of his pea coat along with his latest copy of Whiz Comics, featuring Captain Marvel and his magic torpedo onion.

"Bye mom!" He called loudly through the bathroom door. He could hear the shower running. Not taking any chances, he left the room before putting on his coat in the hallway by the elevators.

"Floor?" The brass-button uniformed elevator operator looked bored and straight ahead, closing the doors after Theo stepped in.

"Lobby, please." Theo tried to sound adult.

Two middle-aged women in fox furs alighted from the next floor. One stared at Theo with baleful, saggy eyes. She cleared her throat. "Where's your mommy, little boy?"

Theo ignored her. She reached over and nudged his shoulder. "Hey, lady. Watch *ya finghas!*" He did his best Bugs Bunny impression, as loudly as he could. "I'm *da papah boy*, if you wanna know! *Wheah's YOUR mommy?*"

"Hummph!" The woman made a face and shook her head, making the partridge feather on her Dorothy Lamour chapeau wiggle. Her equally decked out companion gave Theo the fish eye.

Theo tried to stand straight and not giggle or burp from the elevator's rapid descent, floor after floor, ding, ding, ding, ding...

"Main floor lobby." The operator announced, opening the doors. The two women exited in step as a parade squad. Theo made for the big brass revolving doors and propelled himself onto a powdery sidewalk. He took a bite of arctic, outside air and shivered more in excitement than cold. Cars honked and slushed by, buses growled, people flowed around him in all directions – shoppers, workers, women and men, few children, no one paying him any attention, except for Lena, who appeared alongside him, skipping, holding his mittened hand, apparently not feeling winter's bite in her blue dress, white socks and Mary Jane patent leather shoes. Captain Marvel was free! He would unpeel this torpedo onion mystery and find pop.

7 THE FLYING DUTCHMAN
OF THE INTERNET

This was the last time he was going to do this. The sameness was getting to him. The sublime view from his table at Greens didn't move him. Forget that the Golden Gate Bridge never wore the same dress twice – dazzling in myriad refractive effects or sauntering in stoles of wispy fog. "When I'm out on a spree, fighting vainly the old ennui..." The Cole Porter's lyric suited him this afternoon, memorized from his LP collection. Sameness of everything, not just these semi-blind first dates with Internet sweeties.

He gazed over iffy bobbing boats, determined supertankers, and glistening turquoise swells at the distant span. He time-traveled to the not-so-distant past when the Ohlone fished from tule rafts before the Spanish showed up with their crosses to bear, before white Victorians climbed San Francisco's hills. Then he fast-forwarded to the improbable, spires and domes, aliens and earthlings, that he had drawn for video game posters as a mercenary artist with once-high aspirations.

These days, he conjured storyboards for yet another

RPG shooter in a gleaming East Bay high rise, the latest being Flying Dutchman 2, with quantum-cannon space galleons. His job used to be fun. They were on a double deadline for the next Odyssey and new Flying Dutchman Ghost Ship RPGs for Disney. But Arlo's concentration was spooky as seven hundred head of cattle on loco weed. He spent hours on everything but his assigned tasks. The old restlessness laid clammy hands on the back of his neck. Stop it, he'd say to himself. You burned too many bridges. You're no more the boy wonder.

Then, all of a sudden he would be adrift in sappy fantasies about strolling a beach with a smart and appealing woman of undetermined visage who had his back – not becoming an old guy with a studio apartment walking a three-legged dog. The dark clouds of aborted relationships would part, allowing him a warm moment on the sunny side of love.

Every seven years, the Flying Dutchman comes ashore to find the one true love that would lift his curse. So goes the legend. But what if that were part of the curse, luring him to founder unrequited on the craggy cape of good hope every damn time?

Such considerations informed his online dating criteria, and after many false starts, Iolanda seemed to fill the bill. She never mentioned relationship in her blurb: "Seeking no-strings gentleman of the world, with a brain, sense of humor and style, not afraid of a free-spirited woman. Friends only, the rest for later, depending."

He had dropped her a bon mot – something about string theory – she returned the serve – something about second-stringers – then back-and-forth they went for a few weeks, easy as badminton, with pictures, on to their real names, emails and a Skype clincher.

Arlo scanned across the dining area to the yuppie Zen restaurant's Fort Mason entrance. Still no sign of a lone woman who might be his date who would be scanning back for him. He shifted back to the bridge's towers and sunny bowed span – not wanting to be caught staring needfully at the door. And, in that way that San Franciscans are wont to do, flashed on what it would be like to jump off – that long way down to unforgiving water, an eternity before the final eternity. Like the gamester world, he realized that the Golden Gate – itself seeming as eternal as it is ethereal – was changing in imperceptibly profound ways. He wondered who would be the last to leap from it before they installed those long-debated suicide safety nets beneath the orange railings of its walkways. What was the count? Coming up on seventeen hundred since 1937 – a bizarre part of its history, about to end – so hoped those earnest engineers and committees.

He took out his phone to check the time and was about to text her, when he heard a cheerful voice from across the busy restaurant. "Yoo hoo, Flying Dutchman." She teased, using his screen name, and there she was.

She looked more angular than in her OKCupid.com profile photos. She sat and asked the waiter for a tall glass of water--you had to ask these days, because of the drought. She downed it in one take, as if she'd been herding goats in the Hindu Kush all that morning. Then she fixed him with wolf gray eyes. She toyed with the glass the way he imagined she must posses the neck of the cello propped against the chair beside her, silent in its chaffed brown, faux alligator case. Her hands were bony, long fingered, tawny and balletic, with clear-lacquered nails trimmed short, like her feathered amber hair.

"You seem surprised." She leaned back, comfy in her body, and twirled the water glass absently. "Am I what you expected?"

"Well... " She had caught him short. He did so much better with intermediated characters in idealized forms behind plastic screens – no warm, uneven skin, no scent, no breathy lips and aqueous eyes staring back at you. He recovered. "Actually," he recovered himself. "I'm not surprised that you look appealing – even more so in the flesh." He didn't say the rest – about the keenness of her expression that faded alternatively into a walled melancholy, followed by a quick, off-putting smile as she caught him looking at her.

"You're cute, but full of shit. I'll take the compliment, though" She looked him up and down. "I thought you'd be taller. You look taller in your photos – slim and all that – but you're not really. And your hair is a lot redder. I'm going to start calling you 'Ginger Man.' Do you have a hot temper?"

He sat up more in his chair. "I only get mad at objects, not people. Not usually."

"Do you play poker?" She fingered her linen napkin.

"Not a gambling man."

"Wise choice. You're a marching band of giveaways – tells, as they say."

He twitched. "I mean. Not usually." He squirmed, peeved at himself for wiggling.

"I'm making you nervous?"

"No. Not at all." He cleared his throat.

"It's okay. I do that. People tell me everything. My cello students. I'm like their shrink."

He grinned, and sipped the pricey Petite Sirah he'd ordered. "I took the liberty." He tipped his glass to her. "Want to try it?"

"Thanks. I'll stick to water. We play a matinée this afternoon." She let a beat go by. "... but after the opera, maybe ..."

"That would be great..." He beamed, then caught himself. He glanced at her cello case.

She patted it as if it were her half-grown child. "My constant companion. She gets her own airline seat."

"Must be expensive." He took another sip.

"I rarely go anywhere without her."

"Even on dates?" He grinned.

She flushed a little, for the first time. "Of course!"

She laughed. "I'll bet you're fantasizing about getting both of us in bed together."

"That would be interesting, I confess."

"Actually, what with the matinée, it's simpler to go straight to the opera house from here, instead of doubling back to my flat."

"You drove, I take it." He kept thinking about her naked with that cello now, and she seemed to be smirking like she knew that.

"I never leave it in the car. The cello, I mean."

"I can imagine."

"It's not mine, really. It's a Scarampelli – difficult, but has a voice I love, and I know her well.

"Who's is it?"

"Belongs to a Pacific Heights widow, my benefactor – on loan to me, as long as I perform. Only a few hundred Scrampis left in the world."

"I'd love to hear you play it. Solo, I mean."

"Of course, she's not a Strad. Those are for Yo Yo Ma. But I play recitals a lot, as you know from our emails, besides being in the orchestra."

"What are you playing today?"

"Wagner. You know. We're doing Der fliegende Holländer." She exaggerated the German, like doing Mike Meyers doing Dieter Günter in an SNL clip.

"You should come! Get down with your namesake! Greer Grimsley's the Dutchman, great resonant baritone voice – and, you know, he's a heartthrob, the golden circle of patronesses from Marin to Russian Hill to Hillsborough will fill the box seats."

"Does this Dutchman float your boat too, as it were?"

She smirked. "Not my type. I find lead singers too full of themselves, frankly."

Iolanda's disarming spontaneity gave him no time to calculate. She came at things obliquely, questioning and curious. Their crisscrossing conversation stirred him as much as the honey hollow of her neck where the soft collar of her no-fuss white cotton blouse fell open so casually.

The waiter came and took their orders. Arlo went Spartan for radicchio with white beans, walnuts and figs – all organic straight off the Zen farm, said the menu. He was tempted by something heartier – the chili maybe – now that he could read Iolanda in real time, sitting there, reading him as well. She was earthier than he had imagined, like the tones of her instrument, but he stuck with the salad. Iolanda rattled off something the waiter bent to hear, wrote down and hurried off.

Another perfect San Francisco October day unfolded out the big windows as they continued to converse, summer fogs had been replaced by early autumn's dress blue skies. Sailboats and motor yachts bobbed dreamily in their marina slips. The bay stretched beyond them to the blood orange Golden Gate Bridge beckoning from across turquoise swells and whitecaps as the afternoon wind kicked up.

"I'm being rude," he said. "Let's switch chairs so you can enjoy this gorgeous view. I'm hogging it" He started to rise. "You can see the towers of the Golden Gate Bridge clearly from my side."

She went pale. Her mouth tightened. She motioned for him to stay seated. "No thanks. Really. I don't want to look... I mean, It's all right. I've seen it all before."

"It's why I picked the place."

"I figured." She sniffed, pulled a Kleenex from her small shoulder bag and blew her nose. "Romantic and all that."

"You don't like it?"

"No," she said. "I mean, yes, I like the place. I'm just not into... well ... much into bay views. I guess that sounds strange, living in the city and all that." She stopped. Her face went deeply sad for a moment, her eyes unfocused. Then she smiled at him again. "Let's change the subject"

Iolanda asked him more about his former wife, Sharon, whom he'd mentioned briefly in their online correspondence. "Did she go for caviar, tofu or bacon?"

"Depends if she was stoned. We did a lot of that back then."

It was becoming hard to hear her. He wished he'd picked a different place now. The chattering and clattering – every table filled by now – echoing off the high beamed ceiling of the old pier shed that housed this spiffy California Zen eatery. Arlo's eyes wandered out the giant window at every lull. Wheeling gulls escorted a trawler towards the wharf. Out beyond it, sharp white triangles – the manicured sloops of Sunday sailors – leaned impossibly leeward, tacking and dodging monumental container ships plying the channel to and from the Gate at deceptive speed. Wet-suited water-kiters bounded across waves like skipping stones, pelicans skimmed the swells in single file.

Arlo took comfort in mapping trajectories and plausible vectors – the part of himself he hadn't shared with Iolanda, more to take a break than to prevaricate. While he was waiting for her, he had actually counted the rectangular panes of the floor-to-ceiling window as he had waited for Iolanda to show – a transparent matrix that afforded the clientèle – even those seated way over by the wall – the spectacular bay view for which they came – twelve times ten panes, each Windexed diamond-like. He carried an antique compass in one pocket, and his smartphone in another, bristling with apps, set on vibrate. Multidimensional concordance could be such a comfort.

They were well into their lunch by now. She savored some kind of organic crepes thing with strawberries and blueberries clustered like skiers around a Matterhorn of hand-whipped cream – something Arlo's daughter, Casey, would have ordered on one of their weekends.

He watched Iolanda's capable hands pouring blackberry syrup and bulldozing cream and berries onto pieces of crepes – a surprise order – that she shoveled into her wide mouth gleefully between sentences. At least she wasn't one of those women ashamed to eat heartily on dates.

She'd gone into high gear now with their lunch all but done. She asked him about his job, and didn't get much.

He asked back: "How is it to play in an orchestra? That would be pure fantasy fulfillment for me – actually being part that sound – of making all that exquisite music."

"Right now, for me, it's exasperating," she snapped back. "I hate my music stand mate. They pair those of us in the string sections to share stands, read off the same music scores – the opera's orchestra pit, you know – it being so small." Iolanda demolished her crepes relentlessly while she complained about her music-stand-mate, a misogynistic old-timer, she said. "He pencils his smudgy fingering notes all over the music pages making them hard for me to read, not to mention, making it impossible to put in my own notations. He has fatter hands. We finger and bow differently. After I complained to him – very nicely, mind you – he starts scooting his chair, inch-by-inch, during performances, so that he crowds my space and practically elbows me. Next time he tries that I'm going to kick his chair out from under him!"

Iolanda's orchestral miasma drifted into his consciousness and pixilated all those triangles and rhomboids she had conjured earlier.

"I like that."

"Him doing that?"

"No, you kicking his chair – or his ass." He grinned.

"Probably would get me canned."

"Complain to the union."

"The old fart is shop steward, if you can believe that."

"Maybe he's Wagner reincarnated into being a second cello in San Francisco as punishment for being such a son of a bitch."

"You give mister fat-fingers too much credit."

"He hated Paris," he interjected, surprising himself.

She put her fork down. "What?"

"Paris. Didn't Wagner write The Flying Dutchman in gay Paree while hiding out from Prussian creditors?"

She sipped coffee. "Prussian creditors. Ze vill blitz das deadbeats mit panzers."

"I read that in a book about Impressionists, as an aside." She must think I'm trying to show off, he mused, his lips pursing.

"Show off," she said, grinning and pushing bites of crepe around her plate again. "The Paris Opera."

"Paris opera?"

"They didn't buy Der fliegende Holländer – not enough joie de vivre – so Herr Wagner packed and went back to Deutchland."

"...uber alles." He plucked a fig from his salad. It tasted of raspberry vinaigrette.

"I'll bet you put the cap back on the toothpaste before you start brushing." She smiled. Crimson berry syrup on her teeth gave her a vampire look. He imagined the taste of kissing her. "You're OCD," I can tell. You have to pin the tail to every donkey, just right."

"Well, I wouldn't call myself a ... " He fell silent. Guess she's right.

"What did you mean when you wrote me that, 'I'm a recovering romantic'?"

"Love is a mental illness - falling in love, I mean. I've sworn off. It never ends well."

"I know what you mean. God save me from clingy men – worse, possessive ones."

"Now that we have that settled." He crunched another bite of radicchio bravely. "Who invented this stuff? Self-flagellating foodie health monks?"

A tall figure appeared out of nowhere and stood by their table. Not the waiter. The man sported a red-and-white running suit on a lanky physique, a red headband encircled his longish blond locks, darker than the pale stubble on his face, his pinkish skin flushed. Arlo looked up at him, but the man stared only at Iolanda through orange tinted sunglasses. "Iolanda! I *thought* that was you."

Iolanda ignored him for a long moment, then glanced up and uttered his name flatly. "Jake."

"What do you know? I stopped to buy some Tassajara muffins at the bakery counter – I know, an indulgence." He held up a white paper bag with the Greens logo on it and swung it back and forth as evidence. "And here you are! ... Good to see you looking so well."

He shifted on his feet. Without being asked, he sat down opposite the cello, next to Arlo, who shifted uncomfortably. "Do you mind? Really did a hard run, out to the bridge – against that wind – then back."

Iolanda shrugged. Jake didn't look at Arlo for permission. "Muffin?" he said, opening the bag and putting on the center of the table.

"I'll pass," said Arlo and downed another fig. He raised an eyebrow and nodded to Jake. Finally, he asked Iolanda, "Is this the guy?"

Iolanda nodded, then looked down her fork and pushed back her chair. "Oops. It's late. Gotta go." She stood and took hold of the handle of her cello case like a mother about to hurry off with her child. "Bye, Arlo. Thanks for lunch. Let's talk later." She didn't say goodbye to Jake.

Arlo half rose as she left. He flagged the waiter for a check.

Jake shrugged. "Gotta go too. Nice meeting you – Arlo?"

Arlo sat back down and turned to him. "I don't think the lady's interested, Jake." Arlo was surprised by the edge in his own voice. So out of character. Really, this was none of his business.

Jake scowled, "I think you should butt out."

"Just giving you some friendly advice."

Jake muttered, "asshole," and stood up, knocking his

chair back. People at the other tables lowered their lunch forks and stared as Jake stormed off. He left the muffin bag.

Arlo paid his bill. He saw no sign of Iolanda or Jake outside along the Fort Mason pier or the parking lot.

He dropped her a note when he got home. "Kind of a bumpy start, but I enjoyed your company? Dinner? A little adventure?"

She messaged back, "Okay. I'm free Tuesday night."

Iolanda avoided looking at the Golden Gate Bridge even when it was in plain view, which wasn't often, given that she rented a flat in Noe Valley and spent most of her work time at the War Memorial Opera House and the San Francisco Conservatory of Music where she taught – both nestled among the city's famous hills where one could see neither bay nor bridges.

But every May 31 for the past five years – on or about Memorial Day – Iolanda would take a green and white Golden Gate Transit bus from Fifth and Mission Streets downtown to its northbound Golden Gate Bridge toll plaza stop by the bridge's southern anchorage. From there, head down, paying scant attention the art deco magnificence and engineering trapeze act of the structure and views that drew the tourists – she would take the pedestrian path that led up onto the bridge and across it on the side facing the city. Iolanda would walk, still head bowed, to one of the observation niches just beyond the south tower, where the walkway and railing jut a few feet outward and tourists often pause to snapshot the resplendent panoramic view of bay and cityscape. Still, Iolanda ignored the view.

She would stand there and imagine her daughter's thoughts and feelings in the moments before she disappeared. Had her daughter climbed over the railing and lingered on the steel ledge, in the manner of many suicides, or had vaulted the rail, took a few steps the leaped off like a high diver? Had her arms been outstretched, or in front of her? Had she panicked on the way down, flailing in terror? Iolanda shook, and sobbed into the wind and the incessant traffic noise around her, letting another year of sorrow out over the water, only to feel it begin to fill her consciousness again.

Bridge police had found her daughter's pricey mountain bike leaning against the railing at that spot. A chill marine mist had crept through the gate under the bridge deck. That particular May 31st happened to fall on a Tuesday. The usual summer season foot traffic of sightseers was thinner than it had been Monday, the legal Memorial Day holiday.

A vacationer from Atlanta did notice somebody climbing over the railing just beyond the South Tower and called 911. Police found no jumper and Coast Guard cutters failed to spot a body, as they crisscrossed in the fog beneath the bridge. A day later, however, Linda's helmet was discovered by a hiker, washed up at Baker Beach on the ocean side of the Gate, along with her silver-and-black fanny pack containing her student I.D., lipstick, a mobile phone and sixteen sodden dollars, one for each year of her life. Linda apparently had left no note. No body was found, but, though rare, it has happened with jumpers in the past. The police investigated. Reports were filed. The county coroner ruled death by probable suicide.

Linda had met a man that day, Iolanda had learned later – Seth something-or-other, a thirtyish, self-involved stock analyst from Charles Schwab. The cops tracked him down after checking Linda's cell phone calls earlier that day. Morgan confirmed they started over the bridge together, but denied she was his date. "Just friends," he backpedaled. "We rode together once in a while. I ride with a lot of people. I was across the bridge before I saw she wasn't behind me. I figured she had just gone off on her own."

Iolanda kept replaying that last morning. She and her daughter had argued over Linda's perpetually chaotic bedroom, strewn with clothes and half-eaten snacks, then escalated, predictably, into arguing about boys and men.

"Where are you going? I don't want you seeing that biker," Iolanda had said.

"Chill, Iolanda! He's old news."

Iolanda's jaw tightened. "You didn't answer my question."

"I'm going over to Sid's to study history."

"Do I know him?"

"Sid's a girl." Linda blew and rolled her eyes. Linda had taken to dating bad boys sure to rile her mother – then, without telling her mother, older men.

Iolanda felt nauseated, clammy, simmering in rage and shame. Her daughter had transformed from a pleasant, studious school girl to mercurial delinquent overnight since she had returned from a month with her estranged father down in Newport Beach, sailing with his music business friends no doubt.

That was Jake, with whom every encounter proved toxic. Jake was very successful. His company had an office in San Francisco and a high-rise condo for entertaining and business trips where he stayed occasional visits, but he had ignored his daughter for twelve years since divorcing Iolanda.

Then, on her 15th birthday, Linda had decided to look up her father. He didn't embrace her, but he didn't push her away either, and he gave her lots of presents. Iolanda fumed at the way Jake acted the role of bereaved father after Linda's disappearance. Even now her ex-husband kept popping up in Iolanda's life as if they were connected again in their grief. Iolanda fumed at each encounter – for example, Jake coming to Arlo's table at Greens – but rage and sorrow choked her every time she tried to tell him off.

Iolanda regretted every word of her last conversation with Linda.

"Straighten up your room before you go. I've got company this afternoon,"

"Is your asshat boyfriend with the pimp mustache coming over again?"

"Marcello is *not* my boyfriend. He's a second violinist in the orchestra. We're going over a piece."

"He's all over a *piece* all right." Linda already had donned her silver-and-black, Oakland Raiders windbreaker and was walking her thousand-dollar Trek Mamba mountain bike that Jake had given her for Christmas – down their railroad flat's long hallway towards the door. *Ten years their daughter doesn't exist for him, then Jake gives her a bike, too much bling and a cash card to get herself in all kinds of trouble.*

"Give me this 'Sid's' phone number, please. And don't forget your helmet!"

"Oh, mom! I'll text the number to you. Gotta go." Linda was out the door.

"I love you. Be careful!" Iolanda rushed to the door and called out, but Linda was already gone. She never texted "Sid's" number.

Even after five years, Iolanda could not keep herself from half-consciously expecting Linda to show any day. Her pulse would quicken when she spotted a teen who looked like Linda on the street. Sometimes she would and follow one, just to make sure. These episodes were less frequent now, but her Linda still showed up in dreams, always alive and well, and as a little girl.

The sliver of uncertainty about her daughter's disappearance infected and somehow inflamed her grief. Whether by suicide, or abduction, running off, or any reason, she had still lost her daughter. She prayed Linda had not jumped, but feared something even worse had befallen her, then raged at the thought of Linda choosing to vanish without a word like that, then agonized about the girl caught up in some addiction, or cult, or God knows what.

Worst of all, Iolanda re-lived her every failed moment with since her daughter had been in diapers, every ill-considered word, every false start and misunderstanding of her too brief motherhood, when she had felt like it would last forever and there would always be time to correct mistakes.

They say tragedy can deepen creative expression. But Iolanda played on as capably as ever. No more or less inspired than usual, her practiced hands took up the cello, lachrymal eyes on the score, somnambulist mind finding no solace.

She kept her budding romance with Arlo cordoned off from her tragedy. She needed this break, she told herself. She hid the facts even as their intimacy deepened and dating evolved towards a relationship that both of them avoided defining for now. She simply liked being someone with someone who looked at her with sunny eyes instead of concern and pity. She maneuvered to his place rather than hers for their lovemaking most of the time, thereby avoiding reminders of Linda, keeping their experience dreamlike and disconnected from her past. They weekended in Santa Cruz and Carmel and Lake Tahoe. He didn't ask why she never looked at the Golden Gate Bridge.

He was so shy – slim, pale, freckled with unruly curls the color of fire that changed with the light. He wasn't handsome, but unusual and his softly spoken dry wit turned her on. She was falling for this guy, and that was never intended. She told him she had no children. He asked her once about a framed photo of Linda he saw one evening when he had picked her up at her flat. She told him the photo was of a favorite niece – a lie that would make the truth all the more difficult to reveal to him when the time came.

Arlo kept hinting that he wanted Iolanda to meet his own daughter. She kept putting him off. She wanted them to keep dancing free. Meeting Arlo's daughter would surely evoke memories of her own and bring her grief back to a boil – something she would not want to impose upon either this kind man nor his kid, who had complications of their own.

Omissions and prevarications can seem facile with casual dates, but come to reckoning with unforeseen involvement, and she was becoming more and more unbearably invested in Arlo now.

Arlo wasn't sure exactly when Iolanda broke things off, or if it was to be permanent or what burned out lovers euphemistically call "a break." She faded from his life like a full moon moving behind clouds. She excused herself from one date after another, always plausibly. Then she phoned him early one Saturday morning to announce she would be flying to Tokyo the next day with members of the orchestra for a guest appearance. She didn't explain further. "Be back in a few weeks, sweet man." she said with simulated lightheartedness, baffling him with the endearment at this point.

"A few weeks?"

"Going to do some sightseeing. Might as well."

"What about Casey?" A while back – before the fadeout – he had planned to introduce Iolanda to his daughter during that week while Casey was on one of her scheduled stay overs.

Iolanda responded in a barely audible voice: " … I can't. Our plane leaves tomorrow."

"And you're just telling me this now?"

"I'm so sorry, Arlo." She paused again. "Let's talk about after I get back. Okay? We'll get together."

But Arlo didn't hear anything from Iolanda in the long weeks that followed.

His habitual post-fling diffidence failed to kick in. The Dutchman didn't sail off to cyber-sea and the usual dates in every port.

He pined like a schoolboy over the few photos he had of her. He made a point of driving by the opera house or her apartment whenever his intended destination accommodated the rationalization that it wasn't stalking.

He put on his best face for Casey, a blessed distraction from the blues. When his daughter was not visiting, he worked long hours in Emeryville and sometimes slept over on his office couch when he would miss the last BART train back to San Francisco. Weeks turned into months void of Iolanda. But she pestered his thoughts and dreams.

The Dutchman tried to sail off again. He chatted with a few dating prospects online, but turned away each time, then stopped searching altogether.

Seeing the Golden Gate bridge now reminded him of that first brunch date with Iolanda at Greens eatery. He became even more of a ghost in his own spare apartment, just his place to bed down, shave, shower and work from home, desk and drawing table in disarray, little except dubious take-out leftovers in the fridge.

On sleepless nights he browsed the Net, fishing for curiosities, exploring histories, gazing at images and watching clips aimlessly, until, inevitably, these days, he found himself browsing through stuff about the opera, bringing Iolanda to mind over and over, despite growing irritation at himself for doing so. One night, after typing Iolanda's name into Google once again, he came upon an archived news item that brought him up short: "GG TEEN JUMPER MYSTERY"

He zoomed in on close-up of a teenage girl with wavy blond hair. He recognized the face instantly from the portrait of Iolanda's "niece." The caption read, "MISSING : Linda Cardoso Brolle, 16, daughter of music mogul Jake Brolle and SF cellist Iolanda Cardoso." He re-read the article, then everything else he could find about the case.

Impulsively he grabbed for his phone to call Iolanda, then realized that if she had wanted him to know, she would have told him. His stomach clutched, his throat constricted, his mouth went dry – dark sensations he had felt as a boy when his mother was dying resurfaced.

The revelation and mystery obsessed him in the days that followed. He drafted countless email to Iolanda, never sent. He searched frantically for more information about Iolanda's daughter. Did Iolanda believe her daughter missing or dead? Had she hoped, then grieved, then accepted it? He read stories about people who had miraculously survived a bridge jump, and one about the single, verified faked bridge death: One Chris J. Christensen had been a jeweler and newly elected member of the San Francisco Board of Supervisor who left his jacket with a suicide note in it draped over the span railing in 1948.

No body was found. He was declared drowned. But years later, a reporter found out that Christensen had run off to Texas with a sailor, and opted for faking his suicide rather than either parting with his seafaring lover or the pair of them facing exposure as a homosexuals in those days.

Arlo got to speculating and even making up game scenarios about a special world where everyone who had perished at the Golden Gate, turned out to be still alive in a parallel universe, including the eleven workers who died building it.

One afternoon he dozed off at his desk and dreamed about tow-headed Marilyn DeMont, the five-year-old girl who jumped off a bridge girder in 1946, because her father – an elevator repairman – told her to do it, then jumped himself. Then he woke up, shut down his computer and went out for a walk. Nap dreams are the worst.

One morning, on his way south, to Palo Alto for a lecture at Stanford, he had to turn off the I-280. Perhaps it was synchronicity that he exited at Colma, the cemetery town just south of the city. He had been listening to Mozart's c-minor piano concerto and he just broke down. He pulled onto a side street, stopped, and sobbed convulsively, as if mourning every lost child in the world, and probably himself as a boy.

His doctor prescribed Prozac. He smoked weed instead. It helped, but not a lot. Browsing at City Lights Bookstore one afternoon, he ran into Wicksley again – his ex-priest, poet, and fellow Galileo High School alum.

Wicksley freelanced JavaScript coding to afford living in the city and having time to hang out in North Beach.

They crossed busy Columbus Avenue to Specs' Twelve Adler Museum Café. Wicksley, listened to Arlo's troubles over drinks, then rendered a diagnosis in faux Viennese. "It zeems you hav developed an inconvenient heart."

"What do I do, Wicks?"

"Admit you're in love, for starters."

"I suppose so, but what good would it do me? She's slammed the door to all that..."

"Admitting your heart is broken gives you access to it, instead of walling it off conveniently – as you've been doing for years. A heart is a magical thing, not just a pump – a terrible nuisance that makes you fully human."

"I get why Iolanda pulled away," he told his new shrink a week later. "It's her way of avoiding pain. No wonder she avoided meeting Casey!"

"And what else do you feel, Arlo?" His shrink, Dr. Emma Bean, held forth from Mill Valley, meaning he had to cross the Golden Gate for their appointments. Emma regarded him intently through motherly amber-rimmed glasses. She was one of those Abraham-Maslow-Carl-Rogers humanistic psychologists who believed in "positive engagement" with her clients. She had been a consultant to his firm's game developers at one point when they were bent onto enriching some of their characters. He had looked her up quietly after that.

"You're doing good work, Arlo." Emma said that a lot.

"Why did I have to fall for somebody with so many complications, if I was going to let myself get involved in the first place?"

"Everyone has complications, Arlo. That's the ticket price of real intimacy."

"But hers seem insurmountable."

"Do you think you have to rescue her? She doesn't need that. Does this situation remind you of something?"

"Yeah. I get the picture. As a kid, I thought it was up to me to save my mother from dying, if only I could pray hard enough, be a good enough boy, not ever get her upset."

"Maybe you're just the right person for this Iolanda. You've suffered losses too – your mother, then your marriage. But you can't save and she has to want you in her life somehow."

"That's just it., I think she does, or she would have broken it off more cleanly instead of fading away."

Dr. Emma scribbled a note on the yellow pad in her lap as she rocked in her funky brown leather Barcalounger. Her office, a 1920s bungalow nestled in redwoods and ferns off Shoreline, was done in early thrift shop, with a couple of stuffed leather chairs, no couch, a messy desk, a jungle of giant aspidistras and a boxer's heavy bag for punching phantom nemeses and toxic alter egos hung from a chain over one of its thick wooden rafters.

"Maybe you could express that in a positive way," she said. "Offer her your friendship – unconditionally. Then hope for the best. If she accepts, fine, but tread lightly. If she refuses, you'll grieve, but you'll have gained from this experience, Arlo. Believe me."

He nodded, but his calm resolve evaporated as he drove home across the Golden Gate. His mind rollercoastered up and down probability curves and through a kaleidoscope of detective novels and mysteries. He entered the tunnel of Hitchcock's Vertigo. He would spot a young woman resembling Linda one day on Market Street, follow her like acrophobic detective Jimmy Stewart and discover her living under a different name in a rundown apartment building, like Kim Novak, presumed a suicide. No. Scratch that. He would discover that Iolanda never had a daughter, or that human traffickers had kidnapped Linda. No. Too cliché.

Arlo got into playing detective himself. He didn't tell his shrink right away. Too crazy, he thought.

He went to the Hall of Records and read the coroner's inquest findings. With a little digging, he was able to connect with SFPD Detective Sergeant Noel Parquin, who had investigated Linda's disappearance, and had subsequently retired to Auburn in the Sierra foothills. As a pretext, he told Parquin he was a mystery writer. Parquin, enthused, said he was writing a crime novel himself, and asked about Arlo's literary agent. "No problem! I'll mention you and text you his contact info." Arlo rationalized that maybe he would write a mystery story about all this. He had to be discreet for now. He wondered uncomfortably how Iolanda would feel about him poking around, and didn't know why he was doing it himself.

"The father," said Parquin. "I'd talk to him – Jake Brolle. I pegged him for a hustler. Off the record, he's being investigated by the feds, some kind of RICO money laundering probe. I only talked to him by phone. Linda Brolle's disappearance wasn't a priority, really. Turned out little Linda was seeing an older guy. A local stock analyst named Seth Knox. He lied through his teeth. Said that he wasn't banging that girl – scared shitless. I didn't like the smell, but there was no budget to perusing the case further."

"What about the mother?" Arlo asked, tentatively.

"Iolanda. Unusual name. Classy woman, but frayed at the seams. Sad case. I think she still hopes desperately that her daughter is still alive, but won't talk about it."

"Do you think that as well?"

"Nah. She probably jumped. But maybe she was encouraged – maybe given a shove. Maybe she was pregnant. We'll never know. The tide was flowing out of the bay at the time she would have jumped. You know how swift that is. It could have dragged her body clean out the gate into the Pacific for the sharks. But what's the harm in her mother keeping hopes alive?"

The Sunday after that conversation, Arlo went to Baker Beach, on the rugged Pacific side of the bridge, where Linda's things had been found. He could see the South Tower of the bridge looming to his right just beyond a steep rocky hillside covered with brush, cypress and Monterey pines that blocked a view of the city completely.

He related his various private-eye fantasies to Wicksley later that day at Specs. They were meeting there often now, with Arlo fudging his work hours. "Miracles do happen," said Wicksley.

"You mean, Iolanda's kid could still be alive?"

"I don't know about that." Wicksley signaled the bartender for another Negra Modelo. "But this is the first time I've heard you obsessed with someone other than yourself."

"Asshole!" Arlo had to laugh. He ordered another for himself.

Wicksley smirked stared absently across the bar. "Did you ever think that maybe the Flying Dutchman needed to discover 'true love' in more than one sense?"

"I don't think I'm Iolanda's 'true love', Wicksley."

"That doesn't matter. The Dutchman breaks his curse by learning how to love truly, rapture, risks and all. That's the 'true love' meant by the legend."

Arlo took a swig. "Richard Wagner meets Carl Jung meets Erica Jong. You've read too much Joseph Campbell."

Wicksley ignored the jibe. "Without that ability, he continues to struggle endlessly through blinding storms of willful ego."

"Thank you, Father Wicksley. Have you taken up the cloth again?" Arlo put his hands together prayerfully.

"Write her a letter." Wicksley banged down his beer bottle, opened a bar napkin and spread it out and slid it over to Arlo.

"To Iolanda? Forget it. She won't even answer a text message."

"No. To the *Tooth Fairy*." Wicksley slid a ballpoint pen from his shirt pocket and clicked it in and out rapidly under Arlo's nose. "I bet you never thought writing her a real, low-tech pen-and-paper note delivered by the U.S. Postal Service. It's romantic, pal."

"On a Spec's bar napkin?"

"Why not? If you don't do it right here and now, you'll chicken out. I know you." Wicksley waved the bartender over and asked if he could find them an envelope. The bartender shook his head. A tall, slouchy, stubble-bearded guy scooted over several empty stools, pulled a square white envelope from his jacket and handed it to Arlo. There was a jokey get-well card inside.

"Don't you need this?" Arlo held out the card.

"It's okay." The man waved it away. "It was for a guy at work, but he died."

"I got a stamp," volunteered the bartender.

The envelope was addressed in neat block letters, no return address. It looked like a party invitation. Iolanda opened it, and gingerly removed a bar napkin from Specs. She saw that it was covered with fine ball point writing. After a moment, Sshe found this amusing. It broke the ice. She guessed it was from Arlo. "If it starts to bother me, I'll stop reading," she told herself, unable to contain her curiosity.

She sat at her kitchen table bathed in the morning light of her south-facing window and read, then re-read the note.

"Beached Dutchman, whose ship has sailed, seeks earthy harmonic friendship with enigmatic cellist he can't do without. If you want a grounded guy who knows the score but will never crowd your music stand call me. We'll start again, with maybe brunch, but no distracting views, because, as you should know, I only have eyes for you, dear. You know the tune. One, two, three... Arlo."

She turned Arlo's saloon song this way and that on her table, with a slow smile, then felt her own tears as they dropped on the tissue one by one, blurring the ink. After several false starts, she called him, hoping the number still worked.

"Arlo. hi," she said softly and had to clear her throat. "It's me. Would you like to come over? ...Please? We'll talk.

8 SATAN, THE MOVIE!

What are the odds I'd find myself on this desolate palisade with a dead man in the trunk of a rented Buick? I check my mirrors, headlights off, clammy despite the chill in the pale of a gibbous moon silvering the inky vastness of ocean before me. No one around. Time to get on with it.

I hear – almost feel – the muffled, rhythmic pounding of surf far below. Up here, gusts keep nudging the car. My nervous, irregular breaths urge me to fuck it, just drive off the damn cliff and be done with everything.

I see myself, plummeting behind the wheel screaming, weightless – too late to change my mind – crushed against jagged rocks, exploding, then engulfed in massive waves that restore order as if nothing had happened. Blub, blub. Time and tide go on. The moon still shines, fish swim, soon to take up residence in the wreck and feed on my remains. Yum.

Would I have an out-of-body experience at the end to witness it all, and maybe right beside the man in my trunk? My spotty education in graphic novels and video games prepares me only for the irony of my situation.

I have never believed in luck, one way or another, unless you consider the astronomical improbability of popping up at all in a fourteen-billion-year-old universe, with no do-over, like now, my life down to one existential moment.

Some hold that wherever your head is at when you die becomes your eternity. Would it be like that for me? What about the guy in my trunk?

Why do I hesitate? Anything to avoid the onus of extracting said stiff from the trunk and, one way or another, commending it to the briny deep. Should I say some final words, salute and blow a bosun's whistle as I send him over the side ?

In daylight, this is one of those spectacular spots where tourists pull their campers off Pacific Coast Highway to ooh and ahh, and click photos that reduce their awe to a thumbnail. It looks much like the bluff where Frank and I killed a Dodge minivan.

Frank, his Laila, and myself – misfit musketeers, we called ourselves back in high school – caravanned up Pacific Coast Highway to the bluff, Frank driving my car with Laila. I followed them in a rusted minivan, burning oil, that we took off the hand of a tweeker for twenty bucks. A motley procession of invited kids trailed us in ragged procession, most from our school.

The whole thing had been one of Frank's schemes – a "Living Dead" party! Be in a movie that Frank was making, was the come-on. He already had his own camera and was filmmaking (if you could call it that) back then in high school. "Frank Kim Stein's *My Mother, My Zombie!* was the working title of this one."

"See a screaming ZOMBIE MOM's Car plunge of a cliff and explode! Costume optional. Munchies on sale" (the latter, for sure-fire profits, considering the sure abundance of medicinal weed. BYOB. You'd get a contact high whenever the wind shifted. A modest "donation" bought you a slip of paper with directions to the location and the time the filming would commence.

In his own way, Frank had been into micro-financing long before social media and smart phones. Setting the tone, Laila wore zombie makeup and tattered clothes, as did a number of her girlfriends.

Frank Kim didn't fit any categories or run with any crowd but the ones he gathered for himself, with no shortage of female admirers, despite being a not particularly handsome, wiry, Chinese-Korean-Mexican kid from L.A.'s poly-ethnic Westlake District where gang turf abutted the gated condo encampments priced to sell.

Not being particularly handsome myself, I admired Frank for blowing past that and making people see him the way he wanted. A talent I lacked, starting with knowing what I wanted myself. Except for Laila. I wanted her. Badly. Not that I thought I had a chance. Maybe somebody *like* her, but no one could compare to her in my teen-crush eyes back then. We located and drove onto our location – a flat, off-road apron perched on a palisade, obscured from the highway. The kids partied while Frank, all business, set up and started shooting He ran around taking a lot of jumpy hand-held stuff using filters and off-lighting for creepy b-movie effects. Frank had a Quentin Tarantino passion for B-movie tropes. A couple of guys and I rolled the van close to the edge.

We stuffed blow-up dolls that we had crudely painted as zombies inside the van, packed it with fireworks and on Frank's cue, a bunch, screaming and pushing, got it rolling and over the edge while Frank's camera rolled. The van did a slow-motion tumble, banged and smashed loudly to the bottom, broke up and sunk slowly into the churning water below. It didn't explode, as we had planned. Frank lighted and tossed a red road flare through the open back of the doomed minivan. It glowed and smoked at first. We thought it wasn't going to work, but just as we heard the van hit the rocks in the darkness below, the flare set off a box of fireworks Frank had placed in the van's back seat with spectacular effect. We all cheered, except Frank who stood perilously close to the edge, keeping his camera rolling.

Not everyone of our merry band braved the promontory's edge for a full view of the stunt, but we all heard the final crash, and all cheered boisterously.

"Death to minivans!" I shouted brainlessly.

Laila screamed and did a dead-shuffle holding an ax smeared in ketchup, snarling into the camera in her chalk-face, black-eyed, bloody lipstick, made up like a zombie mom risen out of the flaming wreckage bent on vengeance – Frank's idea for a closer.

No retakes possible after the grand finale, so Frank put the lights and high-end digital cameras he had "borrowed" from the school film lab back in my car.

As the party thinned out, four burly bikers I hadn't seen before walked up to Frank. "We want our money back, asshole." One held a tire iron to his side, another looked like he was packing.

Frank gave them his best grin, and didn't look at all perturbed. "Hey, dudes! What's the deal? We did the scene! Didn't you see the big plunge?" He rolled one hand over the other, made crashing noises – "Grrrr bang-bang-bang, crunch, boom, kaboom!"

They stared at him. The fattest one, a red wooly mammoth of a man, got right up in Frank's face. "Thar weren't no, 'kaboom,' asshole. Where's our kaboom? Where's the bomb, the big ole explosion?" He made an exploding gesture at Frank.

"Well, crash, there was a *crash*... Lots of noise. I'd call it a pretty terrific stunt, all in all." Frank grinned and stood his ground. "If you came too late for the main event, guys, that's not my fault. We did the stunt when I said we would. No refunds."

"Bullshit!" The big one spat on Frank's dusty running shoes. "You wuz supposed to be in the fuckin' car, flying off the cliff."

Frank shook his head and folded his arms. "No. My announcement said: 'See plunge to their doom in a spectacular car crash!' We did have zombies on board. I can show you my footage. Just not me. I don't play a zombie. I am the director." Frank put a thumb to his scrawny chest, savoring each word.

"Hey, let me get the camera. We'll get you guys in the film. Great scene... You're perfect!" Frank make framing gestures at their faces, and started to back away.

The tallest of the biker quartet, an older guy a long, gray-blonde pony tail and tree trunk arms bulging from his sleeveless leather jacket, grabbed Frank by the shirt, lifting and slamming him against the side of my Honda sedan. "Money back, or drive this one over!"

I cleared my throat. "Hey. That's my car, not his."

The shortest of them with a bulbous nose, built low like a fireplug grabbed me by the arm. "Okay, then you drive the car over the cliff, wimp. We don't give a shit."

Laila lurched from the shadows, snarling, still in zombie character and makeup holding her ax high. She howled through dripping fake fangs as if to sink them into the bikers' ample flesh.

Frank jumped in mock horror. "Watch out, dudes, she's fucking crazy, killed five people, escaped from Camarillo. Nothing can stop her. She's got superhuman strength! Run!" He turned to run, waving at the bikers, but they stood rooted and wide eyed. I pushed aside the one closest to me and opened the car door for Laila. Then Frank and I went to jump in, but my timing was off. The biggest one punched me in the face. I felt blood – real blood this time – running from my nose, all over my shirt.

That was when the California Highway Patrol cruiser showed up off the main road, on a routine check, and flashed its lights at us. "Lucky bastard," I told Frank, afterward. "Those thugs would have stomped you flat."

Frank just laughed. "Can't win if you don't play."

There were a lot of questions. Turned out Frank

didn't have any film permits. Lucky for us, Laila drew on her law school knowledge and did some lawyer-like explaining, without giving anything away – tricky considering the zombie makeup. She said we came from a costume party.

And lucky for us, the cops paid more attention to her breasts than anything she said or anything else around us. She even got the bikers off. Nobody mentioned the minivan wreckage at the base of the palisade, half-submerged and obscured by the rising darkness – and no moon up yet – out of sight, out of mind. Frank landed on his feet, just as he seemed able to do no matter what.

"Shit, Frank. I'm still shaking, but you're like ice, dude." I liked using "dude" then. "You have a deal with the devil, or something? Your soul for luck?"

"My next picture. Great idea, Max. Thanks."

The three of us rode in silence back to L.A. I drove. Things got quiet after a round of congratulating ourselves on being black belt smart-asses. With the trunk full of gear, we had to stuff the portable camera light stands in the passenger side. Laila rode in the back seat with Frank. They sat apart, Frank laughed, doing a blow-by-blow of the whole experience, including the bikers, and estimating the take, leaving out, of course, expenses for my gas. I could see Laila in my rear-view mirror doing a slow. Then she leaned forward. "Frank! Would you please shut up a minute?"

Driving on, in silence, I felt her hand gently on my shoulder. "Max, I'm sorry. But I have to tell Frank something right now. Do you mind?"

"Hey, no. Cool." I caught her eye in my mirror then looked away, focusing as best as I could on the road, but all ears. Oh-oh... Things hadn't seemed right between them lately. A deluded, naïve child in me, fantasized about me ending up with Laila if they broke up, then dismissed the thought.

Sure enough, she was calling it quits, right there in my

back seat after what Frank had thought his triumphant moment. She told Frank that she had been seeing her ex-boyfriend again. Roger. I had only met him once, but figured him right away for a preppie prig. They had become study buddies in the bar exam course she was taking. "Roger and I want to try things out again. You know, I met you on the bounce. Timing is everything."

He started to make his case, but dropped it, and went cold. He could do stoic well. "Gotta go your way, I guess. Like we all do." He made a Clint Eastwood squint.

Old boyfriend? I felt like she was dumping me too. Adios, three musketeers.

We didn't see much of each other after that. Laila was there when Frank showed his zombie mom movie, but then so were a bunch of other kids. Herky jerky, but funny. It helped him get into film school.

I went off to University of Chicago – feeling out of step as always. I took my degree in comparative media studies. I had read that the field "prepares students for jobs that do not exist yet." Good enough for me! Turned out that's the new norm. Until they manifest, I could move in with dad and his girlfriend. No? Mom then. Luckily, she got the house.

Later I heard from a mutual friend that Laila passed the bar, and got herself hired by a fancy entertainment law firm in Century City. I thought about her a lot in spite of myself – golden, coming out of the surf, eyes turquoise green shifting to blue like the ocean, laughing – at me, with me, I never knew, perfect teeth catching the light and that little twist to her lips.

Occasionally, I would find some excuse to phone her and talk a bit, but never say really how I felt.

As I arrived here tonight, steering slowly along turnoff to the spot where I now find myself, I noticed a sign caught in my headlights briefly before I clicked them off. It read:

NO DUMPING
$500 FINE

I imagine that applies to human as well as automobile bodies, biodegradable or not.

The run-up to my predicament started one summer afternoon three years ago when Frank – always Frank – walked into Musso & Frank's Grill, no connection, on Hollywood Boulevard, intruding on my L.A. Noir daydream of sipping a martini with John Barrymore, Orson Welles, or Charlie Chaplin, Raymond Chandler, Bukowski, or Faulkner and the other ghosts show inhabit the joint. I had taken to writing, by then, between spotty work for a Hollywood public relations firm, mostly video game clients. At a place like Musso's – its dark wood and worn red leather oozing Hollywood gone by – I could dwell in my own fantasy game playing out my noirish writer fantasy much more easily than actually getting any writing done back at my desk.

A pudgy, crimson-caped Satan with prop pitch fork followed Frank, and to my mild surprise, stepped up to my booth with him. Odd devil looked more like a lost Disney dwarf than a fallen angel.

"Max!" Frank made like he was surprised to run into me. "Mind if we join you?" I gestured my ascent. Satan slid into my booth first, slouching to the middle. Frank followed, sitting opposite me.

"His Satanic Majesty, Lewis C. Farr III" He motioned to Mr. Redsuit. None of the lunch crowd even peeked at us. This was Hollywood Boulevard. A suited-up Chewbaca could just as well have walked in and ordered Wookie Kibble broil and gravy.

"Jass call me Lew." He offered a limp hand and raised his half-drooped eyelids at me. He sounded like a crow on a cold morning.

"You related to the Lewis Farr the media mogul?" Anything's possible in Hollywood.

Frank shook his head. "We don't talk about it."

"Casheth out." Satan squinted, high forehead furrowed, as if trying to remember some long-forgotten verse.

"No money?"

"No, casheth."

Frank helped. "Cast out."

"Dishowned!" Satan munched.

Frank talked out of the side of his mouth, as if our companion couldn't hear. "Nasty divorce. Lots of drama. His mother ran off with him as a child. Anyway, you know the old story: not the son father wanted...We don't talk about it..." Frank gave Satan boy an avuncular pat on the arm.

"Been there, myself." I cast him a sympathetic nod.

"Like I said, we don't talk about it..."

"Oh. Okay... Now. Moving on." I looked over at Frank resumed his pitch. Frank gave me the cut sign drawing his index finger over his throat. My waiter arrived. Satan ordered a mushroom Fontina cheeseburger on the special, with a glass of Petite Sirah. The waiter wrote on his pad. He seemed to have no trouble understanding what Satan said. Frank ordered a Cobb salad.

Somehow, I knew I'd get stuck with the check, but I was hooked by now. It wasn't that Frank couldn't afford lunch, even considering his recent ups and downs. Right out of film school, Frank had landed assistant directorships on a couple of well received films, including one by Wayne Wang. Frank scored well with – Mom of the Dead – his first feature, made on the cheap in Canada. Fan and critics loved it on the festival circuit, and though it never got much theater distribution, it became an instant cult film.

But the sequel – big mistake – flopped badly enough to pull the first down a notch with it. Frank went from boy wonder to boy goat and he wasn't even thirty. I wondered if Frank's lucky streak had ended.

When their orders arrived, Satan hit his with Tabasco. "Nice touch," I told him. "But I would think the Prince of Darkness would want something bloodier than a mushroom burger."

""Shrooms iz fine. No meat fo me!" He shook his head. "...is bad fa da healt." I could barely understand him, talking through his mouthfuls in a Ted-Kennedy-meets-Rosie-Perez-meets-Larry-Moe-and-Curley mashup dialect. He gobbled with the gusto of a pit bull puppy, talcum pale, with his chubby round cheeks well into it. His gelled, purple, spiky hair made his black goatee look fake.

"I wuz an altah boy, once, yo know. Befoah I ...."

"Fallen angel, get it? Great angle." Frank beamed and did his finger-framing thing on Satan in profile. "Amblin's interested. I've got Elijah Cook, Jr., reading the script. This is big!" Like everything Frank hyped. But this seemed too much of a stretch even for him.

I didn't acknowledge Frank. Can you make money posing for tourist photos on the boulevard, what with all the other costume characters – you know, Spiderman, Captain America, the Hulk, Sponge Bob?"

Satan did a fist pump. "I am a man a da people." His nasal tenor added incipient hysteria to his tortured syntax – hell for grammarians, elocutionists and literati. Later, I learned he had grown up with his mother, on the move, never settling in one place for long – home schooled. Along the way, he had vacuumed a pastiche of regional idiom and tropes layered over unattended speech impediments.

"She did da best she cud. Da kids tank I'm keel, doe. Some a deem 'aspect devil candy – Red Hoots – but I don gaveled dat. New god fo dye teed. Makes' fatties too."

Frank sailed on, in full pitch mode. I could tell. He seemed to compress his wiry frame, a lynx about to pounce on some unsuspecting rabbit. In this mode, he looked more Korean and less Mexican. Straight, ebony hair swaying over each ear as he chattered, startled-lemur eyes aglow with contagious enthusiasm. He barely touched his Cobb salad.

Frank looked at me and cupped a hand to the side of

his mouth, as if Lew, aka Satan, wouldn't be able to hear what he had to tell me. "Savant syndrome. You'd never guess from the way he talks, but this kid is a genius with a pen. He draws brilliantly, lays down fantastic stories, frame-after-frame and nobody knows how. He's up for an Eisner..."

"Michael Eisner?" I feigned ignorance hoping Frank would lose interest.

"No, The Will Eisner Award, the Oscar of comics. He's up for best new comics and best graphic novel – 'Satanix! Defender of the Damned!'"

"Das me!" Satan straightened pridefully and did a fist pump. I noticed he never made eye contact.

"He's riding the kiderati wave. Huge! He's an overnight meme, a postmodern psychotropic Hellboy – ripe for development, a movie, TV series, video games, the works! And, my dear Max, I've optioned the rights!"

I didn't ask how much Frank offered him, or where he'd get the money if he did. I noticed that Satan dipped his fries in ketchup ritually, three times before each bite. I stared at his hair, glistening slick purple and lacquered into spikes from each side of his rather massive head. "Nice do," I told him.

"Tanks!"

Frank sailed on: "Satanix becomes a force for good in spite of himself after Wall Street takes his business and outsources his job. He's neurotic, of course, subject to panic attacks and plagued with bad habits. But he finds redemption and lots of raw sex with Lucy LaSalle, a super-punk-hot-ninja hacker who wears baggy clothes by day and Spandex by night. He becomes, ta-ta! Satanix 666, Devil Avenger! Show Max a copy..."

Satan put down his mushroom burger, wiped his fingers on the table cloth and handed me a glossy copy from a wide pocket in his crimson cape. "Check it out, Mr. Max guy."

"I got a blogha, too," sidewalk Satan said. You can

161

opt in if you want." He points to a URL printed on the back cover of the novel.

"You can write?" He could barely talk. Idiot savant, maybe. I arched my eyebrows, playing along to speed things up. "Give me the elevator pitch."

Frank took the cue. "It's a movie-in-a-movie. I have this action movie star fallen on hard times, up to his neck in gambling debts and back alimony, his kids hate him, heartbroken, teams up with Sidewalk Satan, played by himself... to make a comeback as Satanix... "

"And?"

"Drunk one night, he offers his soul to 'Satan,' to get a break. All he asks is a bit of luck, a reversal of fortune. See what I mean? Remember, Max? This was your idea. You said it to me back when..."

I squinted. "Oh, yeah, but... I was only ... "

"And bang, next scene, everything goes his way. He becomes famous again. But then, *bang,* just when he wuz about to win an Academy Award..."

"He gets religion?" I ventured. Leave it to Frank to go over the top every time.

"No. He gets *paranoid.*"

"I follow. ... I guess."

"So, he goes back to Hollywood Boulevard, but he can't find his Mephistopheles anywhere. It turns into a noir thriller. There's a deadline on his contract and his number's up soon, if he can't find Satan..."

"Who has, unbeknownst, become the head of Fox Entertainment. Right?"

"Great ideah!" Satan sent a bit of Portobello flying, and slapped the table.

"You've got a winner, there, Frank." I hated myself for conning him like that, but knowing Frank, I didn't want to argue, or touch a raw nerve. "Maybe it's two movies," I brightened, trying for a soft landing. "Like, the Satanix thing, you could sell as an animation, and the fallen star thing, like something for Sean Penn or somebody."

"Two moobies!" Satan clapped his hands together and rubbed them back and forth. "Ya cud make boat a dem."

Frank lit up. "A two-picture deal. That's it!" He rapped on the table.

"You know I do dat contract thing... paht a my act. I buy ya soul for whatevah ya want … s'a promo gimmick. People love it."

Like a magician sprouting fake bouquets, he whipped a paper pad from yet another cape pocket and laid it on the table. He tore off the top sheet and passed it to us – a printed "Soul Sales Agreement," it read in bold across the top – then lots of fine print, then blanks for "consideration" and "tendered offer" and below them, for signatures and dates, very legal looking. "Fo esample," Satan said, and penned "LOTSA LUCK" in the appropriate blank, then signed with a flourish at the bottom – all in red ink I suddenly noticed. He slid the sheet towards Frank.

"Jesus!" Frank eyeballed it.

"Know him long time – sweet guy. We met long time ago at da Desert Inn."

I thumbed the novel again. "That in your book?"

"Paht a da package. Believe in Satan, ya believe in da rest. Right?"

"My! Getting theological, aren't we?"

Frank looked up from the contract. "See? It's Hellboy for smart people."

Satan pointed to the bottom line "Just fill in yah name and countah-sign at the bottom, and da wohld will be youah oistah!"

Frank laughed, then signed it, his bounce redoubled now.

Satan slid the sheet over to me."You gotta witness it."

"Sublimely ridiculous," I said. I signed, "Stephen Vincent Benét" with a flourish just below Frank's name.

In a flash, our cherubic Satan folded the sheet into yet

another pocket. "Dats it! Next stop, fat city fa you guys. And I'm gonna be in da moobies! Two moobies! No Al Pacino! Me playin' me!"

Then Frank got to the point, finally. "You know Marvin Shales. You could get him to look at my proposal for this. It's great. I've already done it up. Tell him Spielberg's interested. This could be an HBO series! "

My father had roomed with Shales at Yale, a very long time ago. I didn't have any pull with the guy, really… A year earlier, I happened to have worked on the promotional campaign for his latest movie. I interviewed him for a story I planted. I wasn't about to feed him Frank's hype. "Frank, just because I …"

"I know. Just because we're friends! Thanks. I knew you would do it."

"Send me your proposal so I can read it. I can't guarantee… I don't even know if he'll take my call, Frank…" I gave myself a graceful way out.

"No problem. You underestimate yourself, Max. You can do it. I know you can…"

Two moobies indeed: Frank hit the jackpot shortly after that while I was still fudging about trying Shayles on Frank's Power Point pitch, though better than his spiel at Musso's. Even with brains you need luck in this town, and somehow, he got it back.

Frank called me right away. "I got a development deal for HBO. They want me to do a pilot. It's an embedded marketing deal. They had a deal with Devil Foods looking for a vehicle. That's how it's done. I went to them first about their Hot Chips. I got Lew wearing a product patch on Hollywood Boulevard now..."

"Do I have to wear one too?"

"Hey, Max, whatever you want, baby! You did it! You cinched the deal for me. HBO got wind Shayles liked my pitch, and made their move first."

"I didn't do anything, Frank."

"Hey, pal. Don't sell yourself short. You're a player. Anyway, please let me thank you. What can I say?"

I made like Brando in *The Godfather* doing his hoarse voice, with cotton balls in his cheeks. "Some day, and that day may never come, Bonasera, I may call upon you to something for me."

I saw Laila about six weeks after that — for the first time since the day of the teenage zombie moms that she broke up with "us." I didn't expect I'd get a rush, but I did the moment she walked into the firm's reception area. I tried not to feast my eyes on her as she led me back to a private office. Her high-school girlishness had given way to an assertive womanly grace, it seemed to me.

Warm smiles and a hug. I felt tension in her, something more than the momentary awkwardness of meeting an old lover. I commented duly on the high-rise vista of hazy Pacific shoreline to the west and dark hills to the north. She chose an overstuffed black leather sofa with a glass coffee table, rather than parking at the commanding desk opposite and clear of working clutter. Turned out, she had steered us to her boss' office, the managing partner out shilling for the firm, as usual.

I expected Frank to be there when I showed up. She had called me regarding him and a case. But no Frank.

Laila got out a file and showed me some letters sent to Frank from an attorney representing Lewis C. Farr Industries, demanding they cease-and-desist "the Satanix Project." The letters alleged potential copyright infringement and libel.

I whistled. I could see the backers dropping Frank and his sidewalk Satan like hot rocks, product marketing deals or not. But, I couldn't figure why. "Farr?"

"Oil, coal and right wing, Christian radio stations."

"He's a crackpot. Reclusive. Scary guy ... "

Laila nodded, glancing round the room as if she thought it bugged.

"I got news for you. The nut-case sidewalk Satan that Frank played for a bank shot in this is probably old man Farr's son – or maybe grandson. Frank either got some of that trust fund money, or put lil' Lew C. Farr III on his project to give investors the impression he's backed by Farr money."

"Sounds like Frank."

"So, he contacted you when he got these letters? For old time's sake?"

"Yes, but I can't handle it off the books and I don't want to refer this to these sharks at my firm unless I know more. They'll just tell me to get coffee while they milk it. Anyway, I don't know if Frank could afford them and he sure doesn't want to bring HBO into this."

I sketched her the Musso's lunch meeting. "Other than that, I don't know much about it. My guess is little Lew's Satanix comix contain a strong element of piss-off-his-daddy and daddy doesn't want it escalating from an annoying comic book to a viral scandal or a ludicrous meme. It's a stealth drone, preemptive strike.

Guys like Farr live by preemptive strikes. Do unto

others before they *even think* of doing unto you."" Next it'll be carpet bombing."

"Frank thinks this is just harassment. Like, screw them if they can't take a joke. A law suit will make good publicity."

"Probably got a point. But he could also meet with a bad accident."

"From what I gather, Frank's not using much material from the Satanix comic. You know Frank, he loves mashups and twists. In life too, I found out."

"Laila, I'm not a lawyer, but I don't see any grounds for suing. Hell – as it were – you see stronger stuff all over the Internet and cable, on Adult Swim..."

Laila turned slightly more towards me, I thought. "Farr and his lawyers don't have to take us to court. They can paper Frank to death and ruin him and his project in little time."

I gave her my most earnest look. I didn't want to be talking about Frank with her. I casually put my hand on hers. "So. What can I do for you?"

Laila gave my hand a friendly squeeze. "Talk to Frank. I need more to go on. I think if I talk to Farr's attorney, I could find out what they want and work something out.

She pulled a copy of Satan's "soul" contract from the folder she had open on the table. I was surprised to see it.

"You remember this? This Satan guy said this is your signature, as a witness."

"Yeah. It's a joke. And do I look like Stephen Vincent Benét?"

"Zombie Vincent Benét!" She was loosening up.

"You'd be Zombie Daniela Webster."

She smirked. Then serious again: "Did you sign it?"

"Well, yes. I did."

A bit of the old Laila surfaced in her grin. "Smells like Farr fils et pere frying up their personal shit. I'm willing to help but I don't want to get in the middle of that just because Frank likes the drama. Maybe if you talk to Frank again – and maybe that Lewis kid – you can get me something more to go on... so I can talk down the Farr lawyer and keep this contained."

"Mmm. Max Falco, shrink to the stars." We kidded back and forth a while, and wrapped up the business at hand. "I guess I haven't been much help."

"I appreciate your coming..." She was slipping into formalities again.

She inched forward on the couch, making to stand. "Got to wrap this up, Max."

I strung it out. . "It's been great, seeing you, Laila... I think about you a lot.... fondly... as a friend... Well, more... You know..." I had heard that preppy Roger had long departed her life for Long Island and a proper wife. Maybe now...?

"I think about you too, Max." She paused. "We had such fun.."

"How are you doing here at the firm, Laila?" Hollywood adolescent culture on steroids; boys with brains, but you know where. Too much swagger. But I like the law part – copyright, entertainment, literature... A girl's gotta walk softly, and carry a big dildo around here."

"I love you when you talk dirty." I finally got a laugh out of her.

"Can we...?" *Lunch*, I was going to say, or dinner, or make love. *Say something, Max.* "Can I phone you?"

She put down the file folder. Then she leaned over and kissed me... doing what I had been too timid to do myself. She seemed amused by the risk of someone walking in. I appreciated that, but kept an eye open. "Wow!" My face flushed. That was all I could muster for a moment. Then I recovered my wits and kissed her back, gently.

She pressed a finger to my lips. "Shh." She looked down in soft focus at the plush carpeting. After long minutes of silence, she glanced up and met my eyes.

I raised my eyebrows, inquiring, then, making the next move, I said. "Let's get together – not here – for dinner?" I didn't want to scare her off. "No pressure. It will be nice" My mouth went dry. She stood up, all business again, and gave me the official handshake. I always loved her hands, capable, but they could dance too.

She escorted me in silence back to reception. Her face lit up again, just as my elevator dinged. She seemed to remember something she had to do. "Friday, I'm free," she said.

I didn't know what to do except grin. "See you then, Laila," I said, as the doors closed on me. I was so excited I forgot to press a floor. The doors opened again. She looked back at me, head tilted. "Oops!" I grinned and hit the button for the sub-basement underground garage.

I didn't feel bad about not talking to Frank. I tried to phone him. "Frankly, I'm not answering, for whatever reason. But you can leave a message. Thanks." Click. I did, plus texted the gist of what Laila wanted.

He messaged back cryptically, "everything copacetic..." I felt excused from my assignment. Fine.

I asked Laila if she'd be comfortable with Frank as best man at our wedding three months later. I confess some perversity in it, rubbing in a bit of puerile triumph. I still couldn't believe this all had happened, and so fast; I was so damn happy. Laila and I made up our own romantic comedy, pals who didn't realize they were made for each other all along. When Max met Laila. If they asked me I could write a book... how to make two lovers of friends, Frank Sinatra on my car radio tuned to bygones.

We tied the knot in the garden of a small Spanish colonial hotel in Carmel, where her parents lived. Frank seemed uncharacteristically subdued at the reception, but I floated above any possibility of rational thought the whole time. I noticed at one point, late, Frank sitting with Laila at one of the tables off to one side, leaning into inaudible conversation, but then she returned to my side to finish off the rituals with a toss of her bouquet and we were outta there.

Neither one of us go for resorts, so we honeymooned first at the Huntington Hotel on Nob Hill in San Francisco. We rented a car for a week-long getaway up the Redwood Highway. I felt happier than I had ever felt in my life at that point.

That's when things got hinky.

I hadn't bothered to even ask Laila about several, lengthy phone calls she took out of my earshot during our honeymoon. But on the way back from Mendocino, she wanted to take a miserably curvy inland road that led down into the hot Sacramento Valley to Winters, a small aggie town about 50 miles from Sacramento – hand-lettered signs on our approach offered walnuts, fresh freestone peaches and vine-ripened tomatoes. A banner over the main street touted, "Earthquake Festival, Aug. 21."

A rangy, middle-aged woman welcomed us into a peeling, Queen Anne Victorian after introductions. The house sat well back of a wide, barn-like, metal-roofed structure with a sign that read "Conway Supplies: Pumps Is Us!" An old orchard of towering walnut trees protected the house on all sides. The dry summer wind rustled their leaves continually and caused branches to brush against the house like cats scratching to get in.

"'Scuse the mess," she said, inviting us to sit around a circular walnut table. Statuettes of Jesus and the Apostles gazed on us from credenzas and bookshelves all around..

She disappeared into the kitchen briefly, moving with a dancer's lope and the poignant beauty of an autumn rose. A silver chain with a plain cross swung out over her pink and turquoise floral print dress as she poured us iced teas from a frosted glass pitcher. Its glint picked up the silver of her hair, which she wore in a distracted bun with vagrant strands lending a waif-like aspect to her lean face. Her luminous cobalt eyes, large and round from far away with secrets, caught me staring at her pendant and maybe taking in the rest of her, entraining my unsanctioned desires.

Laila slid a folder and notepad from the shoulder bag she brought with her. She set her phone to record. The time between Laila's questions lengthened as the woman related her story.

Okay, I won't say the honeymoon was over, but I couldn't help fidgeting, and stirring my tea furiously so the glass dinged as I downed my second tall glass and suddenly had to pee but didn't want to ask, like a kid at school raising my hand while the two of them talked on... I should have been paying more attention, maybe even contributing to the conversation, except this wasn't a social call. It was work – making this a working honeymoon. Finally, I cleared my throat and inquired about toilet use.

I took a long time in there, admiring the antique copper fixtures, claw footed bathtub, Moorish tile designs and polished walnut cabinets, washing my hands several times, combing my hair... Satisfied I'd made my point, I strolled back to the dining room where the two of them still talked: "Lord, knows, I raised and protected him best I could. But when a boy starts becoming a man, he wants to know his father to know himself, I suppose. I couldn't keep the truth from him anymore. Maybe I did the wrong thing."

"No, you were right, Mrs. Lewis." Laila laid a reassuring hand on the woman's bare forearm.

"It's Mrs. Conway now. Anyway, just call me Rosemary, please."

"Sorry. Of course." Laila pulled her hand away and sipped more tea.

"It's all right. He's a good man. I don't want him involved."

"No need for that."

"I didn't mind my boy going off to Hollywood to find his way in the world. He always had smarts and a prodigious talent, inherited his father's brilliance, no doubt. He had to explore his soul on his own and his art has been a way of doing that. I'm proud of him."

Trying to be polite. I gave her a verbal pat: "I'm sure you are, Ms. Con... er... Rose..."

Laila cut in: "We think your statement can help your son, so that he can continue to develop his art – and his talents."

The woman looked at Laila hard, leaning slightly into her, a back-off, don't-patronize-me look. Laila smiled wanly, took refuge in her iced tea, then looked up all sweetness. "Of course, you know all about it. If you had wanted to sue, you could have done all that a long time ago."

"And I'd be a rich woman too. But I never wanted him to sink his claws into that innocent boy. He's a dangerous man, evil, avaricious, possessive. So I laid low and kept on the move with my boy as he grew up to be his own special self, no matter what."

Laila wrote on her pad, and then looked up. "And now?"

"Now, I don't worry about him so much what with Jack on his own. That's what I always called him, you know, 'Jack,' not Lewis after his father. I understand Jack's taken to calling himself that now."

"Do you think that's what's behind Mr. Farr's trying to shut your son's picture down?"

"You can bet on that... the devil claims his due. He thinks I sold my soul to him for all the riches he could bestow – just like everyone around him – and for the 'honor' of bearing his child. Not so! My Jack doesn't mean to do so either. He mocks his father with his art. You'll see."

Laila put on her best closing smile. "Then, you'll help our case?"

"I'll help Jack. God help us all." The woman looked around at her brick-a-back, seeming deflated. It was time to go.

She filled my arms with bags of walnuts and garden tomatoes as she went out her door and trudged back to the car. Laila gave her a warm hug. "Thank you. We'll see you in Santa Barbara then?"

The woman hugged back lightly. "Yes, dear. See you there. But you two be careful."

"I didn't find out she was crazy until she got pregnant. We were married only six months. Said I was some kind of devil forcing her to have Satan's baby." Lewis C. Farr, flanked by three Armani-suited lawyers, a clerk and a stenographer, puffed his Havana and ignored the no smoking signs discreetly placed around the third-floor, air conditioned Spanish colonial conference room of Becker, Brand and Myers' Santa Barbara branch offices.

Laila sat expressionless, yellow-lined legal pad at the ready, not taking notes yet. The deposition hadn't started officially. I sat far down the conference table from them both, trying to look small, and not like Laila's new husband. I looked out the conference room's curving latticed windows towards the palm trees and porticoes of Mission Santa Barbara set against chaparral-covered coastal hills. Frank hadn't arrived yet. Neither had Satan boy, or – as I had been briefed to expect – his mom.

Smoked billowed from Farr as he ranted on, no one daring to interrupt. The nerve of these people summoning him into town from his hilltop mansion not far from the Reagan Ranch, "It must have been a virgin birth, or the mailman knocked her up, because she went into deep freeze from our wedding night onward. Maybe it was that mealy, fucking priest she ran off with. How was I supposed to be paying her child support while she was in hiding? I got an annulment, not a divorce. You know what?" He leaned towards Laila, blowing smoke her way. "You know what?!"

"What, Mr. Farr?" Laila looked cool and straight through the white, aromatic smoke into his squinty, coal-black eyes, probably noticing the same vague, father-son resemblance that I saw when Farr first sat down – except daddy didn't have purple hair, the goatee, and he knew how to weaponize words.

"I think you're all nuts. And you're wasting my time. You're not going to like what happens. This is a nuisance suit and none of you will get a dime." He laughed. One of his lawyers, the eldest, with the best blow-dried coif, cleared his throat. "Okay. Okay. I'll shut up now." He laughed again. "Nuts! All nuts! This is a joke!"

Frank came through the double, glass doors. He was clad in the brown robes of a Dominican friar, with sandals, and a silver Crucifix dangling from his neck. He looked like a visitation from the controversial early California missionary Junipero Serra himself. "Bless you, my children," he waved a sign of the cross and smiled beatifically. "Don't mind the get-up. I had to come straight from a location shoot over at the mission here, a brandy commercial. Work where I can get it."

Farr scowled and didn't get up. "Jesus Christ," he muttered.

"Amen, brother." Frank nodded and sat directly opposite him.

I wondered if Lew would arrive in his red Satan costume and was disappointed when he arrived a few moments later looking uncomfortable in a cheap blue suit. "Hi dad!" He greeted Mr. Farr, who maintained his scowl, puffed and exhaled another cloud of smoke.

Farr Industries' lead lawyer opened up a leather folder and reached into his jacket for glasses." Let's cut the theatrics and get down to the business at hand. Shall we?"

"We have to wait for Mrs. Conway." Laila didn't flinch.

Satan Boy brightened even more, making his purple hair spikes look even perkier. "Mom?"

"Jesus Christ." Farr intoned, belching smoke.

"Amen, brother!" Frank gave him the old finger benediction again.

Farr slapped a hand loudly on the table.

"Please also tell Mr. Farr, no need for theatrics." Laila bitch-smiled at Farr's lead attorney with this.

"Let's cut to the chase here before we get into a tedious deposition." Farr's legal eagle literally looked down his aquiline nose at Laila. "We have a plain case of legal harassment here, but we won't go into that."

"No, better not go there," Laila hissed back.

"Your client Whateverhisnameis over there...Father Frank... for today... " He waggled a dismissive hand at Frank. Has counter-sued my client alleging conspiracy to libel and deny him free speech, among other charges..."

"And don't forget Mrs. Conway's suit." Laila purred.

"Preposterous... a million back child support, ten million in damages, and so forth. She's not even here, so we can set that aside. What will it take to settle this matter?"

The receptionist opened the conference room door for Rosemary, a time-warp, Twiggy angel in white mini dress, Henri Breton wide-brimmed hat and feathery cropped Sassoon haircut right out of the Sixties, and looking youthful somehow too. She locked those baby-blues on her boy, whose indigo hair seemed to stand even higher on end. "Mom!"

"Jesus Christ." Farr slapped the table again, and froze as she locked on him. Then they were into it. The stenographer could barely keep up with the yelling.

Farr played to the crowd. "She didn't raise him, she ruined him – out of spite."

Rosemary kept on him. "You thought you'd drive me to suicide. Well I'm stronger than you..."

Baby Satan tried to interject. "Mom, dad... please!"

"It's always the kids who get hurt," Frank shook his head. Then I realized that he had a phone camera stashed up his monkish sleeves. If I knew Frank, he was getting it all, grinning fiendishly.

"I'm going to take you for everything you've got and ruin you!" Rosemary herself sounded possessed...

Frank made a sign of the cross with a free hand... "Exorcism's R Us... at rock bottom prices..."

Both Laila and the opposing shysters stood up trying to restore order.

"Wait till I feed this to the tabloids..." Rosemary turned disappointingly shrill. I thought she'd gone over the top, but I noticed paparazzi gathering on the street below. Rosemary laughed hysterically.

Just then, a cloud of pinkish red billowed from under the long table in all directions. The steno screamed. Frank had rolled a smoke bomb on the floor from under his robes, still running his mini-cam with his other hand and shouting, "Cue hellfire!"

Farr knocked his chair back." That's it. We're out of here." Enveloped in a cotton candy cloud, still clutching his cigar, he stormed towards the door, followed by his entourage, hacking and coughing.

"Not so fast, you evil bastard!" She kicked off her low heels and sprung from a chair to the tabletop holding a black semiautomatic pistol with a custom, fuchsia grip.

"Wow, mom, *kewl!* A ten-shot Sig Sauer Moshquito Pink, top-a-da-line in ladies' shidearms. Gotcha pack'en one in my comicsh too!" Baby Satan was beside himself, clapping his hands. Everyone else froze.

"Jesus Christ." Farr exclaimed again, and looked up at her. His cigar continued to smolder in one hand. "Nuts! What did I say I say? You must always act with total *commitment, no matter what!* You too!" He pointed to his presumed son.

"Mrs. Conway..." Laila climbed on the table and was at her side, lowering her pistol arm. "Go!" She shooed Farr and the other attorneys out of the room. They obliged quickly. Mrs. Conway collapsed sobbing into Laila's arms.

"There goes your case." I groused to Frank. "He calls the cops and it's all over." I turned to Baby Satan. "and your ma goes to jail."

Frank smirked and put his camera back into the sleeve of his monk's habit. "He won't. The tabloids and the cable news channels would blow this up and serve it hot for weeks, maybe months. And great for my picture too!"

Through Mrs. Conway's sobs I heard... "I'll kill that Satanic sonofabitch before I let him take my boy and destroy him like every one else." Laila waved Frank and me out of the room now as well – along with the steno, leaving her along with Rosemary and her "baby."

"I'll wait downstairs in that cafe on the corner," I called to Laila, wanting some distance. Not the honeymoon I had envisioned.

"This is all going into my new film." Frank nearly danced down the corridor to the elevator and all the way down. "I'm calling it 'Rosemary's Boo Boo,' for now anyway. Sensational!

Frank patted my back. "See. That asshole Farr's gonna back off pronto, now. He's a reclusive fanatic with a lot of dirt to hide, miles of bad shit to do before he sleeps – politicians to buy, markets to rig, lesser beings to screw, and competition to crush, water to buy up and pollute... Doesn't want any 'Satan Sex Scandal, Week 10, exclusive from CNN' ...

"Yeah, yeah, Frank... but that won't stop you either. Right?"

"All for art and art for all! The true artist won't be denied!"

"I don't know which of you is the more ruthless, but I'm with you, Frank. Fuck'em if they can't take a joke."

"Gotta get this costume back and upload all that hot stuff in my camera, pal." Frank practically sprinted off. I waved, but felt too drained for a goodbye..

Laila took her sweet time coming out. We walked without a word to the car, down the street fluttering a parking ticket in the salty breeze. I didn't ask her what happened to the others.

For my money, at that point, we could have made home the ninety miles south to Santa Monica. But Laila already had booked us what was supposed to be a romantic stay at the old Montecito Inn, nestled between seashore and rocky San Ysidro Mountain outcrops, off the busy 101. I wasn't in much of a mood. But Laila played it light, and by dinner and dessert on the patio of our Mission-style luxury room she had me laughing again... with a tease and an "I'm sorry, but wasn't that a scene? Frank. Again!"

"We should learn. No?"

"Como no, darling."

We got all cozy drifting towards sleep and morning sex, when Laila sat up and said she had left her overnight bag down in the car. It had some thyroid pills in it she would have to take in the morning. "Would you be a dear, Max, and..?

I was a miffed when I discovered the car unlocked down in the hotel garage. The attendant had left the parking key in the ignition, carelessly, so I didn't need mine. I looked in the front and back seats of the rented Buick in the semi-darkness of the garage, cursing the flashlight I couldn't find either. I worried someone had stolen the bag from the open car.

Then I checked the trunk. There it was, her makeup back tucked to one side. And.... a large formless mass in some kind of ... What? Laundry bag? I looked around. Nobody in sight. I found the draw strings and worked the bag open slightly. I couldn't make out the form in the darkness, but I definitely felt... oh shit...hair! A head bobbed limp. My mouth, independent of me, let out one long, screechy man-scream, as I jumped back. "What the fuck?"

I looked around. No one yet appeared out of the shadows of the garage. I stepped forward and squeezed the bag at strategic spots, here and there, not having the stomach to look inside again. "Oh my God!" I saw a glint next to the spare tire well. The flashlight. I opened the neck of the bag again. My hands shook so much I couldn't keep the flashlight beam steady, but I saw enough. "Oh, God. Oh, God.... Frank... Frank... You dumb sonofabitch. Your luck just ran out...." was all I could keep repeating to myself, tearfully until I retched dinner over the back bumper and my shoes.

Not knowing what else to do. I slammed the trunk and stepped away again, surprised to find myself holding Laila's overnight bag in one hand as instructed. I strode upstairs and let myself into our room. I needed Laila. I needed a lawyer too, most likely. Shit. Losing Frank was bad. Being framed for his murder was worse. It had to be Farr, more likely some thugs-for-hire... Maybe Laila would be next. And what about the lovely, crazy old Rosemary and her baby Satan? Unless he or she did it. Not likely, I thought.

Laila lay peacefully asleep on the big four-poster in our room. I put her makeup bag down in the bathroom and eased myself next to her, trembling. She groaned, smiled in her sleep and kissed me dreamily. I kissed her back softly, then sat up slowly. This wouldn't do. I won't be left holding this bag.

I figured I had a few hours. Whoever put poor Frank there figured the body would be discovered in broad daylight, with me practically in flagrante delicto as a bellman opened my trunk and dropped our suitcases on his toes from the shock.

I didn't have a plan, only a sweaty impulse to put distance between myself and Laila. I felt protective. What had happened would it the fan, inevitably. I didn't want her to be implicated. There would be no sense to it.

I don't know how many miles I drove, instinctively north, maybe because that was away from where we lived. I branched off the wide 101 onto Highway 1's two lanes hugging rugged cliffs against a spectacular shore, that people take up to Big Sur, the long way, scenic, winding over impossibly arching bridges over rocky, crashing surf shores, spanning from one palisade to another. I negotiated the hairpins, eyes on the road, without letting the grandeur distract me.

As I drove, I thought, just what would I do if I got as

far as Big Sur and Carmel. What would happen when Laila woke up back in our room with no me there? What would Frank do?

He'd dump the body and probably get away with it. The thought brightened my mind for the first time, bringing giddy elation and guilt with it. Dump Frank? Off the bloody cliff in the end after all, poor Frank. And he'd probably want me to film it.

So, here we are again, Frank and I, come full circle. I'm Hamlet at the wheel now in the dark parked on a palisade, a dark sea raging below, half way to nowhere. Max, a man of inaction.

Bump.

What was that?

A car has rolled up behind me, lights out same as me. Two shadows behind the windshield. So this is how it all ends. Farr's boys here to whack me too. Well, that takes care of my decision. I hit my mobile to leave Laila one of those final, "I love you," messages she could keep on her phone to play over and over after I'm gone to remember me by, tearfully. Oh, the drama!

Tap tap. From my side window, a dark figure silhouetted in faint starlight, tapping out a final message? Why not just shoot me and get it over with?

"Maxsh?" I think I hear him. I lower the window. Yup. And he's back in his red costume. What the....?

"Maxsh, itsh me a Ma." I see the slim woman now towering behind him. I get out. I may have wet my pants a little.

"We've been trying to catch up with you for miles. Max..." Rosemary's voice is soft and reassuring as the bubbly hiss of a receding wave on sand. "Pop the trunk."

I comply. There's Frank-in-a-bag as before. Satan Boy shines an LED light on the body, as his mother pulls the cloth bag down off the face, which is pale white, but looked none the worse for wear, as if Frank were sleeping off a hard night, maybe.

"Ish he?...." Satan boy pressed a finger against Frank's cheek.

A thought crossed my mind. No. "I don't know, I'm not a doctor, but I'd say... Why do you think I'm all the way here. You've got to know, I didn't do it. I didn't do anything to Frank. I never would. I just found him like that in my trunk and panicked." I realized that my explanation sounded completely idiotic.

Mrs. Conway slipped the bag down and all the way off, as her son supported the body, under the arms, and holding the flashlight in his teeth. It was Frank all right, still in his monk's habit.

"Ego te absolvo, domenicus, vobiscus, probiscus, arminium, pliticae, moribundi, extremis...." Satan babbled in flawlessly articulated fake Latin.

"Jesus." I rubbed my face with both hands.

"Him too." Rosemary responded sweetly, rubbing a hand over Frank's forehead, smoothing down his hair.

"Et cum spiritu tuum." Satan Boy bowed his head up and down like one of those dunking duck things you find at novelty stores.

"And Tums for the tummy." I added.

Frank's eyes popped open. Nothing but a rigor mortis twitch. "Nice trick, Rosemary. Do you two conduct séances?"

"Shh!" Rosemary put a finger to her rosy lips.

"You can't do this," I said. Then I looked at Frank. "Okay. This is going to be Zombie Frank. Right?"

Rosemary looked at Sidewalk Satan. "My boy is half angel, albeit fallen angel, you know. So anything is possible," Rosemary cooed just as Frank started to hack and cough and convulse.

"Holy shit!" I jumped so hard I could have thrown myself back over the cliff.

"What the hell happened to you guys?" Frank was shouting at Rosemary and devil boy, ignoring me for the moment.

"I'm sorry." Rosemary held Frank's face in both hands and stared into his eyes. I stepped back and put my hand inside the open car window to turn my lights on, causing the courtesy light in the trunk to go on too.

Frank sat up more, still too weak to climb out of the trunk. He pointed a shaking finger at me. "You! Was that you driving this piece of junk?"

I nodded.

"My God, Max, didn't you hear me kicking and screaming back here in this trunk?"

"Sorry. I didn't hear anything. I guess I was too freaked."

"Where's my camera?" He fished in the baggy sleeves of the brown habit, and felt around the trunk. If I lost that..."

"Farr is right! You're all nuts!" Exasperated, I slapped a hand to my forehead like a silent film ham.

"I gashed it!" Satan Boy pointed to the other car. "Youze dropped it on da boat."

"Boat?"

"The marina."

Mother Rosemary wrapped her arms around herself and started shivering as the night wind picked up off the cold ocean. "Let's get out of here..."

Reluctantly, Frank rode back with me as we headed south again behind Rosemary and her devil-may-care son."

"I don't get it." I looked straight ahead. "I think I better take you to emergency to get checked out. That's quite a bump." I noticed the swelling and discoloration over his left eye, lit up by my dash lights.

"I'll be okay." Frank tilted the passenger seat back and shut his eyes.

"I don't think you should go to sleep till you're checked. You probably have a concussion. So, who hit you?"

"Farr's muscle... on his yacht... down at the Santa Barbara marina. I tailed him and snuck on board, to get more footage."

"Are you a filmmaker or have you turned paparazzo?"

"Little of both right now."

"How did you escape?"

"The guard --- or maybe deckhand --- locked me in a stateroom after he slugged me, waiting for his boss to show. He was headed down to his yacht after the drama in Laila's office."

"You saw Farr again?"

"No, I was in a sort of twilight. I would come to every so often, then pass right out again."

God, Frank. You damn fool."

As we merged onto 101 heading south towards Santa Barbara again, Rosemary's car accelerated and was gone. I didn't care to chase them.

"They must have smuggled me off the boat in that laundry bag."

"Who?"

"Devil Boy and mommie dearest."

"You saw them?"

"Heard. When I regained consciousness for a little while."

"They boarded the yacht?"

"Yeah. And I heard the shots too."

"Shots! Shots?"

"Momma pumped her ex full of holes, while Satan Boy cold cocked the guard. Strong little bastard. You'd be surprised."

"He's full of surprises that one. Then they got you out?"

"Broke the door. First I thought Mommie Dearest meant to whack me too, but she was all smiles. Farr was bloody all over B-deck. Only thing was, Satan Boy had me crawl in the laundry sack. Said better if no one saw me leaving the yacht. Put me on a dolly and wheeled me off like dirty linens. That's all I remember."

"Then how did you get in my trunk?"

"I don't know, but I think he and Rosemary meant to take me to you at your hotel, chickened out and dropped me in your car."

"Lucky --- or maybe unlucky – the parking attendant left it open."

"I might have suffocated in there. Didn't you see me

before you drove off like a madman?"

"I thought you were dead, Frank. Really. Sorry about that. But have you thought, my friend, that you've been the cause of a lot of craziness yourself, in this affair, not to mention murder and mayhem?"

"I'm a doer, not a doubter. When the Muse beckons, I follow." Frank struck the best heroic pose he could under the circumstances, banged up in his monk's habit sitting in a rented Buick. I wondered about damages when I would have to turn this car back to the rental agency.

"You realize, of course, that Rosemary and your Satan Boy are on the lam by now. They're wanted for what the tabloids will call the 'crime of the century.'"

"If she gets caught, she'll plead insanity and get off. She's bat-shit!"

"Does she really believe thatFarr was the Prince of Darkness?"

"That guy Farr? Hell, he was a lot darker."

"Good riddance either way. You're one lucky son of a bitch, Frank, like I always said."

Laila screamed and shook me awake when she discovered Frank asleep on the sofa in our suite, a few hours later, with a bag of ice on his forehead. "What happened?"

"It's complicated, honey." My mouth full of cotton, I covered my head with my pillow. But I could not escape her cross-examination. The three musketeers were together again, under dubious circumstances, ordering pancakes and eggs from room service, though there'd be no sorting this all out that morning. XXXXXXX

9 FIFTY SHADES OF SNOW WHITE

Statement of Queen Meana Regina, Her Royalness of Grimmland, sworn by the bailiff of this Imperial Tribunal, as duly recorded by Dinkle the Scribe and signed by the accused, on this Day of our Lord, 12 Avril 1213 -- said accused Regina having been charged with the following: first- degree vanity, aggravated envy, general cruelty, conspiracy to murder, and attempted regicide with malice fouleste against the person of Her Royal Highness, Princess Snow White, plus poisoning apples with malicious intent and eating a pig's heart on Friday:

Yes. It is true. Once I could gaze into my mirror and know without a doubt that I was the fairest in the land. But unlike a certain "fair princess," handed her unearned beauty by capricious fate, I had to work hard at it.

Week after week, I spent hours at the Magic Mirror Salon and Spa suffering the body washes, facials, trims, treatments, colorings, potions, lotions, permanents, waxings, scrubs, rinses, creams, blow-dryings, mud and makeup applications at the merciless hands of the royal hair dressers, makeup artists, manicurist and pedicurists, masseuses and personal trainers. Oh, vanity thy name is profanity! And don't get me started about the surgeries!

But I had no choice. My beauty got me where I was

in the first place, marrying the king. It continued to be the only way I could survive and keep my precarious hold power after that, frankly. With all due respect, the court knows full well that only my looks kept me in favor with the king, his fickle court, council, and people.

Above all else, as an outsider queen, it was incumbent on me to enter and win the council's accursed annual Beauty Pageant and Reality Tournament: "Who's the Fairest in the Land?" Thousands from this kingdom and those surrounding flock to it every year, spending all their coins on our bad food, foul drink, tacky tunics and knickknacks.

Most of all, you know, they come to see me, Queen of Vanities they love to hate.

But I could see the end coming. Inevitably, my day would soon be done. And the talk about it occupied every gossip crier in the kingdom. I didn't care about the prize, only the bloody eagerness of the mobs to see me taken down by that spoiled brat princess Snow White soon as she came of age to enter the tournament.

And come of age she did! Don't be fooled by her faux-innocence. She knew that she was hot stuff, wrapping men and dwarfs around her little fingers, batting her eyes and flaunting her budding breasts.

She gets all the men to fall over themselves for her little innocent, damsel-in-distress routine – all pouty with those big, blood red lips, tossing her luminous jet black hair back and forth, until all the pages' and squires' tights and pantaloons bulged.

And not a brain in her pretty head, I tell you, nor an ounce of caring for anyone but herself! Snow White, indeed! Nothing much happens inside that lovely head, but inside that flawless alabaster skin beats a little heart hard and black as coal.

I used to ask myself in my Magic Mirror: If I were born so pretty, would I also have been a bubble-head, with everyone indulging me so I never had to think?

Heaven knows, I tried to instill some sense into Snowy. Unfortunately I was the only one, and she hated me for it.

The twit. That spoiled brat! That scheming ungrateful little bitch! The King and I gave her everything she could ever have wanted and more. I made my servants wait on her hand-and-foot, commissioned her the best tutors, and brought in the most compliant playmates.

I wheedled the King to buy Little Snow White the most expensive toys and to pay the royal tailors and seamstresses to keep her outfitted in fashionable finery. As she got older, we gave her the most exquisite jewelry, and staged the most elaborate parties for her birthdays with ponies and camels and baby elephants and trained monkeys, jugglers, clowns, magicians, orchestras and acrobats. We spared nothing to keep her entertained.

It's not my fault she was so miserable most of the time. I tried to deal with her constant whining and complaining and cursing and throwing tantrums. It's not my fault that her mother died in childbirth.

Contrary to the falsehoods she tried to pass off in her self-serving tell-all book, I didn't "steal" poor little Snow White's father away from her! Quite the opposite. It's not my fault that her mother died in childbirth. I'm not to blame for the king turning his back on baby Snow White right after that.

"He was obsessed with that woman. Even after he took me and made me Queen, he kept referring to my predecessor as "my snow queen," And to make matters worse, his courtiers whispered all the time that Snow White's mother was "the truest beauty, more beautiful by far than that new one the king has married." Oh, I heard them, those sycophants and weasels.

"The King left me to manage the servants and abandoned Snow White to be raised by nannies and other servants who resented her. She spent her childhood practically under house arrest in the royal nursery. She was allowed outside her dank private quarters only when the king told the her nannies to dress her up and present the child in court in order to gain himself sympathy as the "poor widowed King raising a motherless daughter – "and with no male heir. Tsk, tsk." What was I, chopped chestnuts?

"They all said that the King married me only for my looks and to give him a male heir. When no son came along, they said I failed him, but I knew the real reason after what could laughably be called our wedding night."

(Pregnant pause. She looks to scribe Dinkle)

"... Oh! So you're shocked? You think I give a royal ratsy arsey that you're writing all this down, you stupid scribe?

"Go on! Don't stop! Keep that quill going, and don't leave out a word I'm saying, you miserable flunky, or I'll have you locked in the tower and your fingers cut off.

"Such cheek! Not likely, you say? Just because I'm here locked up in irons myself now, you knave? Ha! Don't underestimate me, you pathetic ink-smudged hack. Others far above your station have done so, to their bloody regret!

"You have no idea of what I am capable of doing, you wretched excuse for an poet, a failed balladeer. To think that the King once made you court laureate! And now you're nothing but a common court scribe. What a joke. And I never liked your rhymes, either.

"Where was I?

"Oh yes...

"Believe me, I urged the King to spend time with his daughter, if only to get the brat off my hands for a while. I didn't sign up to be queen mother nanny around the palace. But, I did the best I could.

"What choice did I have, raised in the threadbare, crumbling squalor of my own father's run down, debt ridden castle out in the moors? I grew up just waiting for the day my father would marry me off.

"I had no confidence. I didn't believe I could be a poet, even a mediocre one like you, Scribe. All I could aspire to be was a wife, and marriage, probably to some pretentious lout of a local nobleman who would expect me bear children until I died in childbirth. Meanwhile, I would have to wait on him hand-and-foot. And he would probably beat me in the bargain.

"That was it. But I was a strong-headed girl! By age 14, I vowed to change my fate! I would run away to Grimmland and win a pageant prize! Indeed, I would be crowned 'The Fairest in The Land!'

"Immediately thereafter, a hag appeared, pushing a cart of peddler's wares at the gate of my father's decrepit castle. She told me she would grant my wish of great beauty if I gave her all of my father's gold. He had once been wealthy, but had lost all to gambling and wars. The hag didn't know that. She only knew of my once-heroic father and his castle from ballads still sung by traveling players.

"I agreed, and she gave me a large, gilded mirror she said was magic. She told me that it could make the fairest in the land and give me the powers of witchcraft if I always kept it close.

"She told me that the mirror would always protect me from harm. Nevertheless, here I am, you see, standing trial in this wretched court. Where is my magical protection now?

Scribe Dinkle interrupts to ask what became of the hag.
Queen Meana Regina responds:

"The crone then asked me for the gold. She left the 'magic' mirror outside, exposed to the elements, in a horse-cart in the courtyard. I lured her down into my father's treasury vault under the walls. I feared that once she discovered the vault empty, she'd take the magic mirror back and put a curse on me. So, once the hag stepped inside the vault, I slammed its heavy iron door shut and secured it with chains and an iron bar.

"Fearful she would escape, then curse me and get the mirror back, I ran up the stone stairs to the courtyard. I grabbed the magic looking glass from the cart. I ran out of the castle gate, over the draw bridge, up the road and into the forests towards Grimmland as fast as my legs could carry me, holding tight to my mirror. Massive though it was, it felt light in my hands and its magic lightened my step so that I flew zigzag along the ground like a supernatural swallow, or a bat.

"By the second day I was deep into the woods, A king – who I didn't know then was Snow White's father – saw me alone there as he rode with his hunting party. I told him I was lost and that bandits had taken all I had except the mirror, and that I wished to go to Grimmland to enter the contest.

"He rescued me and took me back to his palace. As you all know, I entered and won the contest and have won it every year since then. And the king, as in all the love ballads, fell in love with me and I with him – at least during that first year when we married.

"If I'd have known that he would so quickly turn into such a pompous arse and that his little princess Snow White would grow into vile adolescent, I would have kept running through that forest right past Grimmland and on to greener pastures. Better to risk being devoured by wild boars than coming here!

"But, I have told this tribunal and I will state it again, I am not guilty. Yes, I had plenty of motives, but I never laid a finger on her snowy white skin. I never touched a strand of her ebony hair, I never, never hired a hunter to cut out her heart and lungs and never offered the princess that piece of poisoned apple that they say she swallowed when she sank into her sleep of death before her prince came. In fact, it's a big lie. In fact, your prince came often to – and in -- the House of the Seven Dwarfs where she worked as a saloon hussy!"

Shouts, hissing and booing from the crowd...

"Order, order! Silence or we'll clear the court!" All seven dwarf judges pound their gavels. "And the defendant will refrain from bad language and insulting the king or be gagged forthwith!"

Queen Meana curtsies towards the bench, and says with mock sweetness: "I apologize, your honors. I will watch my tongue. Oh my!"

She resumes her testimony: "Not guilty! I plead. That choking on a poison apple was nothing but a publicity stunt to promote Snow White's outrageous and libelous book, "Witchy Dearest."

Truth was her prince was broke – a wastrel who spent everything he made at the Dwarfs' saloon. He convinced that whoring blabbermouth to write all those lies about me so they could rake in a fortune when the Brothers Grimm published Snow White's story and King Walt optioned it for his movie.

Snow White counted on a gullible public to swallow every one of her vindictive lies. Sure enough her book went right to the top of the Olde Yorke Times bestseller list and stayed there! They ruined me!

Okay, I confess! (holds hands up in mock surrender.) Once, just once, I told my royal huntsman – and lover at the time – to take the brat out into the woods, like she ran away, and bring me back her heart and lungs for a barbeque dinner. Kidding! It was a joke. Everyone knows I hate barbeque!

I made up the story to tease my huntsman after he killed a boar and brought back to the castle. I had cook make nice pot pies with its heart and lungs, not spit roasted. By coincidence Snow White ran away that very same day. She made up the story about the hunter to cover up the real reason she ran off – because she was pregnant by Bashful who used to deliver coal to the palace. That's how there got to be seven dwarfs and not six. They had Dopey!

The crowd in courtroom erupts into hoots, foot-stamping and catcalls. Again, the judges pound their gavels for silence. The chief judge scolds Queen Meana Regina again. She apologies once more,

193

and continues:

"My lawyers will present this tribunal with a sworn affidavit from the hunter's sister that he confessed to her that it was Snow White who got him to take her far into the forest to find the house of those dwarfs. And that the little slut did him a sexual favor with those gorgeous blood red lips to seal the deal. Snow White wanted to steal the dwarfs' gold and said she'd give the hunter a further reward if she succeeded!

(More uproar in the courtroom. Chief judge Wheezy pounds his gavel and clears the courtroom for the morning...)

THIS ENDS QUEEN MEENA'S TRANSCRIPT

... The following is excepted from "<u>Mirror, Mirror</u>" by Dopey White, subtitled: "What the Brothers Grimm never told you about the brief life and high times of my mother and her court. This passage commences at the point when the Queena Meena tribunal reconvenes after porridge, vespers and the public flogging of a boy named Jack for growing giant beans without royal permission. ...

"Hear ye, hear ye, hear ye! All stand for the reading of the court's verdict!" A green elfin page shouts in a shrill voice. The judicial panel, consisting of all Seven Dwarfs, files into the court chamber. They seat themselves behind a high semicircular table facing the defendant, prosecutors, courtiers and peasants in a gallery at the back.

Without further ado, the chief judge, Sneezy, begins. "After due consideration, this court, under the Royal Code of Grimmland and the Laws of God..." Ahhhh... kerchoo, kerchoo, kerchoo... "finds the defendant Queena Meana Regina, former Queen of Grimmland, guilty of all charges.!"

The spectators gasp then begin to shout and argue. Judge Wheezy wheezes violently and pounds his gavel.

"Order!" He yells out in his dwarf voice, then continues. "In accordance with The Royal Grimmean

Code. I therefore pronounce upon Meana Regina a mandatory sentence of Death by Dance."

Kerchoo, aaaaah choooey, snuff, sniff, kerchooey!

"On this night, the sheriff will take the condemned..."
KERCHOO!

"...to the Royal Ballroom at the Palace and, before the assembled, to be placed in The Royal Executioner's Iron Shoes – of the latest fashion, sized to the prisoner's feet. The Royal Orchestra will commence an endless polka to which the prisoner will be made to dance over burning coals in a frenzy of vanity and envy until she expires! May God have mercy on your soul."

KERCHOO, HACK HACK, SNIFF, SNARF, AWWWW CHOO! COUGH!

Wheezy waves to one side of the courtroom where two men stand.

"Bring forth the Royal Blacksmith and the Royal Shoemaker to fit the condemned for her iron footwear." Kerchoo! "And make sure these are the finest shoes crafted in the latest fashion of the best iron flattering to a queen's dainty feet. Though condemned, Queena Meana remains, after all, a royal personage." Kerchoo!

Without warning, Queena Meana, acting in pro se, stands up without counsel from a table facing the judges. "You honor! Wait. I object. Do I not get a chance to put on my defense?"

The crowd buzzes and gurgles with barely suppressed chatters.
Kerchoo!

"Order." Wheezy pounds the gavel again. "Silence or I'll clear this courtroom!" Ah Chiou! Turning to the defendant, he says: "Yes. Of course, Queena Meana Regina, you may indeed, put on your defense right now that we've put the sentencing out of the way ." Kerchoo! "Proceed!"

Unruffled, Queena Meana Regina opens a folder of papers on her table and speaks out in a steady voice:

"I call as my witness... the Magic Mirror!"

More shouts, excited chatter and murmurs from the crowd and more gavel pounding by Judge Wheezy quiets them down. Mirror, tall and ponderous in a heavy gold frame around his oval, shimmering flatness, takse the witness stand.

The Queen begins:

"Did you, at any time, tell me that I was the 'fairest in the land.?'"

"Why no Ma'am," the Mirror responds. "I told you only that you were fair and sometimes *a ham*. It's a theatrical term that I had picked up from my dressing room days with the players at Avon. It means...well over the ..."

"I know what it means, Mirror!" The accused queen fumes at him. She continues.

"But I *am* the fairest! I am not a ham. Why would you say a thing like that?" The defendant queen presses on.

"I am but a simple mirror, Your Highness! I can only report what I can see and nothing more or less. I have no imagination and I don't see many women, and even fewer queens and princesses. So how would I know if you, or any one particular woman were the fairest?"

The defendant queen rolls her eyes, but nods back a thank you to the Mirror before proceeding.

"And so, following this logic, did you ever tell me that Snow White was the fairest in the land, as you have been quoted in her book?"

"Why, *no*. Never, of course not," answers the Mirror. "Not at all. She's lovely, but actually not my type. Plus I hardly ever saw her, and not at all after she ran off with the dwarfs." He starts to shimmer nervously, which is the way mirrors sweat. "Okay, I'll admit," he adds quickly. "I did once say that Princess Snowy had the sweetest little melons in the land."

The crowd laughs. A judge pounds his gavel for silence in the court. The mirror shimmers faster now. Undulations begin to swirl and flash. "Mirror, mirror, on the wall, get a grip!" the accused queen snaps.

"I only have a few more questions," says the queen. "So, in the light of what you just told the court, do you believe there is any truth at all to accounts of my so-called extreme vanity and murderous envy of Snow White?"

"Objection! Leading the witness!" shouts Lumpy, jumping up from his place at one side of the judicial panel. (He is acting both as judge and prosecutor.) Standing even shorter than Wheezy, Lumpy's nose barely clears the tabletop and that made him grumpy, like his cousin usually was in the neighboring magic kingdom. Snarl, Snarl. Hurumph!

"Objection sustained!" shout all the dwarf judges all in unison.

"I withdraw the question, your honors." says Queena Meana, laughing, having made her point.

She calls several more witnesses, all experts, and she asks them each to pore over, refute and discredit various passages in Snow White's tell-all memoir. By now, not only Sleepy, but the rest of the judges have fallen asleep along with half of the spectators.

The rest fall asleep when she delivered her summary. At the end of it all, the shoemaker and the blacksmith step forward and finish measuring Queena Meana's feet by having her try on wooden mock ups of different sizes.

When they finish, the bailiff tiptoes behind the raised dais to Chief Judge Wheezy, bumping into, Baleful, Slappy, Weepy, Creepy and Mopey as he goes. He pokes Wheezy awake, who goes into another violent fit of sneezing, then pounds his gavel, waking everyone else up.

KERCHOO! "Do you have any final requests before I remand you to carry out sentence?" AH CHOO, he said.

"Only that may have my mirror with me till the end," said Queena Meana Regina.

"Granted!" KERCHOO! Pound, pound, went his gavel. "Court is adjourned!"

AT THE EXECUTIONER'S BALL

The following night, the grand royal orchestra plays waltzes and couples, led by the happy royal couple – the graceful, lithe Snow White queen -- her ebony hair curled and springy under a diamond-and-emerald studded white gold tiara – held by her dashing young king.

The dancers swirl under huge crystal chandelier, watched by royal guards in silken livery standing by each of a dozen arched entryways draped in dark red velvet that matches Queen Snow white's lips. Waiters discreetly tend to the needs of those who remain seated at the ballroom dining tables enjoying the royal wedding repast, including the table of the Seven Dwarfs and their dates – young runners-up in this year's "Fairest-in-the-Land" contest.

At the far end of the ball room, at a giant fireplace across the dance floor from the orchestra and the royal couple, stands Queena Meana Regina, barefoot in a stunning ballroom gown, with a sequined black silk sheath bodice and skirt flaring at the knees. She wears black pearls, black opera gloves. Her fine black hair piles high, with an elegant twist and is covered with a long black satin veil twinkling with tiny diamonds.

Three imperial guards flank her. two of them hold onto the short chains that manacle each of her wrists. The third holds her precious Magic Mirror upright so that Queena can see her reflection as she preens herself, seemingly unruffled, conversing with the mirror and the guards. At one point the mirror and her guards laugh nervously, apparently at some bit of gallows humor by the queen.

The imperial blacksmith, a hulking man who doubles as Royal Executioner, bends at a giant fireplace against the back wall of the ballroom, a permanent grimace on his sweating, dark, heavy-featured face. He wears peasant's boots, tunic, and tights, partially covered by a black leather apron. Using a pair of tongs, he holds the court-mandated pair of high-topped iron shoes over brightly burning logs in the ballroom's marble-and-quartz fireplace.

The orchestra continues playing champagne waltzes.

Then the orchestra stops. All go silent. The captain of the king's guard steps up in front of both Queen Meana and the blacksmith and faces the front of the ballroom. He wears a full white and gold dress uniform, with fringed epaulets and a self-important visored, high peaked cap, set with five gold stars. The captains addressed the crowd, who, by now, has turned towards the fireplace at the back of the ballroom.

The captain unrolls a parchment and reads aloud in an expressionless, stentorian baritone:

"In accordance with the law, we now proceed to carry out the sentence of the Royal Court on Queena Meana Regina, forthwith."

He turns and looks back at the condemned.

She stares silently into her Magic Mirror.

The captain of the guard adds, in nasal tones: "Do you have any last words?"

"Liar, liar, pants on fire!" Regina yells sharply loudly enough for all to hear. "I curse all of you. Know that I am the fairest in the land!"

With that, two of her guards lift Queena Meana straight up off the floor. She keeps her face rigid and her eyes on her mirror, and takes up an indecipherable chant, starting with "Mirror, mirror...," then a series of dissociated syllables. The mirror catches her image and shimmers wildly with the white hot light of the searing iron shoes.

The blacksmith, who has donned his black, heavy leather, Royal Executioner hood, pulls the gleaming hot metal shoes from the fire. With one, swift practiced motion, he swings the tongs gripping the glowing white-hot iron half-boots up and onto Meana Regina's feet. Deftly, he uses the tongs to flip little clamps that lock each bright hot glowing shoe at the ankles.

Queena Meana screams with such force it sets the crystals shaking on the chandelier above and breaks wine glasses on the tables.

The orchestra that strikes up a fast polka that the assembled spectators recognize instantly as "Carrie," a popular song of the time about a jilted teenage girl with lethal telekinetic powers. The guards drop the yowling Meana Regina back down onto the dance floor, feet swinging and jump aside. She runs in widening circles, leaping to the beat of the polka.

Queen Meana Regina spins around and around the dance floor, scattering the royal guests in a glowing cloud of red and white smoke.

The queen screams "*eeeeeeeee…*" in an ear-splitting crescendo, without pausing to take a breath.

Soon, her ear-splitting takes on a gleeful malice. She kicks and leaps, and dips and turns and flashes from one end of the ballroom to the other and back around, faster and faster as the polka speeds up, the musicians unable to control the tempo anymore.

The chandelier rattles more and more, shakes and swings wildly. "*Eeeeeeeeeeeeee!*" she screams as she goes. "*Eeeeeeeeeya!*"

The orchestra plays at full-blast through all the commotion. The musicians play ins evermore frenzied, out-of-control tempos. The string players fall over backwards. The woodwind, horn and percussion players fall over in dead faints. Magically, however, their instruments float over them and continue to play at full volume. The violin, cello and bass' bows saw strings away with menacing determination. Meanwhile, the horns suck their player into their brass mouthpieces and play on, as do the drums, xylophones, harps and timpani.

Snow White clasps her dainty hands over her shell-like ears, and screams, "Stop! Stop! I *hate* you. I've always hated you. Stop! I confess. I lied about it all. And I hate waltzes and polkas!" Unfortunately, no one could hear her above the din.

Through it all comes the voice of Meana Regina, causing Snow White to turn even whiter thatn white in shock! "Not really, my dear, *Whitey*," says the queen.

From out of a fiery whirlwind, the queen continues: "You *did* lie. But it is a paradox, for it is also true, that I would have killed you given half the chance, Snow White, and now I have that chance. And I will kill you!"

With that, Queen Meana's scream modulates into an unearthly animal wail. Her voice breaks all the dishes and glasses on the tables. The ballroom spins as if flying on its own. Windows break, posts, and doorways crack and break. The royal guards fly out the broken windows. The Royal pate, cakes and champagne bottles fly about wildly splattering on everyone in range.

In a moment, the heavy chandelier crashes to the floor and the rest of the marble ceiling collapses suddenly in a hail of glass and stones, crushing to death all souls inside, including Snow White, but except the Seven Dwarfs and their beauty contest dates who, overcome with excitement had slipped under their ballroom's sturdy oak table for some hanky panky just before the chandelier fell.

The whirling dervish of Queena Meana emerges from the smoldering wreckage and dust, spinning and holding her magic mirror in front of her flashing reflected light out over the gardens of the palace. Queena Meana races down the courtyard palace stairs and out onto the grounds along the royal road. Her iron shoes drop off, cool and harmless as she runs. Her feet show no signs of burns.

Queena Meana slows to a walk where the road winds into the royal forest. She stops, puts two fingers to her mouth and whistles resoundingly, in a very unladylike fashion causes the mirror to blush red.

In seconds, a fine black coach drawn by four black horses with driver and footmen, all likewise in black with touches of red piping, comes out of the woods onto the main road, glowing under a full moon that breaks through the scattered clouds.

A footman opens the coach door and bows ceremoniously. Queena Meana hands him the mirror and steps inside the coach."Where to, Ma'am?" asks the footman before he closes the coach door.

"Take me to the castle of Briar Rose," she says. "I want to pay a visit to my cousin Maleficent."

The footman repeats the destination up to the driver, puts the mirror carefully into a luggage boot at the back of the coach and hops on the coach's running board.

Queena Meana settles comfortably into the satin-covered seats inside. She sighs. The liveried driver up front cracks his whip and the horses set off at an easy trot, pulling the coach along the winding road through black forests under the pearly moonlit sky.

Inside, Queen Meana taps on the window of her coach's door at the footman, motioning him inside. He leans to open the door, holding onto the swaying coach with his other hand. "Yes, Ma'am?"

"You're my footman, aren't you?"

"Yes, Ma'am. That I am, Ma'am."

"Then get in here and rub my feet. They're so sore!

I *hate* tribunals. When I am queen of this land again, I shall abolished them, and proceed directly to hangings. It's what my public really wants to see."

10 OUR OWN KIND

1. RED ALL OVER

Damn florescent lights keep flickering, just like the one over his desk back at the *Times*. All this white could make him invisible. Bleached walls, tiles, curtains, bedding, pale as his ghostly face, set off against his black silky, Sy Devore shirt and the dark droplets of blood peeking from her bandages that worry him. Air conditioning blows soundlessly from vents above, morgue-cold in this sterile space, once removed from the smoggy heat of this June morning in Los Angeles. This summer, not of love, 1968, will be very long.

Makeda's monitor beeps in reassuring syncopation with the wheezy snores of a curtained-off roommate. A muted TV oozes soap opera from high on a wall opposite her bed. Makeda hates TV, and would loathe that her picture – a dated, inappropriately smiling high school yearbook shot – keeps showing up on network news, and in the papers, though only below the fold now.

Gingerly, Ben takes Makeda's limp hand, careful with the IV tube. He whispers her name. She breathes softly,

unresponsive. The little girl next to Ben stares up at the
television screen for a while. She holds a small bunch of
droopy spring flowers wrapped in greenish paper. Benny
bought them for her to give to her mother. The girl pulls
on Benny's sleeve to change channels – find cartoons. He
puts his finger to his lips and whispers that mommy is
asleep.

The girl steals glances at her mama's face, its familiar,
normally radiant, sienna tones gone to dun against white
pillows. That scary, odd, clear plastic straw thingy running
under mama's nose looks buggy, or Martian.

The girl can't see much else but mounds and folds of
blanket that look like the Hollywood Hills she saw from
the back seat of Benny's car on the freeway coming here.
The girl looks down at the big rubber wheels of mama's
metal bed frame. She imagines Mr. Toad taking the bed on
a while ride through the dull corridors of this place she
doesn't want to say is a hospital.

The little girl slips her hand from Benny's and sits in a
visitor's chair. She puts the flowers down on a side table
and picks up a magazine with pictures of pretty white
women she doesn't know. Her ponytails bounce adorably
from red scrunchies as she flips pages. She swings her feet
showing off her new red sneakers and matching knee
socks with yellow flowers. She likes that Benny let her
wear her new dress today – all in bright colors just like
mama's.

She likes Benny's porcelain whiteness, accentuated by
his all-black attire - jeans and silk shirt open at the collar.
They make quite a pair, him all lanky like a Halloween
skeleton. People look, and notice her pretty colors, and she
skips and tilts her head this way and that when they do.

She wonders when mama will wake up so they can
leave this place with its smells like rubbing alcohol that
remind her of getting shots, but with no lollipops.

Benny presses against the bed and takes Makeda's
hand, careful not to disturb the IV. The warmth of her

palm heartens him. He even catches the familiar, buttery scent of her through the hospital's bitter medicinal odors. He wants to kiss the softness under her chin.

Makeda opens her eyes, glassy, trying to make out shapes. "He's been shot." She tries to cry this out, but it comes out a raspy whisper.

Benny squeezes her hand gently. "I know. It's okay. You're safe. You don't have to talk. The nurse said your throat would be a little sore after they pulled out the tube."

She squeezes Benny's hand back. Her eyes widen as his face comes into focus. He doesn't tell her that he didn't like the nurse's graven look or what else was said.

The little girl slides off the chair and stands on tiptoes beside the bed again. Makeda bends her head painfully forward to see.

"Oh my God, Keesha! Hi baby."

"Hi mama."

Benny lifts her awkwardly to the crook of his arm. He braces when she reaches out, nearly toppling onto her mother. Benny slides the girl onto the bed, so she can sit cross-legged on the edge, next to her mother. Makeda touches her daughter's cheek, her hand trembles.

"Mama is so happy to see you, my darling. You okay?"

The little girl nods and smiles, worry in her eyes for the first time.

Makeda rolls her eyes over at Ben. "Really? Here?" Her rasp turns to whisper, but she gets her point across.

"I thought..."

"You thought like, let this poor child see mama. Well, mama's not dead yet." She manages a smile at her daughter.

"She's been asking about you, about where you are. She's seen your picture on the TV."

"Jesus!"

"Just for a moment."

Makeda lifts her head, trembling, and manages a

smile. "You ought to be going to school now, baby. Mama's going to be just fine and come home very soon."

She looks at Ben. "What day is this?"

"Friday."

She squints. "Three days?"

"Two and a half."

She looks back at Keesha. "Don't fret, sweetheart. They fixed me all up and I'm just about better." Her voice trails off.

Makeda strains towards the girl She whispers. "Kiss. Kiss."

The little girl puts her arms around her mother's neck and kisses her cheek. Makeda kisses her back. "Mama loves you, baby, very much."

"We should go now. Let you get some rest." Benny goes to pick up the little girl.

Makeda pulls his hand again, stronger this time. "Benny..."

"She's doing fine, don't worry. I'm taking time off work and my girls can help us tomorrow, and Sunday when you get out of here, I hope."

Makeda coughs, takes a breath and rasps softly again. "Ben. Thank you for this. Are you okay?"

"I'm fine. And Keesha's doing great."

"Is he, you know... Did he make it?" Makeda raises her eyes to the TV.

Ben shakes his head.

Makeda mouths a word she doesn't want her daughter to hear, then looks back to little Keesha. "You go with Benny, now, honey. Mama see you soon. Okay? You be good now, Keesha."

Ben raises Keesha to kiss her mother goodbye, and squeezes Makeda's hand again. He leaves holding the little girl's hand. She waves back at her mother one more time. Benny checks for the guard. Gone.

----

2. SIREN SONG

Six months earlier. New Year's Day.

Ring, ring, ring! Goddammit! Who's calling this early? It's barely light. The phone won't stop hurting his head. It pings merrily off the bare hardwood floors and sparse furnishings of Benny's rented cottage.

The cottage was a real find, just below Mulholland Drive– perfectly in the path of brush fires and mudslides. Chipped, Spanish stucco and red tiles, once a guesthouse on an estate that belonged to Charlie Chaplin, now subdivided, a cozy three-bedroom. Benny hears the rain between rungs – staccato against his windows. They said '68 would be wet. That's L.A. – drought or downpour, fame or famine, and junk food feasting.

Benny pulls a pillow over his face and calculates whether he can yank the phone from the wall. No rest for the wicked. The pillow doesn't muffle much except the downpour spattering his windows.

Shit. He untangles himself from his twisted blankets and lurches for the phone. He is goose-fleshed naked and New-Year's-Day hung over. Seems this comes with the still unfamiliar territory of the newly divorced – punctuated by alternate weekend daddy-hood. No score in the first inning.

The ringing stops before he can grab the receiver. Damn. Benny sits back on the saggy edge of his bed. Too awake now to recapture dreamless sleep. He brushes aside an urge to dash onto his tiny patio and catch raindrops on his party parched tongue. I used to love that when I was a kid, carefree and dumb. It wouldn't wash away the sour taste of this morning. He remembers now, why he hates parties. He tells the sparrows twittering in the wind-whipped date palm just outside his window to shut the fuck up! What are you so damn cheerful about? It's

January and gray as my prospects.

The phone starts up again. Fuck it.

No robe. Benny pulls the top sheet over his shoulders and pads out to the kitchenette.

I'm the Sheik of Araby.

All the girls are crazy 'bout me.

He cuts his thumb opening the coffee can. He turns on the tap and watches blood turning pink in running cold water until the bleeding subsides. He fills and puts the percolator on the stove. Can't find cigarettes. He grabs the yellow-and-red, peace-sign mug – with the hairline crack in the handle -- from the cabinet. No cream for his coffee, he uses a splash of his kids' leftover chocolate milk from the fridge. It will do.

The phone starts up again. All right! God damn it. His phone is deep red, a choice of calculated whimsy. Hello Nikita! About those missiles. Sorry, but we've had a little mix up with our nukes over here...

By now, his head clearing, he has a good idea who is ringing him. He's been slow to give out his new number, but Lori already knows it from when he had the kids last week.

He picks up on the fifth ring and fakes a wide-awake baritone.

Lori doesn't sound hostile or blitzed for a change. Her voice is edgy and small. Oh, shit. Maybe something's happened to the kids. Should have answered sooner.

"Uncle Phil died."

Silence, then he hears Lori putting down the receiver, coughing, yelling at her mother, crying, then picking it back up.

Poor Uncle Phil, funny man and the only sane one in her family. "Sorry to hear that, Lor. I know he meant a lot to you. ... Shit, he wasn't that old."

"Heart attack." Her voice quavers.

Uncle Phil owned a hardware and feed store up in Redding, near Mount Shasta. He was the older brother of

Lori's mom – blond, bright and still a knockout. They shared a small town childhood, but she didn't stay in Redding. She hopped a Greyhound out of their woodsy hometown for Hollywood soon as she turned 16 and became Gwen Fox, bit actress, then bombshell spotlighted for a few fleeting years, starring, in half dozen forgotten movies that show up in art house retrospectives.

Along her way to stardom, leggy Gwen worked nights as a hat check girl at the Brown Derby by night, and mimeographed manifestos for the Socialist Workers party by day. That didn't keep her from marrying oil fortune playboy David Granville III and becoming tabloid Cinderella paparazzi bait.

She was a little over for Granville's age limit then, but it was true love – at least until he tired of his brainy non-bimbo wife and went back to teen nymphs pimped by his valet. His lawyers settled quickly in private, to avoid another paparazzi feeding frenzy, or worse – considering possible statutory rape charges. Lori walked away with a considerable fortune -- by her Redding standards, though not by his. By then, the studios had found a new bombshell. Nobody would take her seriously as an actress, despite her underrated acting talent.

Plus, when she split with Granville, Gwen was already pregnant with Lori. Nothing was said about this. The lawyers had photos of her with another man, Sean Bliss, a part-time actor, screenwriter and radical leftist cohort from the old days.

Lori got his surname, plus a half sister, Nola, favored by her daddy and, by providence, with stunning, unearned good looks.

Right around that time – in the early 1950s – Sean Bliss made a perfect red witch hunt target. Never a man of good judgment, he not only attended Communist party meetings, but had traveled once gone to Stalinist Moscow to attend a solidarity conference. It was a free trip. He was young and curious, idealistic and stupid.

When Lori was twelve, she returned home from school one day to discover that her presumed father had chosen to answer a House Unamerican Activities Committee subpoena by locking himself in a Cadillac de Ville belonging to Lori's mother, garage door shut, motor on, garden hose from tailpipe duck tapped into the wind wing window.

In need of a tune-up, however, the Caddy's motor kept dying instead of Mr. Bliss. No problem. He put a Walther PK38 in this mouth and pulled the trigger.

Young Lori smelled fumes when she returned from school and walked into to their rambling split-level house in Topanga Canyon. She heard what she thought was a backfire. She walked back through the kitchen and into the garage to check the car. Lori remembers nothing precisely after that except seeing the blood splatter on the car windows. She fled back through the house, vomiting, and locked herself in her room.

She had hunkered on the floor behind her bed for a long time, through all the commotion, when her mother arrived and called an ambulance. She didn't respond to her mother's pounding at her locked door. She heard her mother screaming, getting an emergency guy to kick open the bedroom door, after which her mother threw a scene. Mom wasn't mad at her Mr. Bliss for shooting himself in her car. She blamed Lori for his death, somehow, for not calling an ambulance right away, as if it would have mattered. Thenceforth, mother and daughter never spoke of this in any rational way. But her mother would bring it up in angry fits as she took more and more to drink.

Lori's phone call, on this New Year's Day, reminded Benny of when he first met Lori. Both of them were 18. The met at a New Year's Eve party on her mother Gwen's Hollywood Hills estate attended by various Hollywood celebs, wannabes and hangers-on. A press agent friend had invited Benny, offhand – Ben, at the time, was on the Hollywood social b-list due to his stint as a freelance reviewer of art films for the *Times*.

Ben saw right off that Lori didn't fit with this crowd either, even though that's where she was living. She busied herself in the kitchen mostly, helping the caterers with snacks. Gwen looked annoyed seeing her daughter carrying trays around. He loitered in the kitchen too, and helped a bit, breaking through Lori's shyness asking her questions about this and that. He preferred asking questions to answering them.

Unlike a lot of other girls his age he approached, Lori didn't react as if Ben were Casper the Friendly Ghost or a zombie. She looked straight at him when she talked.

Ben drew Lori away. They wandered the estate ground along paths through rows of white blooming rhododendron bushes, illuminated by a pearly gibbous moon. They wound up at the tiled, kidney shaped swimming pool on a patio overlooking the bejeweled vastness that is Los Angeles on a blessedly clear winter night. The city – squat in daytime - spread out before them like diamonds on a vast black velvet carpet.

No one was there but them. The pool area was secluded from the main house by a stand of cypress. Perfect. They kissed and explored each other to the faint music of the party from the house up the path beyond the trees.

Before long – damn the cold – they stripped and plunged, laughing and yelping, into the steamy turquoise warmth of the pool. They played like dolphins, all sensuous and silky, skin-to-skin beneath the water, stirring vapors from its heated surface. They hardly noticed the whooping from the house at the stroke of midnight. This was happy New Year enough. They started the year enraptured – oblivious to the sounds of car horns and far off fireworks from the city streets below. They glowed with the passion and glamour of it – two naïve kids swimming in the illusion of luxuriant, Hollywood Hills glamour, with not a clue that life just wasn't going to be like that moment.

They made breathy, fumbling love until they were tired, sated. Then they dried off, best they could with a towel Lori's mother had left down at the pool that afternoon. The put their clothes back on, sat close on a chaise lounge and talked and talked, baring their souls with the fervent, earnest naiveté of youth determined to do it all better than their parents.

It had been her first time, not his, but he was barely experienced himself. She didn't mind his albinism, he could feel it. She asked him direct questions about it as they talked about growing up. She seemed to enjoy sliding her hands along his long pearly body, then holding back instead, with the awkwardness of a young girl who thinks herself homely.

Star-struck, thinking-with-your-dick damn fool, he thought to himself these days, nine New Years later. Regret had replaced romance, followed by guilt for regretting their involvement. Because how could he? Without his meeting Lori, his two darling, rascally daughters would never have been born.

Lori's distressed voice on the phone, wasn't helping his hangover. He sips bitter coffee as she inches to the point.

"I'm going to drive up to Redding for the memorial and stay a while to take care of Uncle Phil's affairs." Her voice changes from cheerful to flat, determined.

"You buried the lead."

"What?"

"Nothing."

Uncle Phil, as he had promised, had left Lori a comfortable inheritance, including his tidy, craftsman house on Shasta Lake outside of town.

"Okay. Great then, I'll come by and pick Linda and Nicole. Pack them some extra clothes. I'll see they get to school while your gone."

"They'll be fine with my mom."

"No sale, Lori!" Contentiousness and mistrust had not abated between them in this, their second year of awkward, joint custody.

"No. It's all arranged. She wants to do it. I'm leaving today."

"What the fuck? You can't just do that without checking with me, Lori? I am their father. They should stay with me."

"Don't start" Lori insists. "I just can't deal with my mother and you at the same time." Gwen's hostility towards Ben – predating the divorce, wasn't news. The whole family, except old Phil, displayed an insatiable appetite for drama. Addiction was more like it.

At least Lori sounds coherent this morning – on the surface anyway. No talk of space aliens or the CIA watching her and transmitting coded messages to her over the television, or of doctors and nurses conspiring against her.

"Look, Lori. I don't want to argue. Just bring the kids

over or let me pick them up."

More silence. Ben wants to slam the receiver down. If it weren't a holiday he'd just call his lawyer.

Lori piped in, her voice softer now. "Benny."

"Yes."

"I was thinking that if the girls stay with my mom, you could come with me, to the funeral...." She let that hang. He said nothing. She went on: "I know you liked Uncle Phil. We could spend time together, alone. It's been so long."

"I can't," he said, but meant, I *won't*. "I've got to work. Busy as hell down at the paper."

"Uncle Phil left me his house and everything, enough to get by without my mom or anyone's help. You could quit the paper, write your novel. We could bring the kids up there in the fresh air, put them in good school You might want to work for the local paper. Think of it."

Benny flinches. He flashes back on those fleeting days of L.A. bliss at the beginning – a couple of self-conscious hipsters in black turtlenecks cruising jazz clubs, poetry readings, critiquing half-understood art movies. Then came a careless pregnancy – but they were young, had high hopes just like JFK used to say. They'd raise kids the right way, with Dr. Spock's help. When the baby came, Benny quit school and got on the paper as a copy boy,, working the swing shifts.

Wide-eyed, clueless, starter parents, they were: The doted on baby Linda's every gurgle. Benny, uncomfortable in his uncertain cheap white shirt and regimental tie, played journalist and aspiring film critic. In slow motion, it all unraveled in ways that Benny did not see coming – or chose to ignore – until chronic dysfunction became melt down. Lori, downing six packs night and day, talking incessantly – first blackouts, then the suicide attempts.

... "Hello? Benny? Are you there?"

"Yes."

"Will you drive up to Redding with me?"

"I can't. You know. My eyes. They've gotten worse. No highway driving at night for me anymore." A transparent dodge: he's perfectly able to drive under all conditions. Lucky for him, his type of albinism involved minimal ocular disability. Medically, they had diagnosed his condition as hypomelanism, a partial lack of melanin, accounting for his alabaster complexion, but deep blue, pink eyes. But he rarely talks about such details, even to those close to him, well aware of this engendering mystery, and maybe even liking it. Better to be a man of mystery than a medical freak, he told a shrink once.

But Lori made Ben drop his guard and feel comfortable about telling her all the details of his life as Casper the Ghost, even the delicate matter of heredity, well before Lori got pregnant, and even though they both said they didn't want ever to be parents. Not that there was any choice by then, except a back-alley coat hanger. The doctor told them what Benny already knew. Chances of passing on the recessive gene in a "mixed marriage" were as remote as it popping up from the union of two "normal" parents.

Though he looked as white as the Pillsbury Doughboy, his was what the specialists called "partial albinism." He wasn't legally blind, could drive with glasses, but was impaired enough disqualify him from military service. The point was moot, being as he had draft deferments anyway, what with college. He had not grown up poor, rural or ghetto or barrio – like the kids most likely to be sent to Vietnam. Then he and Lori had Linda and Nicole and another deferment..

Nevertheless, he felt the draft's hot breath – as did all of his generation of young men – divided over the war and the antiwar protests that had escalated during his first years of marriage – along with the war itself – and along with the war at home between he and Lori.

He was a muddle of self-conscious gestures about it all. It seemed everyone was expected to take a stand.

Benny got his back up and had told everyone he'd sooner go to Canada before Vietnam, a moot gesture. He burned his draft card in an ashtray at a party. It got him a few laughs, nothing else. There were no deferments from a marriage going south, however.

Benny cradles the receiver with his shoulder to pour coffee. He pushes two of Nicole's stuffed animals aside to make room on his garage sale, sea-foam Naugahyde couch. Lori keep talking, persuading, and finally pleading. This is awful.

His bladder reminds him with sudden urgency of the previous night's imbibing and this morning's coffee. He puts his cup on the coffee table and drags the phone with him to the bathroom, pulling its tangled line taunt. He sits on the toilet to muffle the telltale sound, leaves the door open, leaning forward to keep the receiver to his ear. He will have to flush after the call – not from modesty. He just doesn't want to let Lori in on any aspect of his private life ever again. Enough of this intrigue, bordering on child abuse! Enough of Lori and her mother pressuring the kids to report on him and then acting like they are the victims.

Lori goes on about the trip to Redding, and the vision of them re-settling there, a dream Benny knew from experience could flip negative into a horror show at any moment. "Lori, I told you I can't."

"You mean you won't?"

Pause. His patience expires. "That's right, Lori. I won't. No, no and no! Please don't ask me again." He feels bad, saying this to her – even now, even meaning every word of it.

He finishes and returns to the living room . He sips his coffee, tepid now, acrid as his guilt for exploding at her. "You left me, remember. Not that it matters. It just won't work with us. Let's leave well enough alone." A better man would step up – the mother of your children needs you, for better for worse, and all that. He downs the last of the coffee and feels dregs gritting his tongue.

"Things could be so much better, Benny, with a house of our own up there." Now she was all hearts and flowers, on the upswing.

He envisions himself exiled up there, no one to talk with but half drunk loggers and half stoned weed growers. *I would go crazy up there in no time – right along with Lori - call my confessional novel, Folle a Deux. Our double suicide could make it a bestseller.*

He tries a conciliatory tone again. "I feel bad, Lori, believe me. But I can't do it just up and leave. I have assignments." *Not the real reason. Actually, he's grown to hate his job. I'm such a coward. What's wrong with telling the truth?* Benny pushes the receiver hard against the side his head. His ear feels hot.

Lori's voice hardens from meek to manic, spits like a cornered cat. "What you mean, Ben, really, is that you want to stay here to screw all those whore girlfriends of yours, you fucker!".

This is the song that never ends... "Sure, Lori, if you say so. Fuck yes! And oh wow, is it great! All I do is screw starlets. Orgies here at Chez Benny, every night! I'm a regular Hugh Hefner. You should see the pair of gorgeous groupies, I got here right now, sitting on lap while we talk."

"Fuck you, Benny. You never loved me. You fucked my sister; then you went and fucked Viola."

Here we go again.

"Oh sure. There we go! Viola, Viola, Viola. Hello! You dreamed that I was with Viola, Lori, over and over. It never happened. You would wake up and rant about my infidelities with your sister – who wasn't even in town, by the way. Nothing ever happened."

But I wish it had. Viola Sabroza, jazz samba diva who lived next door to Gwen, a man would have to be far gone not to catch his breath in her presence, women too. Her daughter Ella played with his daughters.

"I know what you're doing Benny!" Lori's all-purpose

accusation failed to evoke Benny's natural guilt anymore. "I hate you! Fuck you." She hangs up.

"And a happy, friggin' New Year to you too, Lori," he says into a dead phone.

Same old, same old: Nothing new about this kind of exchange -- but this time Benny senses finality in it, a threshold crossed before it could be noticed, the door back into his marriage slamming forever shut. No more chances to mend – and he wasn't sorry, only washed out. Closing that door brings relief, freedom, but not release. He could never detach himself from their daughters, which meant he could never insulate himself from their mother. Some new accommodation would have to be found. None was apparent or even conceivable to him at this point.

Benny sinks head in hands. He seethes over the years trying the spring over her walls of resentment and suspicion, years of trying to ameliorate her stubborn self-destructiveness. But now he realizes that she had, just now, in that New Year's morning phone call, suddenly open the gates – just for that one moment, a one-time offer. At least it felt real.

But things had gone to far for him – and now, refusing her unequivocally, he had broken her heart as surely as she had hardened his own.

He feels queasy, ignoble. He had responded viscerally, without hesitation. He had not considered her as once-his-wife or even as human being, nor the mother their children, nor any of the practicalities, nor even his own desires. He had seen fire and rushed for the exit in unseemly self-preservation. His life would never be the same, neither would Lori's and neither would the lives of their two girls.

He dials her back – but doesn't want to talk, only to press for what he wants now. "Hi Lori" – like nothing happened. "I forgot to ask you what time I can pick up the girls? I've got extra clothes for them here, enough if you need to stay a week or so, and I can bring them to school until you get back."

"Fuck you."

"Did you tell them that I'll be there?"

"You're not picking them up, Benny."

"The hell I'm not."

"My mother will take care of them."

"That's not acceptable. The court order gives me joint custody. I'm their father."

"Fuck you. I'm leaving today. I've already dropped them at mom's house."

"Don't do this, Lori."

She hangs up again. No calling back this time.

Ben broods for a while. Then he slides one of his phonograph records from the shelves where he keeps his collection – that collection, and the stereo being the only items he took besides his clothing, when he split with Lori. He removes a 1929 shellac of Duke Ellington's Black and Tan Fantasy from its jacket. He likes the weight, how the light reflects off its ebony surface and its burgundy and gold RCA label. There's little Nipper, head cocked to "his master's voice" from a brass, Victrola horn – the terrier he always wanted when he was growing up dog-less with his single mother in Hollywood practicing on their spinet after school, fantasizing about playing a gig at a smoky club – maybe Rick's in Casablanca.

He sets the disk gently on the turntable. Be careful – no telling how many plays left on its scratchy surface. Arthur Whetsol's poignant horn fits his mood. Somehow it reminds him of Uncle Saul – on his Jewish side – who was a studio violinist who also owned a rundown music shop on Fairfax. Benny used to help out there after school, and Uncle Saul paid him, mostly in records and advice.

Saul would fish precious rarities from cardboard boxes in the back. He never knew what – symphonies, opera, jazz, Caruso, prized Rachmaninoff and Busoni performance originals, Mary Garden, whom Saul hinted richly about having romanced once when she toured

Europe. But Uncle Saul never talked about the row of numerals tattooed on his forearm that Benny spied when his uncle would roll up his sleeves. Benny learned about such things later.

Ben grubs a half-smoked Pall Mall from an ashtray, collapses on his sofa and listens to the rain and the music – breakfast of champions. He picks a half-crumpled letter off the coffee table and reads it for the fourth time.

At least it was more than the usual, perfunctory rejection slip – a chatty personal note from his old pal Roger Zwick, scrawled by hand, under the familiar, *Rolling Stone* newspaper-boy logo – but disappointing nevertheless. Why keep reading it over and over? He feels a generational pull, more on the political than on the mind-altering side of the new age, grooving like everyone, with the latest *Revolver* and *Magical Mystery Tour* albums – others.

Just make the music – any kind - as long is you keep it real, and not manufactured, not sloppy, not histrionic. He had enough of that. Benny had been at the Whiskey A Go Go on the Strip when they shut down Jim Morrison for screaming, "Mother, I want to fuck you!"

Okay, Benny owned the Doors album, and grooved on it, "but that was bullshit." Benny imagined a time machine parked in his garage, awaiting repairs, jazz being prematurely declared dead as of the go-go sixties.

"It's just not my time. I don't belong even with those who say they don't belong. I'm not with turning on, tuning in or dropping out. I'm not standing defiant on the barricades; I'm too cowardly to risk my head bashed in Selma, Alabama.

"I'm just not with it, man. I'm not hip. Neither am I straight enough, to be a GI Joe. I feel like John Lennon's *Nowhere Man*. I move with Monk, soar with Coltrane and chill with Miles. I square as Robert Frost with miles and miles to go before I sleep.

----

2. MAKEDA

Friends, Benny, that's all. I made that clear. I said it for myself as much as him. I'm on a diet – no more men. Not till I learn to do better, not till Keesha grows up, or both.

"Sure thing, Makeda." Cheerful, covering disappointment well, he lays back just enough to make it seem safe for us to flirt. "I know you love me."

"As a friend," I add too quickly. He gets away with a lot being odd. Reminds me of a marble statue come to life, but skinnier, and with clothes, cool ones, though it is said that they painted the marble figures back then. I won't say he's handsome, but you want to stare, snaky tall glass of milky white with those crystal blue eyes.

Right off I notice that Benny doesn't oob-eye my tits every chance he gets, not like a lot of men, sneaking peaks, or downright undressing me since fifth grade, walking by dick-for-brains white boys and old men who think black girls are easy in the neighborhood where I grew up.

The quiet ones with easy smiles are harder to read. Like Zeke. So fine to look at and how he could play that horn, but good for nothing else except getting high. Should have known better than to let him slow-dance me onto his DayGlo van to nowhere. Misgivings, but no regrets: Being with Zeke gave me my beautiful baby Keesha. I felt him loving me at the beginning, and it was dreamy, all that attention, sweet boy, really, but a boy not growing up, tuning in and dropping out to nowhere. Not for me.

So ended my get-fucked-up, hipster phase, followed by my black-power-get-militant phase.

Went to my meetings. marched with in the black student union strikes at UCLA, even met Angela Davis , then took up with Alonzo Abbake and ran with Black

Nation before it went to hell, what with FBI's *COINTELPRO* frame-ups, infiltration and provocation.

I took on the name of Makeda then – Ethiopian name for the Queen of Sheba, more to her than the Bible let on, their history tells us. And I stopped using hair relaxer, and went short, proud and nappy. Deal with it.

Brothers did good things, aroused pride, fed poor children and all, sisters too. Can't blame the brothers for packing, and all that anger, but there's a lot more – up and down – you don't read about. They say revolutions eat their young. Put that in my FBI dossier, I can testify it's true.

Alonzo said women have a role in the movement – "on their backs." He was kidding, I thought, but I didn't think it funny. Go ask Harriet Tubman. He told me I wasn't black enough. Brothers won't get anywhere fighting among themselves and keeping their women barefoot. Polishing my warrior's spear isn't a life. The world looked different with a baby bouncing from my sling. Time to move on.

Makes me cry and want to scream that six months after I left him, they gunned him down front of Black Nation headquarters on South Crenshaw. By then I'm working for the paper part-time, keeping low. His obit only made page three.

Abbake Dead in Gang Shootout

We all knew better.

Now, here I am in… well, whatever you want to call it – my mother, woman, bitch, and take-no-prisoners phase – maybe not a phase.

Tell me how I can raise Keesha in this world – and forget about child support. I went back to school. Thank God for grandma's checks, just enough – after the grief I gave her. She knows about it all too.

"Wait until your little one becomes a teenager just like you'll be deserving." Grandma teases me on the phone. We talk once a week now, with her Kilkenny brogue making me homesick, but I know there's no going back. Too much other shit.

Grandma McGiven – daddy's mother Maureen – raised me. Silky red hair I loved to play with. Shot with silver now, which makes it even prettier, like my father's would be now, had he come back alive. My nana says I have her eyes, not just because of the gray-green but meaning how we see things. Practical. Women have to be the ones with sense because the men mostly don't. Grandma came to Boston after grandpa died fighting the Black and Tans back in Ireland after the Easter Uprising. She bootlegged Irish whiskey smuggled in by her dead husband's old Sinn Féin pals during Prohibition. She stashed money to buy property in South Boston that she rented out, right through the Depression. She taught me survival, even though I didn't listen to her enough growing up.

Don't remember much of my father, Kevin McGiven – mama called him Kenny. I have a snapshot of him I carry in my wallet – black-and-white. It's the same one shown on the back cover of his novel about South Boston, all but forgotten after the initial fuss.

Daddy stays young forever in that picture – younger than me, now. Cute in that sailor suit, a Camel dangling from sensuous lips half-smiling. You could tell why the women swooned over him like mama said. He's leaning against a Buick – red, I'm told – in his sailor suit. He wears his sailor's hat cocked like Sinatra in On the Town. I squint to imagine the coppery color of his wavy thick hair.

What a pair mama and daddy must have made, she with those wicked, Creole gray eyes and he with his wavy red hair that I got with daddy's blue eyes and mama's Louisiana redbone skin.

Mama says I nearly was born in that red Buick, out in the desert on Route 66 outside nowhere, Arizona. Daddy was driving with her to San Diego where he was to report for duty. I couldn't wait that long. Daddy raced for miles to find a hospital that would take a black woman, even one about to deliver. They named me Ann.

I don't remember my baby days in San Diego. Mama was pregnant again when they shipped daddy out. The war was nearly over by then. Didn't matter for daddy. A Kamikaze sank his ship. We took a train back to Boston where mama had Leon.

Grandma McGiven took care of Leon and me while mama toured, singing with this and that band. She came home less and less often, more and more fucked up. Everybody in the jazz scene drank too much and did smack in those days. Mama couldn't handle life, but she sure could make music out of it. And sweet Jesus, could she sing – and swing, and summon you with her voice.

I listen to mama's old Blue Note records once in a while. I want Keesha to hear them as she grows up. Lotte Loraine, Lady Blue. Jazz stations still play her records. Never sold much. Neither did daddy's novel, good as it was.

Mama finally pulled herself together five years ago after one last stint in rehab. You don't get gold records for that, but it's harder. Teaches music now, married again, to a nice black man. Millard – a contractor with a big heart. He adores her. I'm glad she's happy, but she and I aren't done healing yet – maybe never. I don't know.

Same goes for my brother Leon. He doesn't know mama like I do. Thank God grandma was there for us – and never mind the looks she got walking proudly in that white neighborhood with Leon and me back then.

I suppose that taking care of Leon and me helped grandma fill the hole left by her son's death so far away. I knew Grandma would holler at him, then cry when Leon joined the Army. Hell. He would have been drafted anyway – with those grades – looking at some trouble with the law as well. God help him – he's in Vietnam now, three months and every time I see the news I hold my breath. No deferments for him. He wrote that they put him on supply detail, as if that is out of harm's way. Nobody is safe over there.

I sang in church choir a bit growing up. But I was not given mama's gift. I got something else that I haven't unwrapped yet. I filled journals with poetry and ramblings I would not show anyone. I don't remember when I went from dreaming to writing about the people in my head – those close by and from far away.

In my fantasy world the weather is more sultry, and I'm not in it alone, I love, I am loved, I go deep with that man whose face I cannot see yet. He is present to me, knows my mind as well as my body... but a fantasy a single mom doesn't' find much time to indulge.

Thank God and grandma I went to college – English lit – not much good for jobs, and never got my degree, but it helped me get this job at the Times. Beats waitressing. I took a writing course taught by Roy's wife Mirabel over at UCLA. She really liked my work. She got me to think of my writing as worthwhile, with possibilities. Roy's is the only black reporter upstairs. He put in a word and here I am integrating the Sunday features desk – part-time and hello.

Better than this, Mirabel gives me hope that it's actually possible to have a good life with a man you love, a beautiful kid, and pursue a professional career.

Sometimes I miss being close with somebody again. But I'm not going for that right now – and sure as hell, not falling into anything just for company, or falling for a man who has too many troubles of his own. I like being on my own now.

Benny does turn me on with that sly warmth. He counts his failings, not what makes him special – maybe because they aren't the usual things. He takes such care of those little girls, without making a fuss over doing it like some men. All good.

But his life is too messy. That's a warning sign that I ignore at my own peril. I'm not sure he knows who he is.

Nevertheless, God help me, we keep getting cozier.

As if Benny and I didn't see enough of each other at the paper, now we're sharing daycare. The other day he asked me if I wanted to go in on the canyon cottage he rents, more room that I have now and I'm looking, but like I told him, maybe, but strictly roommates, strictly friends. Then I thought I must be crazy. I still haven't answered.

----

4. PONY RIDE FOR NICOLE

Benny sits in Sid Malik's high-rise office on Wilshire out in Santa Monica. Sid is on the phone. Benny doesn't mind not being important enough for Sid to have calls held, nor that Sid regards this case a pain in the ass, just so dad foots the fees, grudgingly – family pride and to prove how wrong Benny can get in his life choices.

Benny sinks into one of Malik's burgundy leather chairs positioned so he has to gaze upward to his diminutive lawyer swiveling behind a raised walnut desk with its heavy brass lamp, marble ash trays.

Silently, Ben tries out his mantra. He got it from a maharishi at a self-realization temple off Sunset near Malibu. He and Lori were dating then and briefly into that sort of thing, sorting through half-understood readings of Krishnamurti, Paramahansa Yogananda, Alan Watts and Huxley.

The yogi spoke in an accent thick as dal soup. Each visitor got a brief private audience to get a "personal mantra" after the yogi spoke. Ben's sounded something like: "*Om manipadmi*" or "So-many panties." If he got it wrong he could be chanting up somebody else's karma or screwing up his own. Perfect! How could he attempt to have a religious experience without drowning in ambiguity and guilt?

Sid hung up, jotted something on his yellow legal pad and lit an illegal Havana – contraband of the gilded class. "I checked with the family court. Go ahead and pick up your kids and keep them with you."

"Until Lori gets back?"

"Until we have a court hearing. I've got you temporary order. We're filing for full custody. Might as well."

Lori has had another meltdown. She's drying out in a

Reno psychiatric ward, disposition unknown. Benny found out when the hospital phoned the Times to verify her still being on Benny's insurance.

"I've been trying to call Lori's mother, to pick up the kids just for a visit. But she's been avoiding me. ..."

"Just go fucking go there, Benny. I'll give you a copy of the order to take with you. Take the girls back to your place, Benny."

"What if Gwen tries to stop me."

"Don't do anything by force. Just tell Gwen I'll get her cited for contempt of court. We'll have her fined or put in the slammer."

The next day, Benny drives up Laurel Canyon to Gwen's hilltop estate. It's late afternoon on a Saturday, and hot for early February.

The girls are down at the pool with Gwen when Benny comes up the long winding driveway. Gwen rises from a chaise-lounge, a still-striking Venus in sunglasses, zincked nose, tall frosted glass in hand. Ben nods her a grin from afar. She stares, tight lipped. His feet feel leaden. I like Gwen, and she used to like me. Act friendly. But no getting past that I'm about to be the heavy now in this drama neither of us wrote .

The girls run out the patio gate waving, and come around to the driver's side of his dusty, green-and-white Citroen DS.

Little Nicole's yellow water wings flap as she gives him a wet hug looking like a cartoon bug in purple swimming cap and green goggles. Linda, more reserved, towels off first.

"Let's go kids!" Benny tries to sound as wildly cheerful as a kid-show host, but it comes off eerie. "Woo! Jump in the car, girls

We're off on an adventure."

Nicole squeals. "Daddy! Daddy! Will there be pony rides? Please, let's go on pony rides"

"Pony rides, yes! And a train ride, plus cartoons and a

movie. Popcorn too! Jump in."

In the back of his mind, he told himself that he would discuss all this beforehand with Gwen in some orderly fashion. But he didn't have the stomach to wade into what he knew would be her inevitable bad faith attacks on him in front of the kids. He doesn't want to drag things out further, and be forced to send Malik back to court to argue this all over again. He lifts Nicole into the back seat buckles her in.

Linda puts hands on hips. "We're still wet. I want to change."

"No need. I got all the clothes you need at home. In you go. We'll go shopping for more, anything you want." Shameless bribery. Linda slides in next to Nicole and snaps her own belt in place.

Gwen catches on and races towards them, but too late. "Sonofabitch bastard! Motherfucker!"

Benny is behind the wheel backing down the driveway, brushing hedges and nearly flattening the mailbox as he exits and speeds down the curving road back towards Hollywood.

Nicole throws up her arms in the rear view mirror and yells, "Whee!"

Linda is biting her nails.

Benny hasn't bothered to buckle his seat belt.

----

5. ALWAYS DAMNED ESCALATION

Six weeks later: Sid calls and tells Ben that Lori is back in L.A. She hasn't phoned Ben or the girls directly, seeing as we're at war. "Her counsel said she's fit as a fiddle. They're claiming that her hospitalization was just a case of exhaustion. They want the kids back."

"Just like that? No explanation of how she ended up in Reno?" Benny draws a breath. Keep calm. This had to happen sooner or later. "So. Can we work something out?" He doesn't really want to drag this out.

"Sit tight, Benny boy. It will be up to the court now."

"I'm okay with going back to joint custody like before this happened, Sid. But I need some reliable assurance that she's stable." Benny flashes on the list of complaints in the custody filing he signed, alleging Lori to be an "unfit parent" – necessary wording, Sid had told him.

"Too late for horse-trading now, Benny. Motions have been filed. It's not like some tort case when kids are involved."

"I didn't mean it like bargaining over my kids, Sid."

"By the way, Benny, did you get the copy I mailed you of their response. She alleges that you're an abusive drunk who wants custody to avoid paying child support."

"Lovely. Yeah. Like no red-blooded American male would ever really want to take care of his children. Like my old man used to say, that's woman's work."

"I got to be honest, Benny. Judges lean heavily towards mothers in these cases."

"Why does everything have to be a war? Escalate, escalate, like fucking Vietnam, and the kids are collateral damage."

"Not exactly war. The court assigns a social worker. She interviews everyone and makes a recommendation."

"Can you make sure the social worker gets to see Lori's psychiatric hospital records? She's been in and out of psych wards for three years now, starting when she tried to kill herself because she hallucinated a voice on TV telling her aliens had landed, or a nuclear war had started. Lucky thing she didn't poison the kids with her." Why do I feel like such an asshole for saying this over and over?

"No dice. Doctor-patient confidentiality. Anyway, they're claiming that her overdose was accidental, not a suicide attempt."

"Bullshit. They wouldn't have kept her locked up in the psych ward that long if that were true."

"But we can't establish that in court. Like I said, patient privacy. Her doctors couldn't help us if they wanted. Not unless it was a crime investigation. You know that."

"So, trying to do the right thing, I end up putting my kids at the mercy of some second-rate social worker and a biased judge?"

"You might want to think about a witness who can testify to her erratic behavior, drinking and so forth, maybe a mutual friend."

"God!"

"Can't subpoena Him."

"Yeah. That's right. God's been dead for a long time now."

----

6. AND THAT'S THE WAY IT IS

Benny carries a folded, yellowed clipping of his first byline story tucked behind his L.A. Times press card in his overstuffed wallet. The article runs only six inches– about a high school football mom who stepped off the sidelines to intercept a pass and run seventy eight yards to the opposite end zone, evading referees, coaches, players and seriously injuring a security guard.

Wrong Way Mom Scores

Benny wrote it while a part-time copy boy. Good for a laugh when asked how he got into the business. "Mildly ridiculous and emblematic of my career."

He never told anyone that he climbed up an inky catwalk at two in the morning, starry eyed, to watch the Sunday edition that carried his story run on the presses. Wow, a million people get this paper with my byline.

Benny and his daughters settle into a homey routine. It feels good. No drama. He's glad that he insisted on that two-bedroom cottage. No more dating, no parties. He has Zoya for after school until he gets home from work. It helps now that he can split the Zoya's hourly pay in part with Makeda who drops off her girl, Keesha, on the way to work.

Linda calls him at the office every afternoon with a complaint, but really to be sure he's coming home soon – and please bring this or that treat, daddy.

Benny marks his life with headlines, all of them, not just the sappy entertainment lines he writes for the Sunday features desk:

Viet Monk Self-Immolates
Cong Hits Hard in Tet Offensive
Cronkite Says War Is Lost
LBJ Won't Run Again
Headlines for his imaginings too:

Flunky Fails to Get Raise
Kubrick Film to Star Albino

Headlines and columns create illusory order from the world's chaos. Though Benny hates the copy desk, he masters the minor art or tacking droll, ironic headlines onto stories, wherever he can get away with it. Meanwhile, talks the Sunday entertainment editor into letting him write film reviews, one of his passions, and blessed relief from the desk. He gets the art film beat because nothing from outside Hollywood matters much to the first-string film critic and the industry promotional machine that keeps him on it's a-list. Yojimbo. Yoshwimbo, it's all raw fish to him. Weeks drag on.

Benny is expendable. But the Times has grown so fat with L.A.'s ads that it forever needs more and more content to space out its advertisements.

It's always the goddamn money. Spinning my wheels. Waiting for a raise, waiting for the social worker, waiting for the custody hearing.

"You little bum. All you do is play all day." Father used to arch an eyebrow at Little Benny – the sallow son he wished could make him proud on the playing field instead of burying his head in books.

Taking his father's cue, Benny took to playing hobo – carrying a bindle fashioned from an old scarf and broomstick, chomping a Tootsie Roll like a cigar butt, looking to catch an imaginary box car out of his reality, away from parents, school, dodging bullies: Hey, Milky! Gimme your lunch money. Hey, Milky: What's whiter, you or dried dog shit?

"What do you want to be when you grow up, Benny," relatives would ask.

"I want to be a bum, and bum around the world," Benny would respond, delighting in the shocked looks of disapproval he got. Later he read Jack Kerouac. Still later, he and Lori, shacking up, read guides to cut-rate passenger berths on freighters around the world. "We'll sail to Rio, and Singapore, and Istanbul." But then Lori told him she was pregnant. No Brazil. Just baby Linda, and quit school – for now, he told himself – and get a job.

Story of my life. Continues on Page 19.

"The facts, ma'am, just the facts." Here at the real paper – the owned by the Chandler family that practically invented L.A., and for a while was it's only royalty – catty corner from L.A.'s deco City Hall – right out of Dragnet, the establishing shot in a thousand other movies and cop shows, its shape pictured on every LAPD shield as well. Squinting up at its white tower, Benny can see still Superman flying from a Daily Planet window in the Saturday matinee serials he used to watch as a kid.

"Benny, you still expect good things to happen. You're getting too old for that. Shit just happens. Expect nothing. Just keep moving." His friend Roy told him, only half kidding, and Roy should know. It would be such a relief, also a permission whose prospect brought shudders.

7. THE MAD PROPHET OF SPRING STREET

Here he comes, the prophet of doom. His bombast echoes off the bland glass and concrete of the civic center. Shambling forward, shouting the word of God, he parts lunch-hour pedestrians like Moses through the Red Sea. Every damn day. His booming bass voice could crack tree trunks: "HELL! You're all gonna go to H-E-L-L-! Hell! Hell! You're goin' to H-E-L-L-!" Over and over, louder and louder, he arrives like a bad squall, spiral-eyed, tall and gaunt, with long blondish hair and beard bristling. On his head, He wears a plus-size brassiere on his head, D-cups akimbo like Viking horns, with the straps dangling on each side as he strides leaning forward as if into a stiff wind. He bellows in a peculiar sing-song cadence that can't be ignored. "Ha-hell, ha-hell. You're all goin' to ha-hell, damnation and h-hell. You're all going to h-e-l-l-l-l!"

He's a standing joke inside the Times-Mirror Building where they can hear him going by, even through its massive walls. On this particular day, however, the holy rant stops suddenly. Down on the first floor, Benny sees Preacher Man's face flush to the pane nearest his and Makeda's desks. Preacher Man cups his hands against the glass and peers at them with Apocalypse eyes. His face floats disembodied against the dark glass like Jesus on the Shroud of Turin. His lips move soundlessly.

Makeda drops her No. 2 pencil and proofs. "Jesus … It's him!"

Ben laughs. Thinks she's joking. "Maybe."

She stands, glares at the man, grabs her purse and strides from the office.

"Where you going?" Ben follows down the hall into the gray-green Vermont marble foyer in time to glimpse her exiting the massive brass doors to the street. "What the hell?" He catches up to her on Spring Street, about a block south of the Times. Preacher Man is well up ahead, ranting

235

hellfire again.

"Hey, Makeda. What's happening?"

She keeps walking. Preacher man rounds a corner up ahead. He's nowhere to be seen when they reach the intersection.

"Sonofabitch must have hopped a bus."

"I don't think one runs on this street. He'll be back. What do you want with him anyway?"

"Need to talk to that motherfucker."

"Shouldn't be too hard to find. Beat cops probably know where he goes. I heard he hangs at this cult church sometimes – Orchard, I think."

Makeda keeps walking, eyes ahead.

Ben steps lively to keep up. "Hey. Want to get lunch?"

She slows. "Later, Ben."

"Well. Okay. Guess I'll get back."

She keeps walking.

"Unless you need me. I'll by the sandwich place. Want me to pick up one for you?"

"No. Thanks, Ben. I'm cool. I want to walk a little."

"Okay. See ya, then."

She doesn't return to the office until late afternoon. It's unusually quiet. Ben stands at his desk, phone in hand, pale. He puts down the receiver and looks at her, his eyes vacant.

She interrupts him when he starts to say something. "I know, Ben."

"You heard?"

"I was in a store. It was on the TV."

"Sniper. Fuck! Those fucking bastards."

"Gonna be hell now. We're going to hell, all right."

"I think we ought to go, make sure the kids are okay."

"Nothing we can do here until tomorrow. Everybody's on the daily is working on this. By tomorrow we'll be redoing the weekend editions too.

A tragedy, biggest story since JFK in Dallas, and all

Ben can do is get home at watch it on TV like anybody else at this moment, far from what he had assumed would be life on a big paper. I'm a paper journalist all right, ass in swivel chair, not out there checking sources, getting the inside stuff, banging out the big story on deadline, dwelling in a Walter Burns, black-and-white Hollywood fantasy..

Ben drives them to his place, like on most other weekdays, where Makeda would pick up Keesha and take her own car home.

Moving slowly in traffic, they heard details on the car radio. "It is confirmed now. Doctor Martin Luther King, Jr., pronounced dead at Mercy Hospital in Memphis, the time 7:05 pm central, from a single shot to the head. His killer or killers still at large according to a Memphis police spokesman..."

Ben grips the steering wheel. "Fuck, fuck, fuck!" Ben flicks on the air conditioning. They're stuck in the usual, Hollywood Freeway commuter jam. People are honking. He feels the heat and anger rising. He wonders how many people in the cars around them have guns.

"Are you surprised? Why would you be surprised?" Makeda bums a cigarette from him and punches the dashboard lighter. He's never seen her smoke.

"Soon as he went from civil rights to economic justice, Vietnam and peace, it figures they were going to put an end to him."

"Yeah. How are the going to keep their war going without the brothers?"

"Bottom line. He was threatening their profits now."

"And God forbid, fat old white men who start wars might have to send their own sons to 'Nam."

"You realize we're finishing each others' sentences, Makeda?"

She had to laugh, at least for a moment. "Shit, Ben. Don't know if I'm ready for that."

They fall silent, listening to the reports. Riots have already erupted in major cities. So much left unsaid.

When Makeda and Ben arrive, Linda and Nicole sit on the floor with Keesha drawing on a big strip of off-white butcher paper using colored pencils and crayons. They wave hello. Zoya makes a smile with her wide-spaced, knowing Russian eyes, red with grief, not just onions. Her deep-fried pirozkis waft heavenly comfort as they have through other tragedies for centuries.

Zoya is the refugee Russian woman Benny hired through the Jewish community center for daycare and general housekeeping, taking on Keesha as well now. Nicole loves Zoya. Nicole loves everyone. Linda showed her preadolescent disdain at first, giving way to grudging warmth. Zoya had been a teacher in Minsk.

"Look, Daddy." Linda points to Cyrillic letters she's crayoned in nut brown on the butcher paper, Я люблю шоколад. "It means 'I love chocolate.' Very subversive."

The TV is off. Ben turns it back on, sound low, just to check the news about King. It's not good. The kids complain about no cartoons, but without energy. They go back to drawing, then they a play a bit of hide and seek.

Keesha runs to Makeda. "Can we sleep over, mommy, please?"

Ben interjects softly. "Maybe it's a good idea. All hell is breaking loose out there. You and Keesha take my bedroom. I can sleep on the couch."

Makeda looks at Keesha. "We'll be all right."

Linda and Nicole join in. All three run around the adults, Linda smirks at making the adults uncomfortable. "Sleep over, sleep over!"

"Shh. Be quiet kids." Ben glances at Zoya then back to Makeda. "Let's have the food Zoya was nice enough to fix, and check the news."

"There ees plenty for efferyvone," Zoya gives Makeda a motherly look and steps into the kitchenette as if to demonstrate.

"You stay too, Zoya please, and I can drop you home afterward." Zoya's small apartment is just down at the base of the canyon road in Hollywood. On most evenings, Makeda would have dropped her off on her way home with Keesha, another half-hour away, near La Brea and Crenshaw.

Makeda picks up Keesha and bounces her gently on one arm. "I'm not very hungry, but lets eat, and I'll think about it."

Keesha shouts. "I want pancakes for breakfast!"

Linda smirks again. "With whipped cream and strawberries."

The comforts of domestic routine keep horror at bay for the moment. Ben drops off Zoya after dinner, then cleanups while Makeda gets the kids to bed and reads them a story in the girls' bedroom. Keesha and Nicole nod off together in one of the twin beds. Makeda tiptoes out and has the TV on low when Ben returns. "Looks bad."

Ben eyes the flashing news feeds. He sits cross-legged on the floor against the couch on the opposite end from her. "The fire this time..."

Makeda pats the couch pillow. "I need to be held right now, Benny." He gets up and slides next to her, a friendly arm around her shoulders.

A somber David Brinkley chronicles "burning and rioting in cities across the country."

----

8. YOUR OWN KIND

When Ben was in grade school, his parents would take him on a sleeper train cross country for summer reunions with family in New York and Boston. He would run back and forth through the passenger cars with other kids. He remembers noticing that everyone in certain cars were colored people and asked his mother about that. "Oh, they like to be with their own kind," she responded off hand.

"What about the porters?"

"They like being porters."

Seemed to make sense. Porters seemed to act cheerful. He didn't ask about the white conductors, who always seemed grumpy. In any case, the world of adults didn't concern him much. They had their strange ways, and were different. He'd never heard her utter a hateful word about anyone, black or white.

The explanation seemed to make sense, like his father's theory of why blacks like Joe Lewis and Sugar Ray Robinson triumphed in the boxing ring.

"Black men have thicker foreheads. That makes them able to take a punch better than white men. When an opponent takes your best punch and keeps coming, that's a formidable thing."

"Does that mean their brains are smaller, dad?"

"Not at all, Benny, they just have stronger frontal armor."

Seemed plausible, like so many other things he heard from adults, and not very important. He grew up amid urban whites – Jews, Italians, Irish, Polish. They all had a little bit of color that Benny could have used, but he didn't think of it that way. He was simply himself at home. His parents never mentioned his paleness, and he didn't remember the many diagnostic visits to clinics when he was very young. All the fuss at school came as a surprise, nothing happened in kindergarten. Not until second or third grade did the taunts start. His parent moved a lot, and he always arrived as the new kid anyway – fair game.

He shed beliefs and assumptions like a molting lizard as he grew up, major and minor ones – that masturbation would send him to hell as well as grow hair on his palm, for example – morphing towards intellectualism and revolutionary beliefs reading books – later headlines, TV news, pictures in Life Magazine – but very little through life experience until college and the circles through which he traveled now.

His most piquant discovery of late: Those most excluded had most to say. Hell could forge art, comedy, literature. What doesn't kill us makes us funnier. At the same time, being an American in spite of himself, he believed in the pursuit of happiness by the shortest route possible, setting no store in suffering.

Such speculation conferred no special skills on him, and caused inconvenient abandonment of cheap biases and heuristics – as much as this is possible for any human being. He didn't think much on the notion of "sticking to your own kind," that people kept mouthing, except to wonder: Just who the hell are "my kind," white-mushroom people, ghosts, freaks, all of the above?

He heard his aunt Lala, on his father's side, say to a friend over the phone that "the Jews all stick together." Did that mean his mama's own kind would be the Steins of Brookline, Massachusetts? Why did she let them name him Beniamino, after Gigli, with whom his nonna, Renata, had sung back in Italy, Benito Mussolini's favorite tenor, a fact seemingly forgotten among Italians that Benny knew growing up, but not by the Steins. No wonder his parents didn't stay together. Moving to Hollywood, spared his father the embarrassment of a Jewish – and, worse yet, a chalky son.

It is kiss-tomary to cuss the bride. Benny's mother made him a list of famous albinos in history from eleventh-century King Edward the Confessor on. Bores, all failing to inspire Benny, except for William Archibald Spooner, dotty, nineteenth century Oxford dean of peculiar speech habits. Like Benny, Dr. Spooner didn't suffer usual ocular disorders badly enough to hold him back from academic achievement. Constantly, Ben's mother admonished him never to feel sorry for himself – to thank God for being able to read, though with thick glasses and otherwise see well enough to get a driver's license as a teen.

Mama emphasized the Spooner scholarship and didn't mention the crossed wires that won the dotty dean a place in the language. Perhaps, thought Ben, the professor was not speech-impaired at all, but flipped syllables to keep his mocking classroom buggers alert so they wouldn't "taste the whole worm."

Adults tried not to be annoyed by Benny's habitual spoonerisms. I like butter on my cop porn. That put him with a speech therapist for a while. Miss Marney, a buxomly delicious, laughing, brown lady, just out of college herself, in rainbow beads and bracelets, leaning forward as she coached him.

Benny keeps a picture of dean Spooner, or seen dooner, wrinkled, torn from his high school library encyclopedia in his wallet next to his first news clipping. In black and white it's hard to tell Spooner was albino and not just a chalky, balding professor in a dark Edwardian suit.

Around the time he discovered Spooner, Benny started his hobby of categorizing the skin tones and complexions of people, trying to catch them in his coloring books by blending crayons, later paint sets, and making up his own races – chestnuts, butters, nougats – that was Benny – cocoas, maples, Hershey's, almonds, peanuts, peaches, cherries... Most were mixes, hybrids, alloys, he mused, like bronze. Mutts. Someone on a radio groused about "'mongrelization' of the races," but already he had read mutts were stronger and plants healthier and blue bloods got hemophilia.

What about that, Aunt Lala? "

"Mixed marriages never work. It's the children who suffer, like those war babies. Nobody accepts them."

He couldn't fathom the concept. "What about mama and papa? They don't match. Mama has red hair and she's a Jew, like me."

"You're Italian too."

"I'm platinum."

His aunt gave him a disapproving look. "The things you kids make up, honestly.

None of this made sense to young Benny. He stuck to his own methods of observation.

He attributed traits, vulnerabilities and powers to each shade of named. Peanut-Butter people could fly, for example, but rarely did so because they tended to be acrophobic. Chick Pea people could read minds, but couldn't remember names. The extremely rare Porcelains – to which he belonged, possessed the super-power of invisibility, not by being transparent, but of causing people to ignore or look away from them.

As a dramatically monochromatic being, he belonged at the far end of the human spectrum. People called themselves white, weren't all that white, no more than American Indians were red, or African-Americans were literally black. He liked people's colors, and some he found more sexy than others. He liked curvy women, and favored bronze hues, and not by accident did he find Makeda attractive despite his efforts to stay cool.

Growing up, Benny, oddly, felt the most self-conscious among his own kind. When he was ten, his mother --- always forward looking -- took Benny to a support group meeting for children with albinism and their parents. He didn't like the other albino kids, not because their skin was as white as his, but because he found most of them dopey and ignorant – the kind who only looked a comic book pictures and never read the bubbles and captions, the kind who spit and punched, and who liked Roy Rogers better than Buck Rogers or Flash Gordon, and didn't know that the theme from the Lone Ranger was from Rossini's William Tell Overture.

Reading compulsively, outside school, he shunned the textbooks of the times that left out so much, and implied that slaves didn't have it so bad in the antebellum South, and scripted Reconstruction pretty much in the same terms as D. W. Griffith's racist epic Birth of a Nation.

The sixties came too late for him. The counterculture's superficial celebrations of weirdness failed to impress, as did mainly the ambiguous, over-maleness-in-black-turtleneck Beat Generation.

He didn't care to be hip, but the politics, that was different. He hated the mindlessness of the arms race and the Vietnam War. In 1967, he found himself marching in a demonstration – mainly following a radical, free-love girlfriend-of-the moment -- against U.S. involvement in Vietnam. Suddenly, he was in a crush with thousands of protesters marching on Wilshire Boulevard. It was the week after mounted LAPD had gassed and clubbed demonstrators against a LBJ in front of the Century Plaza Hotel, where the president had been attending a conference.

Benny, usually reserved, felt a catch in this throat at the sight. Ordinary-looking people of all ages moved, shoulder-to-shoulder, spread from curb-to-curb, flowing all the way down the wide Miracle Mile. Like many of those present at such an event for the first time, he discovered that there were many other kindred spirits out in the world who felt as he did, no longer lone dissenters. These, he felt, where truly "his own kind," at least for those fleeting moments.

"What do we want?"

"Peace!"

"When do we want it?"

"Now!" Mounted police rode along the curbs in riot gear, and Ben could see tac-squad snipers watching from the roofs and windows of the high-rise buildings.

"Peace now!" Or as Benny shouted it, whimsically, "niece pow, niece pow!"

The demonstration got little news coverage. Nobody important from the paper made him out in the crowd, UN-journalistically breaking the fourth wall of feigned objectivity. Only his usual cohorts of little consequence marched with him – underdogs all, like he regarded himself and took pains to cultivate.

----

9. LA PALETA DE EZEKIEL

Benny riffles papers on his desk aimlessly. Can't concentrate. He wanders upstairs to the third-floor composing room occupying the long low structure over the presses between the Times and Mirror buildings, ostensibly to check proofs.

He can feel the rumbling of the presses faintly as he crosses the floor, threading rows of Linotype machines that loom like allosaurus skeletons, manned by pale, wizened operators in green eye shades. He moves on through the Mirror Building ad and circulation offices and takes another elevators down, stepping out onto the street discreetly from its back doors.

From there it's up to Broadway where he blends into the crowds of shoppers coming in and out of stores, a mix of white collar workers starting to get out of the offices and Latino's from nearby neighborhoods shopping. Right away he feels better.

A few blocks down Broadway, Benny slips into the cavernous Grand Central Market where he can lose himself in what feels like a perpetual fiesta. He takes in the colors, music, chatter, the smells of iced fish, eyes staring up, chorizos, carnitas, flowers, local and exotic fruits, moist fresh-cut seasonal greens, the panderias with hot doughy cinnamon buns, best of all, crowds of shoppers, brown-skinned, with Toltec eyes, speaking familiarly Mexican-accented Spanish, not much English here, mostly by choice. Peppers, mangoes, pineapples, bananas – spirited vendors outdoing each other calling out bargain offers and inducements.

Everywhere, images of La Virgin de Guadalupe, arms wide with open her green robes and baby Jesus peeking out from her skirts, offering her goddess blessings from the white glass of seven-day candles. Earnest, dark eyes, broad-beamed women with shopping bags, pull prankish kids through the narrow aisles. Benny feels afloat in Spanish – no Muzak, no sterile freezer cases, no wobbly shopping carts, no anonymous checkout stands with bored suburban moms who can't wait to get back in their station wagons.

The Grand Central reminds Benny of when he was very young and his mother still was happy and took him to Saturday shopping in Boston's North End, along with her sister and Benny's cousin Paula. Benny takes and breath and stops for his usual iced tamarind drink at a stand deep enough inside the Grand Central to leave the rest of the world behind.

He takes this kind of break often, buying ingredients to cook at home for his kids when they are with him, and even just for himself. This time, however, something different happens. He nearly collides with Preacher man, brassiere cap at all, spying into a glass case of Mexican dulces.

Benny had not seen him since the afternoon when Makeda chased him. Benny sidles over. Preacher smells faintly floral, not rancid, as Benny would have expected. Preacher Man straightens and blinks.

" Hi. I'm Benny. I work for the paper. You know, the Times. I think you've seen me over by the building on Spring Street."

Preacher stands tall, widens his eyes and raised one hand, pointing heavenward like Charlton Heston playing Moses. "End times!"

"No, *L.A. Times*."

"Thou are the White Angel Gabriel come to sound thy horn!"

"No. I'm an albino, actually.

"All be known of God's word, sinners, going to hell!" Preacher man's voice rises above the din of he market. A few people stare, but most just keep moving past them.

"Just a man with no pigment." Even this nut has to

247

type-cast me. The albino has to either be an angel, or some comic-book nemesis.

Benny waves his press card, feeling foolish. "Makeda, my friend, the woman who works with me, wanted to talk to you. Maybe you saw her come out of the building the other day."

"I know who you are. Do you?" Preacher man then turns to the woman behind the freezer case and points at a pale green, lime-coconut paleta. The counter woman's wide-spaced, dark chocolate eyes regard us with the discreet watchfulness of a psych ward attendant.

Preacher Man hands her a crumpled five-dollar bill. She takes it on tip-toes and hands off the paleta. "You are not going to hell," he tells her. His voice softens to normal now. "He is, one other hand, damned -- straight to lakes of fire" Preacher waves the paleta at Benny and points downward with his other hand. The woman puts the fiver in a cigar box and starts counting out change.

"Keep the change." Preacher waves the Latino Popsicle at her. Either doesn't know how to count, or he's a big tipper, surprising Benny.

"Thank you, senor Ezeequle." The woman hints a smile at Preacher that Benny takes as flirtatious. It dawns on Benny that Preacher Man has an actual name – Ezekiel -- and a life beyond that of being a downtown annoyance.

Ezekiel? That seems apt. Benny extends a hand. "Hello, Zeke. Nice to meet you."

Preacher man sticks the paleta in his mouth and pumps Benny's hand vigorously. "Repent, ghostly sinner!"

"Okay. I repent."

"Come to Jesus."

"May I get a paleta first?"

Zeke the Preacher signals to the woman. "*Sonia, por favor, una paleta por este pobre pecadore.*"

"I was only kidding, but okay, coconut, please." Benny pulls out a dollar, but Sonia waves it away and hands him the iced pop of his choice. She flashes another coy smile at Zeke.

"Thanks, Zeke." Benny takes the paleta. "Can I talk to you somewhere privately for a minute?"

Preacher heads up the aisle and Benny follows. They exit the Grand Central on the Hill Street side. Down the block, Zeke steps into an alley, and stops next to some trash barrels. Benny follows, keeping his distance, just in case. "Okay. This is good."

"Your icy is going to melt." Suddenly, Preacher man seems to solicitous and normal, but Benny remains guarded, knowing manic-depression all too well.

Benny peels off the cellophane and samples his paleta. "Wow! These are good! I can really taste the coconut."

"Coconut!" Preacher Man goes ballistic again, shouting. "The Avenging Angel will appear, breathing fire in the grove of coconuts to announce Armageddon. You're all going to ha-ha-hell!" Off the deep end again, he bellows this over and over down the alley.

Jesus. Here we go again. Benny waits until Preacher's ranting subsides. "Look, Zeke, or whatever your name is; all I want to know is where my friend Makeda can reach you. Do you have a phone or address I can give her? I don't know what she wants to talk with you about. None of my business."

"Coconuts will fall. Coconut Grover. Jesus says kill Kennedy. Going to hell. Those in the orchard will be saved."

"Kill Kennedy?"

"Coconut Grover says we must smite the sinner. And the temple will be destroyed, the nations will be consumed in fire."

"What the fuck." Benny starts to back out of the alley.

"We got the fire already. I'll just be going now."

Zeke pulls something small, black and metallic from under is camo jacket. "Holy or holies! Praise the Lord!"

Zeke looks heavenward into the smog waving the object.

Fuck, he's got a gun!

Benny backs slowly out of the alley. "Okay. I hear you. Praise the Lord" ... and let me out of here.

Out of nowhere, a car pulls into the alley. It brushes close by Benny and stops in front of Preacher Zeke – a black Lincoln sedan. Someone opens a back door. A deep male voice calls Zeke, who gets into the sedan, the door closes and it rolls away.

Benny writes the license of the car on the palm of his hand, not knowing what he'll do with it or why.

----

10. GORDON'S KNOT

The social worker doesn't make eye contact. She frowns when she notes things in her file folder, her shoulders hunched as if someone is trying to peek. She's a plump, fortyish woman in a gray suit, with dyed red hair and wire-rimmed glasses, firing off questions without follow-ups, in a hurry to get through the interview, as if she's already made up her mind.

Benny tries to elaborate and stretch out answers to her dry questions to add nuance, but she's having none of it. He has taken off the afternoon. The social worker interviews him in a courthouse meeting room downtown instead of at home with his daughters. Turns out the social worker has already gone by his daughter's school and met with them privately in the principal's office.

Ben comes away from the social worker's interview with a feeling of dread. No sense going back to his office. It's too early to go home. He heads for the Redwood Inn, lunch and cocktail den of assorted civic center minions, flacks and L.A. Times malcontents.

The décor suggests plush Victorian cat house – lots of red, but no redwood – burgundy flocked wallpaper and leather booths, a vaguely oriental carpet, red leather swiveling bar stools with backs matching the long dark wood-and-brass bar. -

Benny sits at the bar and orders his usual Stoli martini, up, stirred-not-shaken, two olives – a 007 with a Russian twist. The bartender, Jimmy, banters with customers about Dodger games on the big TV. They lay bets on how long Don Drysdale's scoreless inning streak will last. Benny hears the usual gripes about the low-hitting Bums' slim, pennant prospects this year, relying on big Don sans kosher strikeout king Sandy Koufax.

Gordy raises a glass to Benny from his regular spot just around the back curve of the bar. Benny lifts his martini in return. Gordy, who usually stays put, moves to a stool next to Benny.

Gordy gets to it without chit-chat. "Hey, Benny, have you talked to Bechtel?" Clean-cut blond, a long, wavy noodle of a man, Gordy gives Benny his standard ambiguous grin, showing perfect teeth, but his eyes remain as distant alpine lakes set deep. He runs cool and silent in a soft gray-green suit, off-white button-down and understated silk tie slightly loosened just enough at the collar.

"Not since the interview."

"Morgan phoned me this morning. Mentioned you hadn't returned his call."

"Oh, yeah. Been meaning to. Had a lot going on lately."

Gordon's upper lip twitches almost imperceptibly. He drains his glass and signals the bartender for another. "Not good, old chum."

"I'm sorry. I'll call him today."

"Don't worry, you're white enough for them." He slams his drink down – made a funny, and Benny obliges with his usually har-har to albino jokes.

Al comes over and pours Gordy a shot of Talisker Islay single malt, with a water back, no ice. The bartender looks to Benny, who puts a hand over his martini glass. Al moves back down the bar.

"Was he bugged?" Benny lights up a Parliament. Gotta quit. "It's just an assistant copy writing job."

"Pays way better than you're getting now, I'm sure. You're the one always bitching about not having enough to take care of your kids and all. Does it matter? Hell, I don't even know if he's going to make you an offer. But it sounds like it. Just call him."

"Hey, I appreciate you setting me up with that interview – free trip to San Francisco, and all." Benny loves the city by the bay, but has decided it would be too far away from his girls unless he got custody, and even there, there'd be complications about them seeing their mother. He likes to think of it that way, but less nobly, he doesn't like their politics, the sterility of their office – no misfits like at the paper – and isn't sure he'd do well at it anyway.

"You just went for the free airline tickets?"

"Maybe. But I was serious about the interview. I gave it a shot. I just don't know."

"Suit yourself." Gordy popped some salted peanuts from a little wooden bowl on the bar. "I'm cool with that, just call the guy. Okay?"

Benny tells Gordy about his encounter with Preacher Man – well known among downtown denizens. Gordy laughs it off.

"Speaking of nuts, what does Howard Hughes think about the election?"

"Germs! All he thinks about germs. When you have that much money it doesn't matter who wins elections, you're still on top, but germs, they can still get you."

"I thought you were supposed to keep your client's name out of the limelight." The mysterious Gordy, who kept mostly to himself except for buying reporters' drinks without visible means of support, was rumored to be "Howard Hughes' publicity man," meaning paid to keep his PR client's name out of the media instead of in. He had "confirmed" this to Benny one night a while back, as if going along with the joke, but on the square.

"Doesn't matter what I tell you Benny."

"Thanks. Like I'm a nobody."

"Like nobody would believe you."

"Fuck you."

"And fuck you very much." Gordy laughed.

Benny knew it was true. "I might surprise you, Gordy. But that doesn't matter because I don't really believe you're Howard Hughes' PR man. It's the best explanation I've got going for you at the moment. As Sherlock Holmes said, 'When you have eliminated the impossible, whatever remains, however improbable, must be the truth."

"I am the most improbable person I know." Gordy snapped his fingers and laid his hand flat on the bar, then lifted it slowly to reveal a shiny quarter.

"That quarter was already there. I'm not that drunk." Benny laughed. "Improbable is the universe in which I flack for Bechtel Corporation. Anyway, I'd suck at it. But I'm not that noble. I like the money."

Gordy downed the rest of his drink and nodded for another. Hollow leg, this guy. "So, you're going to take the job?"

"I don't know... San Francisco so far from the kids... you know, weekends and all."

"I thought you said your kids are with you..."

"Temporary. The whole thing's a mess."

"You just don't want to go. San Francisco's only an hour's flight from L.A."

"It's probably moot now. I felt bad vibes from the prissy social worker who interviewed me for the family court. I can't say what will happen now. "

"I got news for you. Sooner or later, everybody either flakes out or sells out."

"Words to live by. You're so uplifting, Gordy."

Benny shrugs and takes another hit of martini. He tells Gordon about his Grand Central Market encounter with Preacher man. "And I had a contact run the license plate of the sedan that picked him up. You'll never guess who owns it."

"Jeb Crowley."

"Jesus, Gordy. How did you know."

"Simple, my friend. That crazy John Bircher son-of-a-bitch is the moneybag behind The Orchard, you know, that cult for hippie burnouts. They made Preacher Man a deacon because he know a lot of other hippies. But he keeps going off the reservation."

"You know a lot. Maybe you really aren't bullshitting about being Howard Hughes' man. Can I quote you."

"Never. I don't exist."

"What do you think this lunatic means about Kennedy? I assume that it's Bobby he was ranting on about."

"You never can tell about these people."

"I guess I could tell the cops. Maybe there's a story in it."

"You got nothing. Besides, the LAPD doesn't give a shit about Bobby Kennedy."

"You can say that again."

"Maniacs happen. I wouldn't worry about it."

"Coconuts. He's got coconuts and hell on the brain, that guy. That, Jesus, hell and Kennedy! Why does every nut and reactionary bastard always have to invoke Jesus? Poor Jesus."

Gordy goes silent and considers his drink a while, as if pondering what he is going to say next. "You know, just by way of speaking, I had a drink with Imhoff the other night, you know, that LAPD detective who writes TV scripts. He was bitching about our tin-horn Mayor Sam Yorty, and ubermanfurher police chief Bill Parker refusing to order any police protection for Bobby Kennedy while he's campaigning here in the Presidential primary."

Benny snorts. "No surprising. That red-baiting asshole Yorty has presidential delusions himself."

"It's all a cat-and-mouse game. Yorty wants to keep Kennedy from campaigning in South Central to turn out the black vote. Parker doesn't want his cops down in Watts with Bobby singing 'Kumbaya' with all the black folks. Far as LAPD is concerned it's a free-fire zone for itself and the gangs."

Benny vetted a script from Imhoff once a while back. The detective recently sold a script to a Jack Webb's new cop show, Adam 12. "Imhoff's no Kennedy fan either. He's just ticked because he wanted to be on the Kennedy detail himself. He wants to cozy up with Bobby's celebrity crowd... rub elbows with Elizabeth Taylor at fund raisers and get his photo taken.

"Yorty and Parker would shed any tears if Bobby just went away."

"What if this Preacher Man, or some other nut takes a shot at Bobby?"

"Nothing stopping him. It would make a lot of people happy. They hate Bobby like his brother, only worse – the Mob, Castro, the Cubans, J. Edgar Hoover, Jimmy Hoffa, not to mention the CIA and the Pentagon... Not all you hippie pinkos believe him, but he says he's going to pull us out of Vietnam war. Lot of people around here making billions of dollars from that war... Just because you're paranoid doesn't mean they're not after you."

A shout goes up from the other end of the bar. The bartender turns up the sound on the TV. Vin Scully wraps it neatly up: "It's happened! Drysdale now is one strike away from finishing off the Houston Astros in his fourth straight shutout, tying a National League record..." More cheering.

Drysdale winds up and unleashes his bulk into an impossibly graceful sidearm pitch. "Strike three! Caught him looking," Scully announces excitedly and he crowd roars. Scully ices the cake. "Two more shutouts and he could break all major league records. Looks like he'll face the Giants next, then the Pirates. That would be on Election Day, June 4."

The bartender turns the TV off. He walks over to Gordy and lays down a ten-dollar bill.

Benny smirks. "Hey, Al, don't you know you don't bet against Don Drysdale? Not in this universe."

Gordy puts the ten spot in his pocket. "You snort too much scifi, Benny."

"I Swatch Tar Wreck."

Gordy laughs. "Believes in a future, but all fucked up."

"Where no ban has gone before..." Benny makes a woo-woo sound. "I confess. Really, I can't think of any time I'd rather live than twenty-third century Federation Earth, no racism, no cash, warp drive, painless surgery, and everyone would just think I was an Andorran, but with out the feelers."

----

11. ROY

A little later, Roy Wolfe lights a Camel. Gotta quit these things. Roy's not the Star Trek type. He envisions a dystopic future, if any. He like Benny, but not Gordon. He doesn't like any public relations men, though, he thinks, they shall inherit the earth. He knows Gordon's secrets, not just about Howard Hughes, but about the gay bars Gordy frequents on the sly. Good for him, except keeping secrets can fuck with your mind. I don't trust him.

In any event, Gordy has moved back to his perch at the other end of the bar. He's not part of the circle of Times outsiders that drifts each evening in after deadline. Ben and Roy move off the bar to their usual booth in the back of the lounge.

"Hey, Roy, great pieces you've been filing!" Benny switches to coffee. "Got to go pretty soon, and get the kids."

"Thanks. Just turned in the last of the series." Roy looks straight ahead, eyeballing Paula, the curvy Rumanian waitress, who brings over menus. "Another masterpiece for Chalmers" – mealy mouth city editor – " to de-ball." Roy talks down low like you need to listen – raspy, New York hip, like a Monk improvisation, spare, edgy, ironic. So not L.A.

Roy has just spent ten days on the road covering uprisings in major cities after the MLK assassination – hot, first-hand stuff going where no white reporter, or any lesser one of any race or background could dare go, given the tension of the times. Pulitzer Prize stuff under fire – up close with a Black Ranger gang leader patrolling black-owned businesses amid the burning and looting on Chicago's West Side, for example – being part investigative reporter, part front-line war correspondent.

As usual, the editors cut hell out of what he files. They give him ready excuses about space, or redundancy with other coverage, or legal problems, delays from upstairs, never about race, or their inclination to censor what disturbed them, and he would get the message, subtly, confided in a hallway that the publisher feared what he wrote would incite blacks in Los Angeles. "My job is to report, not to second-guess, not protect the police or politicians, not keep the peace."

He kept his cool. But they seemed to send him out of L.A. a lot more often after that run-in. Perhaps it was coincidence. But it kept him from stirring up more shit in the Times backyard for a while, especially after the enterprising report he confirmed about the LAPD detective who harassed a young black woman in his police car by shoving his service revolver between her thighs. Despite carefully corroborating his sources, they spiked that piece as "too incendiary. It could set off another Watts riot," the assistant city editor told Roy privately.

Again, Roy zipped it. He had learned how to play this game a long time back, as eager reporter for the Paris International Herald Tribune, just out of Columbia J-school. He covered a different war then, in Algeria, then its bloody aftermath in France.

The Times hired him right after the Watts Riots of 1964 when it didn't have but one black reporter and he, an inexperienced hire from the its truck dispatch office. That didn't signal, as Roy found out, any expansion in the paper's curiosity about South Central once the uprising ended.

Jorge, another of their merry band, comes in the door and heads back to their table. "Well if it isn't Pinky and Blue Gum. Mind if I join you losers?"

"Tortilla Fats!." Roy raises a mock toast to the robust Jorge Ramos and motions for him to sit. Jorge waves to the waitress for his usual Negra Modelo. He grins like he's reading your mind, and usually is. He smoothes strands of gray-speckled straight black hair back from his forehead with chubby hands, a boyish gesture, contradicted by the intensity of his brown, wide-set eyes that move about the room, pinpointing everyone and everything.

The waitress is quick with his beer, which he sips straight from the bottle, setting aside the little lime wedge. "Here we are, los dos tokens de Los Angeles Tiempo. Representing America's oppressed minorities..."

"... by drinking as much as we can and staying invisible." Roy waves his glass at Benny. "Los tres, if you count Benny. I bet you're the only real whitey in West Coast Journalism."

Benny joins the toast but says nothing. He can never get comfortable with that stuff.

Roy coughs, put out his cigarette and sips his bourbon and water. "Benny here was just telling me about that crazy sonofabitch street preacher ranting on Bobby Kennedy, waving a gun."

"Well it wasn't that dramatic." Benny coughs, self-consciously.

Jorge pats Benny's shoulder. "Que loco, that one. I need ear plugs when he comes down the street. Hey, it could happen. Anything could. Look at what happened to JFK and now King, and in Saigon, you know every step could be your last, not like here where we act like life is forever."

Roy takes a breath, and talks softly from deep inside, like a growl. "You know what comes into your mind at the moment of death?"

Jorge: "How would you know?"

Roy: "Trust me. In Korea, 1951."

Benny: "Okay. Your girlfriend? Wife? Kids? The best lay you ever had? If you forgot to pay your light bill?"

"None of the above. It's surprise! You're fucking surprised! You always know everybody dies, but you always thought that meant someone else. You can't believe it's you. You say to yourself, 'fuck, so this is it? I can't fucking believe this.'"

"Really?"

"Just felt a thud that laid me out, heard nothing – pain came later. Sniper. Bullets travel faster than sound, you know. You don't hear the shot."

Jorge: "Yeah, but that wasn't really your last thought, as it turned out. Maybe you were surprised because you knew it wasn't your time, Roy."

"It's never anybody's time."

Benny: "You suppose Martin Luther King was surprised when they put his lights out?"

Roy: "He got it in the head. Bullets fly faster than sound. He wouldn't have heard it coming."

Jorge: "But he knew what was coming... What he said to the garbage workers there in Memphis, the night before he got it. 'I been to the mountain'...." Makes your blood run cold.

Benny: "Why does it have to be this way?"

Roy shakes his head and draws on his Camel. "The night guy desk guy, you know ..."

Jorge: "Stumpy Charlie, the one-armed copy bandit."

Roy: "Yeah, Him. He stands over my desk. I'm pounding out copy for deadline. I look up. He puts his good hand over his heart and says, 'Roy? My condolences on the death of Martin Luther King.' I'm like, 'Okay – and Bo Diddly.'"

Benny laughs uncomfortably. "Well, he was trying."

Roy: "Yeah. Cold. I admit it. But he doesn't get it. It ain't my loss. It's everybody's fucking loss, and he don't need to apologize for the white race, not to me. I don't have to be Token Man, pretend-integrating the Times to make anybody feel better. And I don't to go to fucking Africa either, or live in any black power nation. This is my own fucking country as much as yours. I want a nice house, my kid in a nice school. Black folks aren't the problem, the bigots are and I can't fix them. They need to fix themselves."

Jorge applauds. "Nice speech. You should run for President."

Roy grunts a chuckle. "Don't make me laugh. I'm just a reporter trying to do a job digging up shit, and most of the shit happens to be on some places more than others. I'm no civil rights crusader, no hero, not here to free the slaves or make it all right for you white folks."

Jorge smirks: "Don' 'white-folks' me, Kimosabe."

"I get you. But you're already a hero of sorts, just being here. And you're a goddamn war hero too, like stumpy Charlie. Sidney Poitier could play you." Benny gives Roy a quick salute.

"Poitier's too pretty to play me. And I was just a grunt freezing my ass off, trying to stay alive and wondering how the fuck I ended up in Korea."

Benny asks: "Isn't Charlie the one who asked you to come and integrate his church one Sunday?"

"Yeah. I could charge fees. A whole new career."

Jorge makes a priestly blessing with one hand. "Good way to get crucified, my friend. Most congregations segregate themselves better than any Alabama lunch counter ever did. They go to church with your own kind and looking down on all the heathens across the tracks. You got to give one-armed Charlie credit for trying."

Benny flicks his cigarette lighter on in front of his chin. "I belong to Casper's Church of the Friendly Ghost. Woo."

The waitress brings a dish of peanuts. Jorge takes a handful. "I thought you were with Jews for Casper."

"Yeah, that too." Benny turns to Roy. "Hey, great piece on Detroit last Sunday."

"Wouldn't it be nice if I could report straight-on that way on the LAPD. Shitty desk slashes copy bad as Pravda. You'd never know this was an L.A. Paper."

Jorge: "White L.A. They send me to Vietnam so I'm as far away from the barrio as I can get, except on Cinco de Mayo, I can maybe file a piñata report."

Benny: "Minco de Cayo, I go for Dia de Los Muertos myself."

Roy: "At least you're not pigeonholed."

Jorge: "Just corn-holed."

Benny starts to get up. "Well, guys. It's been a bit of heaven."

Roy nods. "Hey, I'll dig around about Preacher Man. Okay? I want to do something on Bobby anyway, if I can get the okay."

"Cool. Thanks." Benny heads off. It's his last full week with the kids before the hearing. And who knows after that?

----

12. RING AROUND ROSEY

Hard to be around Benny since he lost his case. Moody: I feel bad for him, but if he doesn't want to talk about it, I'm not going to press him.

Not the end of the world. He's just back to being a part-time daddy, which is more than a lot of men do, or want. I told him almost losing her kids will get his ex to straighten up, get into AA or something.

We still take our kids out together when our days off line up. But now I'm on assignment.

After a couple of pitches, I landed an assignment from the Sunday magazine editor, Marshall. He's a funny, smart man everyone around there underestimates because he's low key and gently funny. I'm writing a profile for him on Roosevelt Grier, the ex-L.A. Ram star. I don't know anything about football, but this isn't a sports story. It's supposed to be up-close on Rosey being a bodyguard for Senator Robert Kennedy while he campaigns for the California Presidential primary pretty much for all the marbles. Everybody knows Rosey and Olympic star Rafer Johnson are more than muscle. They're helping Bobby connect with black voters who haven't been much in the mood for any of that since Dr. King was killed in April.

The other day, I met Senator Kennedy himself, and later, Ethel Kennedy. Rosey is even bigger than he seems in news photos. But it's been a while since the he and his Rams Fearsome Foursome knocked heads on the gridiron. He and Rafer make a pair of very unlikely stand-ins for Secret Service, which Kennedy doesn't get unless he's elected. But fits the messaging, as they say, and helps Bobby draw big crowds in South Central.

Benny encouraged him to pitch stories, but now he seems put off. I know he was for Eugene McCarthy, then got into all that Peace and Freedom Party stuff for a while.

I went with him to a meeting. No wonder they get no traction. Wrought up, guilt-ridden, rich white college boys fight amongst themselves worse than black nationalists. All they do is jerk off about who is more revolutionary? I'd say, they're crawling with FBI bedbugs too.

I feel bad for Benny. Tried to talk, but he just pretends everything's all right. Heading for a crash if he doesn't open up. I knew we shouldn't have gone to bed together. Sex always makes things complicated, and the better the sex the worse it is.

I got back a week ago. We had a big fight, of course. He going on giving me a bunch of paranoid shit about Preacher Man, and that I should watch out for him on my assignment – some kind of conspiracy. I resent him following Preacher and prying into my life without permission.

I suppose I should have told Benny about Ezekiel being Keesha's father. I suppose I was embarrassed. My excuse was Benny had enough crazies in his life what with his ex-wife. Whatever. I don't need Benny trying to play white knight for me, thank you.

I may never get the back-child-support that sonofabitch owes me for Keesha. But it's worth a try. Zeke dropped too much acid and fried his brains with too much other shit. Then he got religion – in that crazy-ass way of drug burnouts. I found out he's in a cult, The Orchard. I heard he's some sort of deacon with that Orchard bunch. They're getting money from some rich, nutty Orange County John Bircher who wants to save America by turning hippies into holy-roller zombies. Good luck. But if Zeke's getting cash out of this the way I think, it's time for him to pay up.

Whatever happens, it's none of Benny's business. And the whole thing has nothing to do with Bobby Kennedy and some conspiracy theory Benny's babbling about. Shit, I don't need Benny to tell me about all that. Those are the risks. Look at our history, nothing but bombings, lynching, killings in the dead of night. We live with it, especially people of color.

If I didn't know better, I'd think Benny was jealous about my assignment and trying to scare me off of it.

---------------------------------- -

13. SHOTGUN PSYCHOS

You'd be wrong to take Detective Sergeant Jacob Imhoff as just another burned out cop, tough-but-fair, maybe a decent guy, hard to read. Roy could see all that – and knew what else.

They sit opposite each other in a booth at the back of Clifton's Cafeteria on Broadway near Sixth Street, a place with a history, catering to mixed downtown clientele of drifters, downtown workers, tourists, and unfrequented by cops or newsmen. Roy examines Imhoff's fleshy face discreetly for clues. With his graying crew cut and massive shoulders, Imhoff resembles an ICBM emerging from its silo. Imhoff plays on his bulk and striking homeliness, alternating between King Kong and the Jolly Green Giant, menacing or jovial, always imposing.

Roy keeps to himself what he his not supposed to know. Not that he cares about the closet where Imhoff keeps his sexuality hidden, well behind freely thrown epithets about fags and fairies. Roy knows a lot, not all of it useful. He can't leverage this bit of information, nor would he be so inclined. It's more than he wants to know about this man with gun and leeway to do what he likes long as he keeps it on the down low.

Roy trusts Imhoff, warily. Imhoff is more like the bent, worn cops Roy knew back in Brooklyn, not one of chief Parker's scrubbed, storm troopers. Roy can detect Imhoff's contempt for the officious chief, who cleaned up L.A.'s conventional payoff-corruption years earlier, only to replace it with something more insidious – running his force by the Machiavellian precept that it is better to be feared than loved. Parker manages a mobile force, once-removed, from the populace it intimidates more than protects. It works as far as securing upscale areas.

Unlike older cities, Los Angeles suburbanite

communities have the room to stand apart with little overlap between rich and poor. The cops of Parker force, with insufficient numbers to really police L.A's sprawl,, keeps moving in its patrol cars, freeway-alienated to its constituents – pretty much as Angelenos are to each other. They are ordinary cops, some good, a few bad, working stiffs – not the enemy. The sign up to keep law and order, but become surrogates – thrust into an impossible hit-and-miss counterinsurgency with indigenous gangs, abandoning any pretense of protecting of everyday black and brown neighborhood citizens caught in the crossfire. Intimidate first, ask questions later, and if this involves cracking heads and an undercurrent of racism, so be it. Parker and the Prince forgot to ask what devolves from instilling fear so successfully, loathing.

A passage from Howard Thurman's Jesus and the Disinherited comes to Roy's mind about "the ever present fear that confronts the poor," about how living under a constant threat of violence "attacks the fundamental sense of self-respect and personal dignity," how fear of violence boxes in the poor from enjoying freedoms the majority takes for granted – going to school, employment, building social networks, how it engenders seething outrage. "There are few things more devastating than to have it burned into you that you do not count and that no provisions are made for the literal protection of your person." Roy muses at the irony of L.A.'s tin horn mayor putting this interloping New York senator, another Kennedy who would be President, in the same predicament as endured daily by the city's black and brown citizens he aspires to champion – unprotected.

It is Roy's misfortune to be a member of that vanishing breed of enterprising, investigative reporters rather than a talking head. He never lets things go at that. He has to put his nose where it's not wanted and ask rude questions. Roy enjoys it, perversely. He like works the gaps and wedging the cracks in walls. He finds his sources on the dark streets and behind the facades of the powerful. It's a given that the best sources have axes to grind. Practically everyone does, like Imhoff, who has one foot in Hollywood.

"You and I, Roy," Imhoff snorts. "We're in the same business, you know."

"How's that?"

"Entertainment."

Roy isn't big on show biz, but even he knows that Imhoff already is too old to get anywhere with Hollywood's boy-apparchiks. But, what the hell? Roy was doing no better with the gray-faced editorial apparachicks upstairs at the Times. Better to humor Imhoff. "Should I count this as research for your next script"

"Whatever. Now. You didn't just meet me here for the Salisbury steak. What do you want."

"I hear you got fucked again by City Hall. You wanted in on the Bobby Kennedy detail, but Yorty and your boss Parker decided to deny any police protections to JFK's brother, Senator Robert F. Kennedy, who is odds-on favorite to become our next President. Can you confirm that?"

"Fucking fag Gordy's got a big mouth."

"The better to suck your cock with, my dear."

"Fuck off."

"So it's true."

"The part about Yorty pulling the Kennedy detail. Yeah. That's true all right. Bastard."

"Sonofabitch. Why do you think that is? Any talk down at headquarters?"

"Shit. Yorty just takes orders from those wing nut millionaires who pay for his way up the ladder. He's the kind of weasel they like. Does what he's told."

"And they would want Bobby Kennedy running around Los Angeles unprotected?"

"They want him to limit his campaign, maybe lose the primary because of that. Or maybe more than that."

Imhoff shovels forkfuls of Salisbury steak, heavy with translucent gravy, past his oddly sensuous lips. He doesn't chew much. Roy can't read the mood of Imhoff's slit eyes or if they are brown, green or gray, only that they size him up constantly out of habit, watchful as a cat at a mouse-hole.

"So, what do you know about the that nut job who marches around downtown hollering doom, wearing a brassiere on his head, the one they call Preacher Man?"

"You mean, 'you're-gonna-go to-hell.' Zeke Ludlow? Yeah. Don't you guys know anything there in that Daily Mausoleum over there?"

"Is he dangerous?"

"No more or less than any nut job. Maybe he's right; we're all going to hell. Maybe we're there already."

"He's got a gun."

"So what? Maybe he wants to put himself out of his misery.

"Maybe. But somebody told me this Zeke character has been talking crazy about Bobby Kennedy while he waves a gun around."

"Just an act. I wouldn't worry about that asshole. He's crazy like a fox."

"What do you mean?"

"Drop it."

"My source says a black sedan picked him up in a alley, very mysteriously. He says the car belongs to a certain Jeb Crowley. Do you know what's that about?"

"You got nothing there. Probably a friend." Imhoff starts on his mashed potatoes, sipping Jack Daniels between bites.

"Does Zeke have a record. Does he work for LAPD?" Roy fishes. "Off the record."

Imhoff puts down his drink. Roy notices the sweat on his upper lip. "Off the record, maybe."

"An informant?"

"Don't go there. You're out of your depth, boy. He's

just another burned out hippie who dropped too much acid, got into meth, then got god-crazy bible thumping religion."

"Pick your poison. How about another round?" Roy signals a waiter. Booze and mashed potatoes seem to loosen Imhoff's tongue.

A busboy arrives – smallish, trim, Middle-Eastern looking, even-featured, with dark, vacant eyes, black wavy hair. "May I help you?" The man has faint accent that Roy can't place. The name tag says "Sirhan." Imhoff scowls at him.

Roy tells him to get a waiter for another round. "Come on, Imhoff, give me something more here, off the record. Okay?"

"Off the record, Zeke is a stooge for Crowley, and the Rheebus Brother, big John Birch Society backers down in Orange County, got their fingers in everything from missiles to oil."

"What do they want with a loser like Zeke?"

"Just a side bet. Crowley put money in this cult church for hippies, to bring them all to Jesus – his version. Zeke was pastor, but then went off the deep end – I mean the deep end of the deep end – comes down here hollering about the Apocalypse, giving everyone a headache."

"What's that got to do with Bobby Kennedy?"

"Maybe nothing really. But you know Crowley and that crowd hate the Kennedys, especially Bobby."

"Take a number. Get in line."

"Worse, since Bobby's gone peacenik and brotherhood, picking up on Martin Luther King – and the black vote."

"Just politics?"

"Not to them. They're all nuttier than sand fleas. Worse than any Preacher Man, but with unlimited cash, and a lot of weight to throw around." A waiter brings their drinks.

Roy lights a Camel. "Bobby's all over Los Angeles

campaigning. A California win will be his ticket to the White House."

Imhoff tops off his fresh drink with the last drops of his old one. "That is ... if nothing happens to him."

"You're saying?"

"Isn't it obvious. Nobody's minding the store, unless you count the pair of black bookends Bobby's hired as his so-called bodyguards -- for show down in Watts – Rosey Grier and Rafer Johnson." Imhoff snorts, "an over-the-hill football fatso and a track-and-field fairy, couldn't bodyguard my ass. No Secret Service either. How convenient."

"What about feds?"

J. Edgar doesn't ever want Bobby as his boss again." Imhoff leans forward and whispers with boozy breath. "What to hear something hot? This guy, Kyle Olson. You heard of him? He's an FBI factotum - probably helps Hoover unlace corsets after work too. The other day, I hear, at FBI headquarters, Olsen says – get this -- out loud, right in the office, 'I hope someone shoots and kills the son of a bitch' – meaning Bobby Kennedy."

"How do you know this?" Roy draws down his Camel.

"Let's just say a little FBI birdie, who I used to work with here, told me."

"And you say to forget Zeke?"

Imhoff is getting bleary now. "I've already said too much."

"What if there's something to this. You're a cop. What are you going to do."

"If your nut-job Zeke is even serious – which is improbable – he'd just be a fall guy. You don't get how big boys play? No conspiracies, no chain of evidence, no connections."

"Then what? How?"

"They don't order a hit. It's not like some mafia shit. They just pull strings and set things in motion. They open the doors and let the dogs loose. Poke all the wackos in any given town and a dozen of them come out of the woodwork with guns looking glory. It doesn't take much. A little extra cash to the usual hate mongers, pressure here and there. Feed the paranoia out there, and, bang, the crazies go off in all directions like buckshot. Most of them miss, but only one of them has to get through...and, voila, you've got your – ha-ha – lone assassin" – with maybe some backup just in case."

----

14. CRY, THE NOT SO BELOVED COUNTRY

Benny drifts through the election night crowd packing the Ambassador Hotel ballroom. Waves of cheering fan outward from strategically placed TV monitors, louder with each bit of good news. People are smiling, buoyed by Kennedy's mounting lead in the California primary vote count.

The crowd of campaign workers and supporters smells victory as midnight approaches. Misgivings aside, even Ben feels it. He's over the resistance of those who thought Bobby Kennedy a late-comer to the anti-Vietnam War cause. Maybe it's really going to happen. Bobby has enough courage and clout to end the bloody war -- declare victory and get the hell out -- pull the country together and finish his slain brother's work – the New Frontier, chapter two, at last. Benny hasn't felt this buoyant about anything in a long while.

He scans the crowd for Makeda. He just wants to keep watch that nothing happens to her, no matter what. But he feels silly about his paranoia now, amid all these confident, excited supporters, on the verge, they know, of something to powerful to be stopped now.

Benny knows the Ambassador Hotel well, where movie stars, presidents and financiers have stayed since the 1920s. Its storied, lush Coconut Groove hosted legendary entertainers and the Academy Awards during the 1930s. The L.A. Times' even held its own annual awards there privately in the year Benny started worked there. Makeda's mother sang there with Benny Goodman's band and his own mother. The Coconut Grove! Coconuts! Oh my God. Kennedy! Preacher Man's Delphic babble in the alley!

Benny spots a tall, gaunt man moving through the partiers. The man's long, sandy beard is tidy and the shoulder-length hair trim as well. No brassiere on his head.

But it's Preacher Man! What the hell?

Shouts and clapping erupt from those near the TV monitors.

"Did Bobby cinch the nomination?"

A rotund, ruddy man in a blue blazer, red tie and white straw, "RFK-All-the-Way" boater cheers and bounces a Kennedy sign up and down: "Not yet. Don Drysdale has just pitched his sixth straight shutout for the Dodgers – a world record, the big lug."

Benny catches up with Preacher Man. "Zeke. It's me" Preacher Man stares at him blankly. Ben feels stupid trying to sound casual through the din. "What's up? What are you doing here?"

Preacher drills Benny with apocalypse eyes. "Guarding. Ah! The Angel Gabriel come to blow your horn! It ends. Prepare for the Rapture!"

Preacher Man wears a tan slacks and a light green sports jacket instead of his usual camo jump suit. Ben notices a bulge under the jacket.

Benny improvises. "Hey, Zeke. Come on with me. I got a surprise for you outside." He tries for Preacher's arm, but the taller man pulls away with surprising swiftness and slips into the crowd with surprising nimbleness. Benny loses him.

Another roar goes up, this time nearly deafening. "NBC just gave it to Kennedy," somebody yells. People stomp, clap and chant for their hero, some in tears of joy. RFK appears after what seems a long time, and moves to the lectern with his entourage. He looks small and exhausted – sans the Kennedy verve – wearing a rumpled sports jacket, white shirt – collar unbuttoned, his narrow, nondescript tie loosened.

Benny spots Makeda, on her big assignment, well behind Kennedy, standing on the low platform, nearly obscured by a massive Roosevelt Grier, her subject – perfect – and right near Ethel Kennedy. The crowd moves forward, forming a tight knot that prevents Benny from getting closer. Makeda probably can't see him beyond the TV camera lights. He wants to hold up a sign that says something corny – "I love you, Makeda" and "I'm sorry. Please forgive me" Corny - vapid romantic comedy wrap-up lines. What he wants even more is to warn her – and Kennedy and the entourage about Preacher.

Benny can't see him anywhere. "Shit," he mutters, standing on tip-toe.

Someone grabs Benny's elbow. Imhoff! "Back off, Clark Kent." he whispers into Benny's ear. "I got this."

"What the...?"

"Forget the Preacher. He's out of action. But I got my eye on that guy over there, just ahead on the right, by the kitchen doors. Why don't you get this down? It could be your big story, movie guy."

Benny doesn't catch all of Imhoff's next words, except: "Morales … used to be CIA Havana station chief... Bay of Pigs. Hated Jack. Hates Bobby." Imhoff stops. He grips Benny's arm harder. "Oh fuck, he's with another one of them." The man Imhoff calls Morales, in a beige sports jacket, black slacks, Hawaiian shirt, holds a paper sack, like a kid's school lunch, except the bag hangs oddly at an angle.

"Stay out of this." Imhoff lets go and moves toward Morales, parting clusters of people like an ice breaker. Ben tries to follow, but the crowd gets tighter, blocking his progress and his view.

Robert F. Kennedy begins. He sounds tentative, not seeming to acknowledge this moment of triumph. There is too much yet be done. The crowd cheers wildly nonetheless. "I'd like to congratulate..."

"Ken-ne-dy, Ken-ne-dy, Ken-ed-dy!" The chant rises. Bobby pauses, nods shyly … "Don Drysdale." The fans laugh. "I understand that he did it tonight, broke all records ..." Cheers and applause.

It's hard for Benny to hear Kennedy through the noise. "Moving on... tonight... historic..." Benny squeezes closer to catch more, while trying to locate Preacher. He knows Roy is somewhere around too, probably off to the side, up there with the rest of the press corps.

The room goes quieter now as Kennedy gets down to the declaration of victory – albeit understated – that they have anticipated all evening.

"One thing is clear in this year of 1968 as I traveled across this country, I believe that the American people want no more Vietnam..." Loud cheers, applause and sign-waving. Flash bulbs go off.

Bobby warms up, now, flashing a bit of Kennedy charm. "What is quite clear is that we can work together, in the last analysis, and that what has been going on within the United States in the last three years – the divisions, the violence, the disenchantment with our society – the divisions, whether it's between blacks and whites, between the poor and the more affluent, or between age groups or the war in Vietnam..."

Cheering.

Kennedy's voice rises. "It is clear that we can start to work together. We are a great country and a selfless country and we are a compassionate country..."

People seem to lean towards him, hungry for every word. "A compassionate country?" Benny keeps repeating this to himself, his eyes tear up. He scoures the scene for Imhoff, and Preacher, and the mysterious Morales.

Bobby gives everyone his big toothy Irish grin, winding down. "Mayor Yorty has just sent me a message that we've been here too long already...." The crowd sighs, wanting more. "My thanks to all of you.." Cheering rises again, and a tired Bobby calls up energy in his voice concluding, anticlimactically "... and now it's on to Chicago and let's win this." Kennedy gives a shy thumbs up, and his trademark boyish grin, then withdraws toward the back of the room, his entourage following. The mood of the crowd deflates as it starts to disband. Benny feels enormous relief. Nothing terrible happened. Preacher Man is gone. Kennedy is safely away, headed no doubt for his room at the hotel and good night's sleep. Makeda is safe.

Benny wades through the remaining onlookers in the direction of the Kennedy party. He wants to catch up with Makeda. He waves his press card, "coming through" trying to follow Kennedy, who, apparently impromptu, has decided to exit via the big double doors to the kitchen instead of going through side doors the way he came.

Benny spots the braided back of Makeda's head. He's squeezed and swept along a dim corridor towards the bright lights of the kitchen ahead... Everyone talks at once, energized. Like a conga line on its way to a party, they all snake through the pantry and along a row of sinks and chopping tables and stoves from which delicious smells arise from pans and pots bubbling dinners. White-aprons and caps line their way with much cheering... Kennedy, up ahead, ever the tireless campaigner, is greeting and shaking hands with the help.

Pop, pop, pop! It comes deafeningly loud. Benny's ears ring. Everything seems to blur and slow down. A truck back-firing ? Shots! Screams from everywhere. More shots! More screams.

A man shouts. "Close the doors! Close the doors!"

Another: "He's been shot!"

Another voice, yelling, choked. "Oh, my God! No! No! No!"

A woman moans loudly next to Benny, tearing at her blond fashionably coifed hair. Benny falls to his hands and knees and crawls forward. He thinks he catches sight of Grier and Rafer Johnson tackling a smallish, dark-haired man in a white kitchen-help jacket. Maybe he saw this in a TV clip later. He can't remember. His memories will conflate with the public images and coverage in a grand shared delirium.

This isn't happening. In an instant, still crawling reflexively, Benny finds himself almost atop a woman... Makeda! He sits up, gasping, and tries to tend to her. She's bleeding from somewhere. Her eyes glaze, blinking. He props her head against his rolled up jacket. He finds a pressure point to staunch her bleeding, using one hand until he can grab a dishtowel off a nearby counter and make a tourniquet. She sees Benny and tries to smile. Her lips move. He tries to hear what she's telling him... Something about Keesha.

Shouts. "Call an ambulance! Get the police." Yeah, like where the fuck is the LAPD?

"You got a bloody nose. Might be broken." A voice from just above calls out to Benny.

"I'm okay."

Somebody else keeps repeating. "Senator Kennedy's been shot!" The sobs, groans, curses, screams, go on. "Head wound. Blood everywhere," a woman says, staggering back from where the senator lay on the grimy floor, the life oozing out of him.

Benny doesn't remember much in the confusion that follows. Medics arrive. They take Kennedy and others out to ambulances, eventually, Makeda. They won't let him come with her. No room in the ambulance. He stands up, refuses help himself, and walks away while the medics busy themselves with others. . Others are dead and wounded– nobody can agree on the number of rounds or from whence. No Imhoff. No Preacher Man to be seen. Roy is there somewhere, unscathed. After a while, Benny finally sees uniformed police. Then feds, press, everyone asking questions.

Benny makes his way home. It's past three in the morning. He crashes on his couch, waking with a start from time to time, sweating. He wants it to be first light, another day. Sitting up, he waits for the comforting glow of dawn filtering through his French door curtains from the patio, early this time of year – reassurance that the world keeps turning.

Then he realizes what Makeda had been trying to tell him. He phones Zoya, who has been babysitting Keesha.

Zoya already knows about what happened from the TV. He tells her about Makeda and they make plans for little Keesha's care until her mother can return from the hospital. "We pray to God, for her," says Zoya.

"They got him too," Benny says to himself after he hangs up.

----

15. MAKEDA'S ARC

Makeda rips a half-typed sheet from Benny's clunky Underwood and crumples it into a over-filled wastebasket by the kitchen table. "I can't write about this shit!" She hobbles to the small fridge, still using a crutch. Ben has stocked it with snacks, milk and Keesha's fruit juices. She finds a carton of takeout chow mein from last night, and takes to it, cold. She's healing, but it still hurts to move around. She's not that hungry, but if she eats she can take another pain pill. That won't help the writing.

It's a Saturday. Benny has taken Keesha and his two daughters to Santa Monica pier for a few hours. He's been a brick, but she wishes he wouldn't hover around her so much some time. Another sunny, late June day outside.. Why did Leon have die too? Fucking death everywhere. Makeda learned of this from their grief-stricken grandma on the phone. Another pointless horror like the war itself, Leon was decapitation by a malfunctioning chopper blade just outside of Hue as he boarded for Saigon airport and home – his tour, up, but his number as well. It brings back childhood visions of her father's death, which she learned about second-hand long after the fact, covered now by the eternal swells of a timeless ocean. Her father incinerated with hundreds of other young, World War II sailor boys, taken out by one, white-scarved, too-young Japanese pilot, honor-conned into a his suicide mission for an all-but-defeated fatherland. No sun rising for any of them anymore.

And now Dr. King, and not long afterward, a noble, quirky, intense Robert F. Kennedy on a grease-spattered hotel kitchen floor, blood oozing from his bullet-broken skull, the backup brother who stepped forward, called by other martyrs, for his turn. Martyred for what?

Makeda goes back to her typing. Work provides relief

from tears, staring at walls and pounding pillows. Don't try to write, just put down whatever comes. Words pour forth now... It will never make sense, but she can only trust herself to compose her thoughts into some palatable form later – a form that can never capture the unspeakable, but will have to do.

No way that I should not want what comes with this assignment. But I won't feel important from it now, no matter what they tell me. I don't know anything more about what happened than my own panic and pain, as anyone could imagine. What I saw and heard blur with all that has followed. "You're a lucky girl, my Annie baby." mama told me when she visited. God love her the grief we share for Leon, no one famous but he's with them now.

"You can't call what went down, luck." I'm glad I didn't smart-ass her with that. Mama was being so brave for me. After Leon I know she cried for so long, but stayed together, not like the old days when she would have shot up probably.

She surprised me showing up right after what happened at the Ambassador. I want us to go see grandma McGiven too. Soon. Grandma calls almost every day now. Her quiet courage braces me, as does my baby Keesha. Makes me thankful every day I didn't leave her an orphan.

I don't like that this has made me some kind of damn overnight celebrity, for the moment anyway – offers from Rolling Stone and Newsweek, even an agent with a book offer and somebody about a movie. Vultures. Can you imagine? Tom Brokaw interviewed me for KNBC and the network feed. Am I always going to be the black girl who was there when it happened?

Rosey Grier visited me in the hospital, but I didn't take notes. Roy says the Times has to promote me now to make itself look better. The bosses stick with their own kind, most of them anyway except for a few wild cards, bless them.

We find our own kind by breaking wrong rules. Our own kind endures and evolves. Definitions don't stick. You'll know us when you see us. The powerful and the bigots try to pry us all apart, slice us and dice us, set us against each other, divide and conquer.

We give birth to cultures. We make our music and they use it. They try to make reason for hatred rather than gifts we like to share. Form up your tribes. Chose your weapons. There's money to be made in blood.

But I see now that nothing stays the same. We keep living and loving and screwing, and marching and working and moving on. They can't undo the changes. Sometimes they succeed, like right now. It seems they are winning.

But try as they might, they can't keep it up. Blood flows together, people mix and match and make anew. ... blessed are bloodied peacemakers. Everybody says now that what is happened is the end of civil rights, of integration, of the peace movement. Nothing left now but race war, repressions. Why does evil always seems prevail? Maybe this is the ultimate illusion they want to sell us.

I'll stick my neck out and say no. Not always, but just below the surface, life goes on, and its streams are many, of many hues. We sing ourselves, and those who take the trouble to really know each other give and get that little respect Aretha sings about.

Every personal act is a statement, including whom we chose to love, as along as that love is real and not self-serving. You don't read that in the news.

In that, we win – in transcending all the hate and fear, inside and out. No assassins can stop that. I'm here, larger in my life and proud with my Keesha. We shall overcome? Hell, I don't know. As long as I can give Keesha strength to make her own life in the best world I can help make for her. I'll be with and love how and whom I chose. No matter how bad the news, long as we breathe we resist and make anew.

New heroes keep rising up from among all of us, living our lives here on the ground. Life goes on; we abide, with its old rhythms and new dances. "The arc of the moral universe is long, but it bends towards justice." Martin Luther King said that in his last sermon not three months ago before they murdered him. I don't know if I can feel this inside me, right now. Not after all this. But I choose to act is if it is so, for Keesha – for myself too. We go on.

ABOUT THE AUTHOR

Umberto Tosi's novels and nonfiction books include *Ophelia Rising, Milagro on 34th Street, High Treason and Gunning for the Holy Ghost*. His short stories have been widely published in literary journals, These include *Catamaran Literary Reader* and *Chicago Quarterly Review*, where he is a contributing editor. He has published hundreds of articles online and in print. He was contributing writer to *Forbes ASAP*, covering the Silicon Valley tech industry. Prior to that, he was an editor and staff writer for the *Los Angeles Times* and its Sunday magazine. He has held top editing posts at *San Francisco Magazine* and Diablo Publishing Group. He has written more than 300 articles for newspapers and magazines, online and in print. He blogs for Authors Electric and has contributed to several of its anthologies, He has four daughters - Alicia Sammons, Kara Julia Towe, Cristina Sheppard and Zoë Tosi. He resides in Chicago, Illinois.

10695060R10164

Made in the USA
San Bernardino, CA
06 December 2018